PRAISE FOR FIONA VALPY

'Love, love, loved it . . . Brilliant story, I was completely immersed in it, so moving and touching too. The research needed must have been hard to do but it brought the war . . . to life.'

—Lesley Pearse, author of *You'll Never See Me Again*

'A wonderfully immersive novel set against a vivid and beautifully described . . . setting. I loved it!'

—Victoria Connelly, bestselling author of *The Rose Girls*

'A moreish story of love, war, loss, and finding love again, set against an atmospheric . . . backdrop.'

—Gill Paul, author of *The Second Marriage*

D1169070

The
Storyteller
of
Casablanca

OTHER BOOKS BY FIONA VALPY:

The
Storyteller
of
Casablanca

Fiona
Valpy

LAKE UNION
PUBLISHING

Text copyright © 2021 by Fiona Valpy
All rights reserved.

Published by Lake Union Publishing, Seattle

www.apub.com

Amazon, the Amazon logo, and Lake Union Publishing are trademarks of Amazon.com, Inc., or its affiliates.

ISBN-13: 9781542032100
ISBN-10: 1542032105

Cover design by Emma Rogers

Printed in the United States of America

Had I the heavens' embroidered cloths,
Enwrought with golden and silver light,
The blue and the dim and the dark cloths
Of night and light and the half light,
I would spread the cloths under your feet:
But I, being poor, have only my dreams;
I have spread my dreams under your feet;
Tread softly because you tread on my dreams.

'Aedh Wishes for the Cloths of Heaven'
W. B. Yeats

For my friend Lesley,
who listens to the truth beneath the words.

Zoe – 2010

May McConnaghy perches on the overstuffed chaise in the drawing room and fans herself gently with the little booklet she's brought with her. 'Don't worry, you'll get used to the heat. And once they get the air con working again you'll be just grand. When the chergui's blowing like this it creates all sorts of havoc. Wasn't that sandstorm yesterday a pain? They have a nasty habit of knocking out the electrics in these old buildings.' She has a pleasing, low-pitched voice with an Irish lilt that goes with her auburn hair and pale, freckled arms.

The shutters are pulled to, casting deep shade over the furniture to protect it from the blaze of the mid-morning Moroccan sun, the louvres angled to allow in just enough light. Despite this, the air in the room is hot and heavy and I try hard not to scratch at the angry welts on my hands, which have flared up again. I'd hoped the move to a warmer climate might have helped my dermatitis to heal a bit, but it seems to have had the opposite effect. My skin feels too tight where the heat has swollen my fingers and my wedding ring cuts into the flesh. I'd tried to take it off when I woke up this morning but the knuckle was already knotted into a hard, unyielding lump, so I had to leave it and hope that if I run my finger under cold water tonight it'll ease the discomfort. The hot wind blowing in from the desert frays the nerves as it insinuates its way down the boulevards and alleyways of the city, the fine, dry dust hissing and whispering as it scours the patched and pitted city pavements. 'You don't belong here,' it seems to be saying. As if I needed any reminding.

The housekeeper sets a tray of tea things down on the low table between us and nods when I murmur my thanks, closing the door gently behind her as she goes.

May waits until she hears the quiet pad of Alia's leather slippers fade away down the hallway and then says conspiratorially, 'Isn't it heaven having staff? I don't know how any of us will be able to adapt to having to do things for ourselves again when our postings come to an end. Make the most of it while it lasts!' Her laugh tinkles like the clinking of the glasses on the silver tray as I pour mint tea into them. I pass her one.

From the handbag on the floor beside her, May extracts a beautifully wrapped package and passes it across to me. 'These are the best honey cakes in Casablanca,' she tells me. 'You're lucky having the bakery right on the corner. Though it'd be the ruination of my figure if I had it so close by – just too tempting! Now then, most of the information you'll need is in the booklet.' She puts it on the coffee table between us and pushes it towards me. 'The Club's wives' committee compiled it and we all chipped in with the important bits and pieces to help newcomers hit the ground running. It mentions the bakery here, see?' She points one red-lacquered fingernail at the relevant page, headed 'Food and Drink'.

I look at it politely, pretending to scan the list of shops and restaurants.

'And I'll take you around the city one morning to show you where everything else is,' she continues.

'Thank you,' I say. 'That's really kind.'

'Oh, don't worry.' May waves a hand airily and I'm not sure whether it's to dismiss my gratitude or an attempt to stir a breath of coolness into the hot, heavy air. 'It's all part of the deal. I'm on the welcoming committee. It's always good to meet the new arrivals and help them learn the ropes. Morocco can be a bit of a shock to the system at first, but you're among friends here. Us expats stick together. We all know what it's like to be new to a place.'

We only moved into our new home – an elegant townhouse in the French Quarter of the city, rented for us by the shipping company Tom works for – two days ago, after spending our first week in Casablanca in a hotel. Not that there was much to move, just a few suitcases of our belongings. We've left the house in Bristol with everything in it, ready to visit whenever Tom has leave and so we'll have a home to go back to when his posting ends in five years' time, when he'll most probably return to the office at Avonmouth. The HR Department offered us the option of furnished accommodation and since, quite honestly, I have neither the time nor the energy to spend on setting up a new home from scratch in a completely foreign place, I'm happy to live with someone else's furniture. The things here are old and a little shabby, but of good quality.

'Have you everything you need?' May surveys the room with an appraising eye.

'Pretty much, I think. And we can always buy anything extra if we need to.'

'Quite right.' She flips the pages of the booklet. 'Here's a section on homeware shops that deliver. Really the best place to shop for everything is the mall.'

I sip my tea. I've discovered it's surprisingly refreshing in the heat. Then I turn my attention to the little parcel, untying the curled ribbons and removing the wrappings to reveal the cakes within, whose golden sponge is topped with almonds that glisten beneath a honeyed syrup.

'Thank you for bringing these, it's really thoughtful of you.' I offer her the box, along with one of the crisply pressed linen

3

napkins Alia's included with the tea tray. I see her notice the state of my hands and she tries not to wince as she helps herself. My rough, leathery skin and raggedly chewed cuticles are in stark contrast to her elegant manicure.

May's right, the little cakes are absolutely delicious, although the heat takes away my appetite. She chats on, describing the social programme at the Overseas Club where all the expats spend their spare time, playing tennis, swimming and socialising. There's to be a cocktail party there tomorrow evening, laid on by Tom's company to welcome us. Everyone's being so kind. Although the thought of being in a room with my husband and a plentiful supply of booze, in the presence of his new colleagues and their partners, fills me with dread. Hopefully Tom will be able to keep the brakes on his drinking while in public and being appraised by the people on whom his career depends. I'll just have to be vigilant, as usual.

Oblivious to my preoccupation, May continues to chat away. 'I'll organise a lunch at the Club one day next week with a few of the girls. And I'll give you a ring to arrange a morning that suits to show you round, too. Don't worry,' – she shoots me an appraising glance, perhaps realising my polite enthusiasm is a little forced – 'moving's always stressful. Sure, it takes a few weeks to find your feet. We've all been there. But you'll soon get the hang of it all. Casa's not a bad place for a posting in the big scheme of things.'

I'm truly grateful to her for being so welcoming, but she's no fool and can probably sense I'm a bit distracted. The overwhelming compulsion to wash my hands is building within me as I contemplate the prospect of so many social situations. I know it's irrational. I know it's a reaction to feeling anxious and out of control. But it's a compelling reflex and it's easier to give in to it than to fight it. I'm longing to get back upstairs to the nursery to finish unpacking Grace's toys and clothes, too. I feel calmer in that peaceful space at the top of the house, and I'd like to be there when my baby daughter wakes up from her morning nap so she won't be alone in this strange new home. As I sit half listening to May talking about the book club and the other interest groups on offer, I'm picturing the way Grace smiles when she sees me and how I'll scoop her into my arms, my heart filling as she gives that little chuckle of joy. I tune back in, though, when May mentions a crafting club.

'Do they do any quilting?' I ask. 'I have a project I'd like to try but I've never done any before.'

'All manner of things like that, I believe,' says May. 'Personally, I'm hopeless with my hands and I don't have the patience for needlework in any form. But I'll make sure Kate is at our lunch. She's the crafting queen bee so she'll be able to tell you more.'

'That'd be great. And do you know where I might be able to buy fabric and thread?'

'Oh goodness, you're really asking the wrong woman! I suppose you'd perhaps find a stall in the Quartier Habous for those sorts of things. I'll ask around.'

From beyond the shutters the sound of the call to prayer begins, resonating on the torrid mid-morning air. May wipes the last traces of honey from her fingers and glances at her watch. 'Well, that's time for me to be off. I've a few things to pick up before the shops shut. And you'll be wanting to get on too, I should think. Mustn't hold you back from your nesting.'

She gives me a kind smile and an embrace as I see her out into the blaze of light and heat. In the French *nouvelle ville* the streets are wide boulevards, the ubiquitous date palms interspersed here and there with plane trees that at this time of day cast concentrated pools of deep shadow on to the pavement directly beneath their branches. But as you move towards the ocean the streets become narrower and the buildings lower, drawing you into the tangled heart of the medina, the old Arab Quarter. Beyond that is the sprawl of the docks, where Tom's office overlooks one of the biggest seaports on the African continent. From there, he directs the movement of the company's ships and keeps track of the sky-scraping stacks of containers as they're loaded and unloaded from the quayside.

There'll be time to explore all of that later, once that relentless, restless wind has died down again. For now, I wave goodbye to May and then climb the stairs to the top of the house. I wash the sticky residue from the cakes off my hands, giving them a thorough scrubbing twice over before I go into Grace's room. I stand at the window watching a trio of turtle doves, who seem to regard these roof tiles as their domain, as they ruffle their feathers and coo companionably to one another.

Beyond the slates, a sprawling muddle of flat rooftops stretches to the very edge of the sea. Above them, the minarets of the mosques soar into the infinite blue of the North African sky.

We came here looking for a new start. But instead of hope, I just feel emptiness. This is a city perched on the edge of an ocean of broken dreams, shabby and windswept, its once fine streets now down-at-heel. The Hollywood glamour of the days of Bogart and Bergman is long gone, nothing but a distant memory now.

It looks to me like the end of the world.

Zoe – 2010

Every house has its own vocabulary. Our new home on the Boulevard des Oiseaux mutters and sighs to itself at night when the city outside finally falls silent for a few brief hours and the darkness drapes itself over the rooftops, as heavy as velvet. I lie awake listening, trying to decipher this new language of creaks and clicks. Perhaps in a month or two familiarity will make the sounds fade into the background, but for now I'm alert to each one. In the bed beside me, Tom lies motionless, sunk in the depths of sleep.

My mind's still buzzing in the aftermath of the cocktail party at the Club. All that conversation and so many introductions heightened my natural anxiety at being in a social setting. I always find these things such an ordeal. And then there was the added vigilance needed to make sure Tom's drinking didn't reach that point where he tips from charmingly expansive to hopelessly addled, slurring his words and lurching into people. The whole event was completely exhausting, but now I'm both too tired and too wired to sleep. Now it's over I think I can say that the party was a success, though. We got away with it, managing to project the image of the committed young couple, excited at the new opportunities this posting has given them. Tom did a good job of playing the role that's expected of him and his boss seemed pleased, beaming his approval as I stood at my husband's side. I must have looked the very picture of a suitable corporate wife, even if really I was trying to resist the urge to flee to the bathroom and wash my hands over and over again.

Tom stirs slightly, but doesn't wake. The distance between us is a wide ocean that neither of us dares cross. I envy him the oblivion of his quiet breaths. I know he's working long hours in his new job and comes back from the office exhausted at the end of each day, but sometimes he's more animated than usual when he comes through the door and I can smell the musky haze of whisky on him.

The floorboards of the room above us – Grace's room – tick rhythmically every now and then as the wood contracts in the relative coolness of the night, reminding me that I need to find a hammer tomorrow and see if I can do something about the loose board beneath the Berber rug in the middle of the nursery. It creaks loudly when I walk over it and I wouldn't want to risk it disturbing Grace, startling her from her sleep.

At some point, lulled by the rhythm of my husband's breathing, I finally fall into a deep sleep of my own and, by the time the song of the muezzins wakes me, the bed beside me is empty. Tom likes to run and the best time is at dawn, before it becomes too hot and he gets drawn back into the demands of his work. Sure enough, as I tie the sash of my silk dressing gown, I notice that his running shoes are gone from beneath the chair on his side of the bed. He'll be back to shower off the sweat, changing into his shirt and tie and grabbing a quick breakfast before it's time to get to his office at the docks. In the meantime, I'll go and get Grace up, scooping her out of her cot and covering her smiling face with my kisses as another day begins.

Once Tom leaves, my limbs are filled with a restlessness, fuelled by the two cups of strong coffee I've drunk with my breakfast of fruit and yoghurt, so I strap on the baby sling, making sure the clips are securely fastened, and set off for a walk. I have no clear idea of where I'm headed, but my feet turn automatically towards the ocean, skirting the walls of the medina. The wind has dropped today, bringing a welcome stillness after days of its incessant, nerve-fraying bluster. I've thrown a light shawl around my shoulders to help shield Grace from the sun. The sea breeze flirts with its edges, making the fringing flutter. At last we reach the corniche with its beach clubs and lines of palm trees that toss their heads in the wind, and I push my sunglasses on to the top of my head to drink in the sight of the golden sand and the ocean beyond. Close in, the water is awash with light, but the far-off horizon is a smudge of darker blue. I show Grace the waves. She watches the Atlantic rollers a little warily at first as they curl and crash on to the beach. Then she decides she likes the spectacle, gurgling and waving her hands in approval.

'I know,' I tell her. 'It's wonderful, isn't it? We'll have to find a nice quiet beach to take you to so we can do some paddling. We can buy a bucket and spade and I'll make you a giant sandcastle fit for a princess.'

I feel a sense of buoyancy at having walked this far and made it to the corniche under my own steam. Although much of the city is shabby and dilapidated, seeing the beach and the expanse of sparkling ocean lifts my spirits. Perhaps I can get used to life in this new place after all. I remind myself how lucky I am to live in such an affluent area and to have the help of Alia in running my new home. I don't feel completely comfortable with the luxury of having a housekeeper, but she seems to take a pride in keeping the house neat and tidy and to enjoy the cooking she does for us, so I suppose she likes her job. I'd thought I'd be ill at ease having someone I hardly know in my home each day, but with Tom working such long hours it's actually nice having the company.

I watch the waves washing on to the shore and find I'm unconsciously swaying in time to their rhythm, rocking Grace in her sling as she gurgles happily.

I settle my sunglasses back on my face and rearrange the shawl protectively over Grace's downy head as we turn for home. I've walked for miles already and I'm conscious that the sun is climbing steadily overhead, its rays becoming fiercer by the minute. My feet are sore and swollen from the hot, hard pavements and my trainers pinch my toes. The noise of the traffic makes my head ache and I begin to hurry, feeling exposed out here, longing for the sanctuary of the townhouse with its shaded rooms, and a cool glass of water from the fridge. If I had a few dirhams I could flag down one of the little red taxis that speed through the city streets and be dropped at my door, but I've come out with no money. The glare of the sunlight reflects from the white walls around us, seeming to redouble in intensity, and I curse my stupidity. Grace shouldn't be out in this heat – what was I thinking? She begins to whimper, sensing my anxiety. Distress rises in my chest. In desperation I duck into a narrow alleyway, hoping it'll provide a shadier shortcut through the medina. But it's all corners and angles between whitewashed walls and I quickly become disorientated. The urge to get back to the safety of home is overwhelming. I'm half running now; panicking; lost. My breath comes in short gasps. The alley twists and turns and heads swivel to watch me pass, hands reaching out to tug at my shawl, begging for money, urging me to buy something. The clamour of voices overwhelms me as children run by kicking a football, shouting to one another, and merchants pushing handcarts call out their wares. A boy on a motorbike swerves past, too close for comfort, the roar of his engine making me jump. In my alarm, I almost trip over a goat as it grazes on rubbish in the gutter and it turns and looks at me with a disconcertingly blank gaze. A man with a face like tooled leather opens his mouth in a toothless grin and offers me a strange-looking wizened root from the battered ebony box he carries. I swerve away from his outstretched hand, recalling the warning in the booklet May gave me: walking through the medina without a guide is not recommended; beware of pickpockets.

And then a woman steps out from a doorway just in front of me and I stumble into her, apologising. She turns to look at me, her eyes widening in concerned recognition beneath the neat folds of her headscarf.

'Alia!' I gasp, almost weeping with gratitude.

'Mrs Harris, are you all right? What are you doing here?'

'I've been out for a walk, but I lost my way.'

She smiles, momentarily resting a reassuring hand on my arm. 'Well, you're not far from home. Come, I'll show you, I'm on my way there now. We can walk together.'

My heartbeat slows to a more normal pace as she leads me out of the medina, through a narrow keyhole-shaped arch in the ancient walls, and suddenly we're back on the broader, art deco streets of the *nouvelle ville*. I spot the bakery on the corner and we turn into the Boulevard des Oiseaux. My hands are still trembling a little as I fit the key into the lock, but Alia stands back respectfully, giving me space, so I'm not sure she notices.

Relief floods my body as I step across the threshold. I ease off my trainers and heave a big sigh of relief as my aching, swollen feet meet the smooth coolness of the mosaic floor in the entrance hall. Alia closes the door behind us, shutting out the fierce glare of the sun. 'I'll bring you some iced water with lemon, shall I?' she says.

I nod gratefully. 'Please put it in the drawing room. I'll be there shortly.' I hurry upstairs to the nursery to soothe Grace, scrubbing my hands three times over before I change her and wipe her face with a cool cloth, settling her for her morning nap. The pounding of my heart gradually slows and now that I'm back in the safety of the house I feel a little calmer as the sense of being overwhelmed recedes. How could I ever have thought I'd be able to navigate this new city – this new life – on my own?

As I move quietly about the room tidying things away, the loose board creaks, protesting loudly beneath my feet. I pull back the faded rug and see that a length of floorboard has warped and lifted away from its neighbour along one side. I press down tentatively, hoping I might be able to wedge it back into place, but it doesn't budge. There's a knothole at one end just big enough for me to hook my finger into. The wood is slightly rough and it resists at first, but it gives as I tug harder and I'm able to pull it out, wincing and cursing beneath my breath as a splinter catches in the sore skin surrounding my fingernail. In the space between the floor and the bedroom ceiling beneath it, covered in decades of dust, are a little box and a leather-bound notebook. I lift them out carefully, rubbing the box with my thumb to reveal its inlay of mother-of-pearl. A faint scent of sandalwood rises from it, as if it's breathing out a soft sigh of relief after its years of incarceration. My curiosity is piqued by this intriguing find, a forgotten hoard of treasure hidden here – how long ago? Years? Or decades? I wipe the top of it with the corner of my shirt tail and the geometric design gleams faintly, the mother-of-pearl like drops of moonlight in my hands.

I ease open the lid, revealing a small cache of objects. One by one I take them out and lay them on the rug. There's a Star of David on a tangled gold chain as fine as the filament of a spider's web. There's a feather the colour of coral, and a sliver of jade-green sea glass worn smooth by the ocean. Next comes a folded sheet of pale blue writing paper on which is written what looks like a signature in faded sepia ink. And finally there's a hollow wooden stick with a notch cut into it towards one end. I raise it to my lips and blow softly. There's no sound at first but as I adjust the angle and blow into it again it makes the gentle, sorrowful sound of a turtle dove's coo, echoing the murmurs of the birds that roost on the roof outside Grace's room, overlooking the courtyard behind the house.

Very carefully, I set the little collection of artefacts back in the box, wondering at the significance of each one as I do so, before turning my attention to the notebook. The leather is as dusty as the box, desiccated by exposure to the hot, dry air in its hiding place beneath the floor. But I can still see that the cover has been beautifully tooled and I trace the complex curlicues with my fingertips. Curious, I open it. It seems to be some sort of diary. The pages within are covered with looped handwriting and when I turn to the first page I read the inscription there:

This journal belongs to Josiane Françoise Duval.

Private.

Scrawled underneath, as if as an afterthought, and underlined heavily, twice, is written:

GO AWAY ANNETTE!

I glance around involuntarily, as though someone is watching me. These items have been deliberately hidden from prying eyes and for many long years, judging by the accumulation of dust. Should I show them to someone? To Alia, perhaps, or to Tom when he comes home tonight? But no, my instinct is to keep them a secret. I flip to the next page of the notebook and spot a date inscribed at the top: 1941. I've never been one of those people who skips to the end of a book to find out what happens, and I resist the urge to do so now, even if I don't have the willpower to resist reading someone's private journal. I justify it, telling myself I'm the one who's found it after – what? – some seven decades of it lying undiscovered. Its rightful owner is long gone. Somewhat guiltily applying the principle of 'Finders Keepers', I feel I am the self-appointed guardian of these artefacts now. I need to find out more, to unravel the mysteries they hold, before I show them to anyone else. Are they simply a random jumble of objects, or do they tell a story? I hope the answer may lie in the journal. In any case, I realise they represent a very welcome distraction as I carefully place each of the items in turn back in the wooden box.

I slip the floorboard back into its place – it seems to fit a little more easily now, so maybe the cache of treasure it was concealing was obstructing it before – and draw the rug back over it. Grace is sleeping soundly, lying on her back with her arms outstretched in peaceful abandon, none the worse for our morning's adventures. I gather up the box and the notebook and go quietly downstairs.

Alia has set a tray on the table in the drawing room. The jug of iced water, spiked with mint and lemon, is misted with condensation and little cold drops drip on to my hand as I pour myself a glass. Then I curl my legs beneath me on the sofa and, with just one more brief twinge of guilt at snooping in someone else's private journal, I start to read.

Josie's Journal – Wednesday
1ˢᵗ January, 1941

My New Year's Resolutions.

I, Josie Duval, hereby resolve to:

Write in English to practise for living in America.

Stop biting my fingernails.

Be nice to Annette, even when she isn't nice to me.

-x-

Papa gave me this journal for Christmas. We get to celebrate it because he is a Catholic, although he says he lapsed when he fell in love with a certain beautiful Jewish woman. In other words, Maman. But he still likes to celebrate at Christmastime. We light the Hanukkah candles as well, even though Maman has lapsed too. Papa says it's the best of both worlds and we're hedging our bets.

I want to be a writer when I grow up, so this journal will be a good way to begin my career, even though I'm still not quite 13.

I love reading SO much. Annette says I'm precocious because I always have my nose buried in a book. But then she rarely reads anything more taxing than the latest Hollywood movie magazine and I'd rather be precocious than only ever thinking about film stars and boys and hairdos.

I can read a whole book in a day if I'm not interrupted too many times by annoying things like having to tidy my room and go to the shops with Maman and Annette. When we left Paris, I was only allowed to bring one book with me, though. We couldn't bring any of our other books with us, they were too heavy and there was already no room left in the trunk because of all Annette's things. It was awful having to choose and leaving so many of my favourites behind. That was the only time I cried. I brought the copy of La Fontaine's *Fables* that had belonged to Papa when he was a boy and which helped me learn to read when I was little. I've taken such good care of it that it still has its paper dust jacket with the picture of the Town Mouse and the Country Mouse on it. I've read it so often that I know most of the fables off by heart. I'll need to try and lay my hands on some more books now that we're settled in our new home.

It's been a very strange Christmas this year, now we are living in Casablanca. It's hot and sunny here even in the winter and we have had very few presents. It feels like we've reached the end of the line, like if we take one step further we will fall off the edge into the ocean. I can see a glimpse of it from my bedroom window in the distance beyond the rooftops of the city, the wide, blue Atlantic. So near and yet so far. We are waiting here for a ship to take us to Portugal and then from there we can get to America. We just need to get the papers organised. Maman says it's going to take an age.

Paris seems an awfully long way away. Which it is. We've travelled more than 2,000 kilometres to get here and there will be about another 6,000 to go to get to America, Papa says. I can't even imagine what it will be like to travel such a distance, although I can picture the globe on the library shelf back home and remember how I used to make it spin, my finger tracing a line around the curved expanse of empty blue printed with the words *Océan Atlantique*. It's a shame the globe was too big to bring with us. It probably would have come in handy now that we are world travellers.

I wonder where Uncle Joseph and Aunt Paulette and their boys are now. They are travelling too. They used to live in Alsace, near the German border, but Maman received a letter from them a few weeks before we left saying they had decided to pack up and leave because things were getting so dangerous for Jewish families there. We don't know where they went. But I hope they are on their way to America too and we will see them again there, despite the fact that my cousins are practically the most annoying people on earth sometimes. When they used to come and visit us in Paris, I was always the one who was made to entertain them and share my books and toys, even though they are years younger than me, while Annette was allowed to sit in the *salon* with the grown-ups, sipping tea and looking smug.

Our new home on the Boulevard des Oiseaux looks quite like our old one in Neuilly, just a bit smaller and an awful lot dustier. But it smells different here, of sweat and heat and spices and the rotting rubbish that lies in the streets. I don't mind it, but Annette wrinkles up her nose and looks like she's about to throw up whenever we go out. It's a lot better than the refugee camp, though, even Annette has to agree about that. Many of the signs here are in French so we can understand them easily. Morocco is a protectorate of France, or at least it was until France was taken over by the Germans, so now I suppose Morocco has been taken over by Germany too. Papa says there is a new government in Vichy, which has responsibility for here as well, but it's not the proper French government. There are German army trucks on the streets and it feels quite frightening to see them, but they aren't bothering much with people like us. Along with the Italians, they have to defend the desert against the English, who own some other parts of North Africa. So they leave the refugees alone, as long as we are just passing through and we don't cause any trouble.

Maman says 'just passing through' is a relative term. Some people have been here for nearly a year already, trying to get their papers organised. We are going to need exit visas for Morocco and then transit visas for Portugal and entry visas for America. Trying to get all of that paperwork lined up is causing Papa's hair to fall out, he says. It is quite white nowadays and definitely thinner on top so maybe he's right. We're lucky that Maman's parents were American so we have relations who will help us when we get there. And now I think we're lucky that she taught us to speak English as well as French when we were little, even if it was a bit annoying at the time and Annette always used to laugh at me when I got my words muddled up.

I've chosen my room at the top of the house. I have a little bathroom of my own up here so I don't have to wait for ages while Annette uses the big one downstairs. She's so selfish. Maman says it's her age and that when I'm 17 I will spend more time washing my hair and filing my nails like she does, but I don't think I'll ever be that vain. And in any case I bite my fingernails, so there's never anything to file. She's started plucking her eyebrows, too, to look like the photos of Hedy Lamarr in the movie magazines, but I think it just makes her look like she's surprised the whole time.

Annette likes to claim she's 5 years older than me, but she's not, it's only 4 years and 7 months. She spends all her time these days when she's not washing her hair or filing her nails pining for Édouard. He used to take her to dances in Paris but his family stayed behind when the Germans came. Annette says we should have stayed too, because they didn't bomb the city like everyone said they were going to, and Papa's bank has reopened now, even if they have put Monsieur Albert in charge in his place. It would still be too risky to return now, though. Jews are most certainly not welcome in France, even lapsed ones.

Annette laughed when I chose my bedroom upstairs because she says I'm in the servants' quarters and that's where I belong, but I don't care. It's my own private space up here. We can't afford servants who live in nowadays, but we have our Housekeeper, Kenza, because her services are included with the rent. She lives in her own house in the medina and comes here each day. She has a daughter about my age called Nina and sometimes she comes too. We speak French to each other and I think she could be my friend.

I like Kenza very much. She has comfortable curves beneath the long robes she wears and her eyes are wise and kind. She cooks the most delicious meals for us and bakes cakes. She always gives me a little slice of honey cake warm from the oven if I pop down to see her in the kitchen. She calls me *Khadar Ini*, which means Green Eyes in Darija, the kind of Arabic they speak in Morocco.

Annette says having green eyes is a bad thing because it means I'm jealous and jealousy is one of the Seven Deadly Sins. But really I know she's the one who's jealous because her eyes are more of a browny-hazel colour like Papa's and she wishes they were clear green like mine and Maman's.

I love my new journal. Papa told me it's for me to write my life story in. He knows I want to be a writer, and he says it's also good to write things down because then you don't have to carry them around in your head all the time and that it might help me not to have so many bad dreams. It's my best Christmas present. This year we got dresses made of silk because the big trunk with all our good clothes went missing somewhere in Marseille, or maybe on the way to Algeria. Anyway, it wasn't there when we got off the boat in Oran. Maman says we'll need something to wear when we go out now that we have a proper home again, because the one thing Casablanca does have is a social life. The hotels and bars are full of people, some who live and work here and many who are just passing through like us. There are even tea dances at the Hotel Excelsior on Saturday afternoons, so those might cheer Annette up a bit. Even though my dress is nice and I know it must have cost a lot, it was a bit of a boring present. My new notebook and the little basket of sugared almonds were better.

I'm going to go to sleep now. We stayed up late last night to celebrate the arrival of the new year. I wore my new dress and I was allowed a glass of champagne. It didn't taste as nice as lemonade really, but everyone was making a big fuss about it so I pretended to enjoy it. It's the start of our new life too. I'm sad to have left France, but excited to be going to America to meet my cousins there. Maybe when the war is over we will go back to Paris and I'll see my friends again. I suppose many of them will have left too. I hope they are all right and have somewhere safe to go like us. I'm sending them good wishes now. I hope I'll sleep well tonight now that I've started writing things down in my journal.

Goodnight.

Zoe – 2010

The ringing of the phone jolts me out of Josie's world, back to my own. Reluctantly, I set the journal aside and go to answer it. It's May.

'Just checking in. How's the nesting going? Are you starting to feel a bit more settled?'

I'm not sure 'settled' describes how I feel. The experience of my morning walk has shaken my confidence badly, making me realise how completely out of my depth I am here and leaving me with the impression that I'll never get the hang of this new place. As well as that, though, Josie's journal has pushed ajar a door on to another world, one I hadn't realised existed. Other than watching the famous movie, I suppose I hadn't thought much about what Casablanca must have been like in the war years. I glance longingly at the leather-bound notebook lying on the coffee table. I want to read on, to find out more about Josie and her family in those extraordinary times. But, for now, I thank May and tell her that I'm doing fine.

'Grand, I'm pleased to hear that,' she replies. 'I'm phoning to let you know I've managed to get some of the girls together for a lunch at the Club next Wednesday. I hope that still suits? Kate will be coming and she's happy to talk to you about that quilting project you mentioned. She's delighted to have another crafter on board.

And sometime before that it'd be good to go for a drive around the city, like I promised, to show you where things are. We could have a cup of coffee afterwards, maybe? Would you be free tomorrow morning?'

'That'd be lovely,' I say, and I mean it. Distracted as I am these days, I know when I meet people I can come across as a bit distant and stand-offish. The person I've become isn't someone you'd naturally warm to, very unlike the warm, carefree woman I used to be. I am truly grateful to May for the effort she's making to include me and help me adapt to the expat life here. It'll be good to meet her friends too, to get involved in things outside this house. And I know that will please Tom. I imagine how I'll tell him about these arrangements over supper tonight, presenting them to him like a gift. For a moment his expression will relax into a smile at this sign that I'm making an effort, getting into some sort of social life. But then the silence will fall between the two of us again, he'll reach for the bottle and pour himself another glass of wine and the darkness of his preoccupations will resettle itself on his face like a flock of crows coming back to their evening roost.

Even though I expect the lunch will be something of a trial, I'm looking forward to meeting the other wives. Perhaps they'll know something of the history of Casablanca, be able to tell me more about what the city would have been like in Josie's time.

I hang up, having arranged that May will call by at eight-thirty tomorrow morning. Alia knocks softly on the door. 'Mrs Harris, may I clear the tray now?'

'Please do. And Alia, please call me Zoe. Mrs Harris makes me think my mother-in-law must be in the room.' To my ears, my voice sounds forced, trying too hard. There's that sense of awkwardness again at having a housekeeper when I would probably manage just fine without any help in the house. After all, it's not as if I have a job to go to, now that I've joined the ranks of expat ladies-who-lunch. But Alia is a real blessing, with her delicious cooking and the way she keeps the house so much tidier than I would. I'd completely trust her to babysit Grace, too, and in fact I find her calm, unobtrusive presence even more of a comfort after she rescued me from my foray into the outside world. It's reassuring having her here, making my days not quite so lonely.

'Very well, Mrs Zoe,' she replies. I smile. That seems to be about as far as she's prepared to compromise, but at least it's a little less formal than Mrs Harris. 'And would you like me to clean in here today? The dust is bad when the chergui has been blowing from the desert. Even with the shutters closed, it still manages to find its way in.' She runs a finger along the beading framing the wall tiles to show me.

'Thank you very much, Alia, that would be great.' She leaves to fetch her bucket of cleaning things and I gather up the inlaid box and the notebook, heading back upstairs to get out of her way and read some more.

Josie's Journal – Monday 6th January, 1941

Papa has gone to queue at the American consulate, which is where you have to go to get given a visa. But first you have to have the correct forms and write down who your sponsors will be when you get to America. He's already filled those in, but we haven't heard anything for months now. Maybe it's because all the offices were so busy with all the refugees arriving from Europe and then they closed for Christmas. Papa has gone to see if he can speak to someone to find out. Then Maman and Papa will go for an interview and we'll all have to have our medical examinations and after that we get our visa. Once we have the American visa we'll be able to apply for our transit visas for Portugal and then finally our exit permit for Morocco. It was hard enough getting our *permis de séjour* to let us stay in Casablanca while we're trying to get everything else arranged. With all these permits, it's no wonder poor Papa's hair really is falling out. He now has a definite bald patch on the top, which I noticed the other day when I was coming down the stairs and he was standing in the hall below, reading the headlines in his newspaper.

When we left Paris we didn't apply for any permits. It happened quite quickly. Papa came home from the bank one day and told Maman to pack as much as she could. The Nazis had entered France and it was time for us to leave. It was all such a rush that I scarcely had the time to feel anxious.

We went on the train to Marseille and I quite liked that part of the journey. I held on tight to my book, and it was comforting reading the words of those familiar stories. After a while, I put La Fontaine away safely in my bag, and watched the French country-side rolling past outside the window. I pretended we were going on our summer holiday to the Côte d'Azur, just like we'd done the year before. I ignored Annette, who was sniffling into Maman's shoulder because she didn't want to leave Édouard. And I ignored the people crowded into the corridor outside our compartment, because that side of things made me feel a bit scared and I knew I had to be brave. But I also knew that sulking and moping, like some people I could mention, wasn't going to help.

Even Annette pulled herself together a little when we reached Marseille. It was pandemonium. Everyone was scrambling to try to get to the port. Papa paid two men to find us a taxi and bring our luggage. That's where I think the trunk went missing, even though the men assured us they'd delivered everything to the correct ship so that Papa would give them a tip.

We were some of the lucky ones because Papa had enough money to pay for things like porters and taxis and tickets and even to give certain officials a tip to make sure we got a cabin. There were crowds and crowds of people at the station and at the port and most of them seemed to be very frightened and angry. And some of them didn't have the money to make sure they could get on the ship. I don't know what happened to them. Maybe they just stayed in Marseille. Or maybe they decided to go somewhere else instead, like Italy or Spain. There was a family with a girl about my age – she looked friendly and we'd smiled at each other when we were in the queue waiting to have our passports stamped – but they didn't get on the boat. I looked back when we were going up the gangway and there she was, standing on the quay, watching me go. Even though I never really knew her, I still see her face in my dreams sometimes and I wonder where she is now. Perhaps her family managed to get on another ship and one of these days I'll bump into her in the Place de France here in Casablanca. That would be nice.

Our ship finally departed in the middle of the night. It was so late Maman was starting to panic that it wasn't going to leave at all. It was too hot in the cabin, and it smelled of engine oil and vomit, so Papa and I went up on deck. We found a little corner near the back of the ship – there were people sleeping everywhere – and I leaned against him as we watched the lights of Marseille disappear. It was comforting to have Papa's arm around me and to breathe in his smell of cigars and soap, even if we were all a bit dirty and dishevelled by then. The sea was as dark as Maman's black velvet evening gown, but the night sky was full of millions of stars – way more than I'd ever seen in Paris. I touched the little gold star that hangs around my neck and somehow it was reassuring to feel that it connected me to all those stars above us.

Papa told me to try and get some sleep because we'd still have some long days of travelling ahead of us when we got to Algeria. But I think he and I both just stayed awake watching those millions of stars and wondering what lay in store for us when we reached Africa. A whole new continent!

What did lie in store for us was the Aïn Chok refugee camp. But I'm jumping ahead.

First we disembarked from the ship at Oran and had to stand in line for hours and hours in the customs house, which was a bit like being put in an oven to be cooked like a rotisserie chicken. At the start people were quite noisy, complaining and calling out to the officials who were checking papers and reorganising the queues into different lines for reasons that must have been clear to them but seemed quite confusing to the rest of us. But as the day wore on and it got hotter and hotter, a thick, heavy silence fell over us all. Occasionally a baby would whimper, and a woman behind us made a strange noise like a balloon deflating when she fainted and had to be revived with smelling salts and a cup of water, but otherwise there was no noise at all. We just quietly waited and cooked.

At last we reached the front of the queue and had our papers checked. Then we were told to stand in another line for a few more hours. At long last we were allowed to get on a bus. Soldiers from the French Foreign Legion stood alongside it and made sure everyone did as they'd been told by the officials in the customs house. One of the soldiers looked at Annette in a way that made her stand up a bit straighter and smooth her hair back into place. When we got on the bus, two more of the soldiers got on too and sat at the front with their guns. I noticed that Annette opened her purse and put a bit of powder on her nose when she thought no one was looking. That was an improvement, actually, because it was very red and shiny from all her crying.

I slept for quite a lot of the bus journey, which took another whole night. I think it was mostly desert outside so there wasn't much to look at in any case, even if it hadn't been pitch-dark again.

When I woke up, we were driving through city streets lined with palm trees. Maman smiled at me and nodded, saying, 'Casablanca.'

My first impression was of the whiteness that gives the city its name – we drove past low white houses and taller white buildings. But then I noticed that everywhere there were splashes of colour – green, red, orange and pink – from gardens filled with flowers. I felt quite reassured then – it reminded me a little bit of the Côte d'Azur. I pressed my cheek against the dusty glass of the window and looked at those gardens and at the people too as they walked along the streets, women veiled from head to toe in black and tough-looking men in white robes, all oblivious to the busloads of refugees that were sweeping past them. But then we started to leave the city streets behind and the buses drove along a much bumpier road, making dust clouds billow out from beneath the wheels, and there were no more flower-filled gardens, just sand and scrappy-looking shacks where half-starved cats slunk among piles of garbage.

Everyone on the bus got very quiet again then and I didn't feel so reassured after all.

At last we arrived at the gates of the camp. The buses drew to a halt and the dust slowly settled around us. The soldiers got out of ours and went to talk to some others who were guarding the gate. They waved us through, but still no one spoke a word until we pulled up in front of a big building. A few people stood up and began collecting their things together, but the driver told them to sit back down and wait, which made everyone groan. We all just wanted to stretch our legs by then, not to mention badly needing a bathroom. I pictured the luxury of a lavatory and a basin with taps, basic things I'd completely taken for granted in Paris. But when at last we were shown to our place in the hall, there was only a bucket behind a curtain. Flies buzzed everywhere, but especially around that bucket.

Annette crinkled up her nose and she started to cry again when she saw the mattresses on the floor that were to be our new home in Morocco. 'Don't worry, *ma chère*,' Papa said, stroking her back as Maman hugged her tight (I think she might have been crying too). 'We won't be here for long. This is just temporary until they can find proper places for us all. I'll go and look for someone to speak to straight away.' I wanted to go with him, but he told me to stay and look after Maman and Annette. 'Talk to some of the others,' he said. 'See what you can find out about how things run here.'

It was so hot and smelly in the hall that most people had gone outside, so I decided that would be the best place to go and try to find someone to talk to once Maman and Annette had settled themselves a bit. I took my book, so it would look as if I was just casually doing some peaceful reading, and went to try and find a place to sit in the shade, only in the camp there weren't any shady trees or comfortable benches to sit on like the parks in Paris. So I found a patch of hard ground instead, against the wall of the building out of the sun, and sat down and watched some boys kicking a football around in the dust.

After a while, the boys noticed me and one of them deliberately kicked the ball right at me. My reflexes are quick, though, and I managed to catch it. The boys shouted at me to throw it back, but I just glared at them and shouted back, 'If you want it, you'll have to come and ask politely.' There's never any excuse for bad manners, as Maman frequently reminds us. The boy who'd kicked it at me came storming over and demanded I hand it over. 'Only if you don't aim it at innocent bystanders again,' I said defiantly. You can't let bullies get away with that sort of behaviour, as I have learned from my reading.

Some of the other boys came over too, and one of them, with a broken tooth, apologised and asked nicely if I would please return it. I was about to throw the ball to him when, to my absolute horror, the bully spotted my book on the ground beside me and grabbed it. 'A hostage!' he cried triumphantly. 'You want your book back then you give us back our ball.'

I leapt to my feet and let the ball fall on the ground. Tears of rage and pain sprang into my eyes as he held my precious book above his head, beyond my reach, laughing and jeering. He was taller than me and a few years older and a truly horrible specimen. As he waved the book about, trying to make me jump for it, the dust jacket came loose and tore and the hot wind snatched it, blowing it across the patch of bare ground and on to the barbed wire of the fence surrounding the camp, where it got stuck.

I was really crying now. I was about to start hitting the bully with my fists when the boy with the broken tooth stepped in and took the book from his hand. 'Give it back to her. We have the ball now anyway. Come on, the others are waiting to get on with the game.'

The bully turned and spat at the feet of the book-rescuer. For a moment I thought he was going to start on him – and he was a lot bigger and heavier than either of us – but in the end he turned away and went back to join his friends.

The boy with the broken tooth handed me back the book. I wiped my eyes on my sleeve and thanked him. Then I started to set off towards the barbed wire fence to try to retrieve the dust jacket.

'Stop!' The boy grabbed my arm.

I tried to shake him off. 'Let me go,' I protested. 'I need to get that back.'

'You can't. It's dangerous to go near the fence. The soldiers keep everyone away from it, look.' Sure enough, a guard with a gun was patrolling there. 'Let it go,' the boy said. 'At least the book itself wasn't damaged so you can still read it. That old cover is all torn now, in any case.'

The tears came back into my eyes at the thought of losing a part of my papa's book that I had always taken such good care of, the only book I had left in the world. But the boy was right, I still had the rest of it, and I knew I needed to pull myself together if I was going to be able to survive in that camp. He handed me a rather dirty handkerchief so that I could blow my nose and then he smiled at me kindly. 'It looks like a good book,' he said. 'Want to tell me more about it?'

'Don't they need you back on the football team?' I said, not wanting to have anything to do with someone who was friends with that bully.

He shook his head. 'I don't like them much, and they're rubbish at football in any case.'

So that was when I made friends with Felix Adler, who had come to Morocco from Vienna via France. He had a cheerful smile made a bit lopsided by that broken tooth, which he told me was as a result of an accident with a swing in the park back at home. He and his parents had been in the refugee camp for a couple of weeks already. He told me it was called Aïn Chok and that some people had been there for months. But he also told me there was a committee run by a kind lady called Madame Bénatar who was Moroccan but Jewish as well and that Papa should speak to her if he could. She was very good at organising places in the city of Casablanca for people like us to live. Some people took refugees into their own homes, especially in the mellah, which is the name for the Jewish Quarter, even if they didn't have much space themselves. Felix and his parents were hoping to move to such a place soon.

I was happy to be able to report this important information to Papa when he returned and he smiled and kissed the top of my head. 'Well done, that is very helpful to know. Don't worry, *ma p'tite*, we'll find a place of our own to rent.' I realised that money was going to help us again.

But even with our good fortune it still took a while to find somewhere for us to live and be allowed to leave the camp once we had our *permis de séjour*, which Madame Bénatar helped us get. And in the meantime we quickly discovered that the annoying buzzing of the daytime flies was replaced at night by the high-pitched whining of swarms of mosquitoes that liked to spend the hours of darkness feasting on the blood of exhausted refugees. Between the bugs and the crying babies and the whispered arguments between some of the grown-ups in the hall, no one managed to get much sleep.

Felix got teased in the camp because of his broken tooth. Some of those other dreadful boys called him *Croc*, which means 'fang' in French. He didn't care, though. He told me that when he got to America he would get his tooth fixed and then his smile would be as perfect as a movie star's. I didn't mind his imperfect smile really, because the thing you noticed most was the way his eyes smiled too and so that broken tooth didn't seem to matter at all.

A few days after we met, he came over to our corner of the hall one evening. He had something behind his back and he was looking very shy all of a sudden. Then he handed me the dust jacket with the Town Mouse and the Country Mouse on it. He'd managed to get it back from where it was stuck on the fence when the guards weren't looking, he told me, and he'd done a pretty good job of mending it, sticking the torn pieces on to a sheet of old newspaper with some glue he'd made from flour, which he'd begged from the kitchen, and water. I couldn't believe how kind he was, risking his neck for me like that, and I gave him a hug as now I knew he was a true friend. Felix's face went pink with embarrassment, but he seemed pleased that he'd made me so happy, too. I wrapped the cover around my book and it looked good there, bearing its battle scars but back where it belonged.

Most of the time it was very boring spending long hours in the camp with nothing much to do. Papa invented a game for us to play to help pass some of the long hours in the middle of the day when it was too hot to be outside and we had to retreat to our mattresses on the floor of the hall again. It was a bit like I Spy, only there wasn't anything very interesting to spy in the hall, just lots of unhappy people waiting to get out of there. In Papa's version, you said the initials of the things you most wanted to get when you got out of the camp and the others had to guess what it might be. The first time we played, mine was ice cream. Annette's was a bottle of Studio Girl shampoo. Maman said hers was a mosquito net for each of us. It took us longer to guess Papa's because it turned out to be a bottle of Chanel No 5 perfume so that he could give it to Maman to remind her of Paris. She got tears in her eyes when we finally worked it out and she had to blow her nose quite a lot.

Felix had swapped his mattress for one next to ours – he seemed to find my family more interesting than his own and his parents didn't appear to mind – so he played too. He wanted a penknife and some sweets.

When we were finally allowed to leave the camp and Papa brought us to our new home here on the Boulevard des Oiseaux, he had surprises waiting for us. Like a magician, from behind his back he produced a bottle of the shampoo for Annette and the perfume for Maman. Then he showed us our beds and each one was draped with its own mosquito net, even though there aren't nearly so many bugs in the new house as there were at Aïn Chok. And then he offered me his arm and we walked along the street to a café, where he bought me the biggest ice cream I've ever seen, piled into a coupe glass and topped with honeyed almonds and chocolate sauce. He had one too.

I wished we could have offered Felix's family a room in our new home, but Papa said he'd spoken to Madame Bénatar and she'd assured him she'd found them a place in the house of friends of hers in the mellah. When we left the camp, Felix told me he'd come and visit us sometimes, but he hasn't done so yet. I expect he's busy making new friends. I hope perhaps he got a penknife and some sweets for Hanukkah – his I-Spy things.

I think I can smell the delicious scent of baking coming up the stairs so I'm going to go and see Kenza in the kitchen now. I've written so much that my hand is aching, but that is the story so far of how we came to be here. I'll write more another day.

Zoe – 2010

May drives us around the city in her air-conditioned BMW – a far more comfortable way to tour it than my walk yesterday. I'm thankful to give my feet a rest as they're still pretty sore and there's a large blister on my right heel. As she points out the sights, I wriggle my toes in the chilled air emanating from beneath the dashboard. I've left Grace at home with Alia for the first time, but I don't feel as anxious as I'd thought I would. I know my baby's in good hands.

The first impression you get of the city is of chaos and grime and peeling façades. It's only when you look a little more closely that you start to see the wrought ironwork, the old-fashioned signs on the shops and the beautifully crafted detailing that adorns the stonework of many of the neglected buildings. We bypass the medina, where I got lost. I doubt May's car would fit down its narrow streets and alleyways. She points out the Quartier Habous with its Moorish archways, explaining how it was conceived and planned by the French when they colonised the city. It's a newer version of the ancient medina, built for the tourists and the expats so that they can enjoy a similar experience, but with safer streets and a less bewildering layout of shops and stalls.

'So it's a kind of sanitised version of the original?' I ask.

'Well, yes.' May shrugs. 'But you wouldn't be wanting to go into the real medina in any case now, would you? It's just dirty and dangerous.'

I bite my lip, remembering the goat in the gutter and the toothless man selling his strange remedies, and say nothing.

We sweep towards the ocean and I crane my neck to look up at the tower of the Hassan II Mosque, the pure whiteness of its stonework dazzling and dizzying against the blue of the sky. Then we swing on to the corniche, passing the spot where I stood yesterday showing Grace the waves. The beachfront is lined with clubs and restaurants – including the Overseas Club, where we'll be having lunch next week – but May continues on to the mall and pulls up in the multi-storey car park. The existing shopping centre is being replaced by something much larger – May says it's going to be one of the biggest shopping malls in Africa – and the din of the vast building site reverberates on the hot, dusty air.

Once inside, it's much more peaceful as we stroll through the arcades of shops. Canned music floats on the artificially chilled atmosphere and the skin of my arms prickles with goosebumps as we wander past shopfronts displaying brands that are recognisable the whole world over. The glitzy luxury is a little overwhelming and I find myself longing for the simplicity of the bakery on the corner of the Boulevard des Oiseaux in the heat of the sunlit city.

We pass a pharmacy and I pop in to buy some more hand sanitiser and bottles of baby shampoo and lotion. I tend to use them myself too these days, because they're less harsh on my sore skin than other brands.

At last we settle at a table in one of the mall's many coffee shops, ordering cappuccinos and Danish pastries.

'Do you ever go to any of the cafés in the *nouvelle ville*?' I ask.

May looks a little doubtful. 'Occasionally. But you're more likely to get hassled there. In any case, we're usually either shopping here or socialising at the Club.' She gives me a sympathetic smile. 'I think we all have quite a romantic image of Casa in our heads when we first get here.' She laughs. 'That movie has a lot to answer for! But we very quickly find out that Humphrey Bogart and Ingrid Bergman are long gone and it's a completely different city nowadays. You've seen enough of it yourself this morning to realise it's now mostly urban sprawl, much of it fairly shabby and unattractive. The port has become far more important, commercially speaking, since the days of Bogart and Bergman – after all, none of us would be here otherwise, would we? Casa is just a big, commercial city these days. The romantic notions very quickly wear off, you'll find, and then the familiarity of places like this' – she waves a hand to encompass the bright lights of the shops, the piped music, the chilled air and a man in grey overalls who's sweeping the already pristine white marble floor tiles – 'becomes a comfort.' She pauses to stir the froth in her coffee cup.

It's not so much the Casablanca of movie fame I want to explore, although I don't say so to May. It's Josie's world that's captured my imagination. But it feels like something private and I'm not ready to share it with anyone else.

May takes a sip of her coffee and blots the foam from her mouth carefully with a paper napkin so as not to smudge her lipstick. 'If you want a little more local colour then we could organise a trip to the Habous. But the best places to go to experience traditional Moroccan culture are the other cities, like Fez and Rabat. You and Tom should plan a few weekends away maybe. How's he getting on in the new job, anyway?'

We move on to discussing husbands. May's is something high up in insurance, associated with shipping, so she knows all about Tom's role.

Once we've finished our coffees, I glance at my watch. I'll need to be getting back for Grace shortly, although I'm sure Alia is a completely trustworthy babysitter. May insists on settling the bill and then drives me home.

'Let me know if you're planning a weekend in Fez,' she says as we pull up at my front door. 'I can give you the details of the loveliest riad right in the centre. It would probably do you and that handsome husband of yours the world of good to have a romantic getaway.' She reaches over and gives my hand a little sympathetic pat.

I smile and nod, and thank her for showing me around. But, as she drives away, I can't help wondering about that gesture and what she might have heard about us.

Josie's Journal – Thursday 16th January, 1941

Maman took Annette and me shopping in the Habous this morning, which is a place where there are lots of different kinds of traditional shops all crammed together. Before we left the house, though, she told me to take off my necklace.

'But why?' I asked. I've worn the little gold Star of David ever since Maman gave it to me for my twelfth birthday last year. It belonged to her once, although she stopped wearing it when she married Papa. She'd noticed how I especially used to love it when she let me play with the things in her jewellery box while she was putting on her make-up and doing her hair, as long as I was very careful and put everything back neatly afterwards.

'Because it's best not to advertise things like that these days,' was her reply. 'We're not a particularly religious family, in any case, so there's no point looking for trouble.'

I didn't need to ask her what kind of trouble. I've seen the same stars painted roughly on the doors of certain shops and houses, along with the printed notices pasted on to walls and even some shop windows saying that, by order of the Préfecture de Police, Jewish businesses are to be avoided and Jewish people have to obey certain rules. It frightened me a bit the first time I saw a notice like that here in Casablanca. But Papa told me that Morocco is ruled not only by the Vichy government but also by a Sultan called Mohammed the Fifth. He is a kind person and as well as being a Sultan he is also called Defender of the Faith. He has said that <u>all</u> the faiths are to be respected in his country. He told Marshal Pétain and the Nazis, 'There are no Jews in Morocco. There are only Moroccan subjects.' It cheered me up a bit when Papa told me that because whenever I saw the notices I thought about Felix and how the smile would go out of his eyes if he read those hateful words. I hope he knows what the Sultan has said. Papa says kindness is one of the most important things in the world but a lot of people seem to have forgotten that nowadays. I gave Annette a meaningful look at that point but she just ignored me as usual.

When we got to the Habous, Maman gave me some pocket money to spend however I wanted. I spotted a beautiful wooden box on one of the stalls, inlaid with mother-of-pearl in a design a little like the tiles on the floor in our house. First of all, the man behind the stall told me it cost way more than I could afford. But Annette gave me a nudge and told me to haggle a bit. The man thought it was quite funny that I asked for a much lower price and at first he refused, but he let me hold the box and showed me what excellent quality it was. I agreed that it was indeed, but then I showed him all my pocket money, which was 5 francs. He told me to ask my beautiful sister to give me some more money but Annette said, 'No way!' I put the box back down on the stall then and started to walk away, but the man saw how disappointed I was and he called me back. 'Okay, okay,' he said. 'We have a deal.'

I'm so happy with my beautiful wooden box. It smells like the Habous (the best bits, not the stinky goat hides and the places where stray dogs have peed) – which is to say of soft spices and fragrant oils. Maman says it's made of a kind of wood called sandalwood and it will always have that smell. I've put the gold star necklace in it to keep it safe while I can't wear it. I think it's a very good place for it.

When I got home I showed my new box to Kenza and Nina and they agreed it was an excellent purchase. Next time I get some pocket money I'll go back to the same stall and buy another one like it for Nina. She and I are friends now. We still mostly talk in French, but I'm teaching her a few words of English too. You never know when it might come in handy. Her eyes are as warm and kind as her mother's and she laughs a good deal, especially when I tell her what life used to be like in Paris before the war turned everything upside down. I used to have to go to deportment classes where I had to practise walking up and down with a heavy Larousse dictionary on my head. She finds that very funny. Once, when everyone else was out at a tea dance, I showed Nina all Annette's bottles and jars lined up on the shelf in the bathroom. Nina tried on a little rouge and I put on some lipstick. We both found that completely hilarious.

She and I like playing hopscotch in the courtyard behind the house. It's nice and shady there. There's a pomegranate tree and the air smells of the jasmine that scrambles up the walls and over a trellised archway. I brought my skipping rope with me from home and we take it in turns to see who can keep jumping the longest. I'm winning at the moment, but Nina is getting pretty good at it so she'll probably overtake me one of these days. I let her take the skipping rope home with her sometimes so she can practise.

After we've finished our skipping and hopscotch, Kenza gives us lemonade and soft cookies called *ghoribas* in the kitchen. That's one of my favourite times of day.

When Papa got back from waiting in line at the American consulate he looked tired and a bit preoccupied, but he says he quite likes spending time in the queue because you meet all sorts of other interesting people with stories to tell. People have come here from all over Europe, escaping from the war. Some of them will have had a hard time, I think, with all the unkindness that's around at the moment, but Papa doesn't tell me those sorts of stories. Instead he told me a funny one about a lady who had managed to travel to Casablanca with her little dog, which was a poodle called Minou. Both Minou and the lady had the same hairstyle, although the lady's was a delicate shade of blue and Minou's was pure white. She was giving the American officials a hard time because she was demanding a visa for her dog as well as for herself. The story was funny up to that point. But you can't actually get visas for dogs, that's why so many of them get left behind and become strays. Then the story became quite sad because I think the lady and Minou will have to stay here in Casablanca for ever. At least the lady will be happy to be with her dog. I'm very glad Minou won't get left behind.

I hope they won't be sent back to France, though.

I asked Papa if he's ever bumped into Felix's parents at the consulate but he hasn't. He says he'll keep an eye out for them, though, next time he goes.

After some mint tea, Papa picked up his hat and told Maman he was going out again. When she asked him where he was off to, he said he'd met an interesting man at the consulate who had told him about a group that meets in the mellah to discuss current affairs. Maman raised her eyebrows quite high at that and told Papa to be careful if he was planning on spending time in the Jewish Quarter. He just smiled and gave her a kiss, saying she shouldn't worry so much and he'd be back in time for supper. But I could tell she really was still a bit worried, even though I can't see what's wrong with talking about boring things like the war if Papa really wants to. We already hear more than enough about it on the radio every day in my opinion. We're supposed to listen to Radio Maroc, but sometimes Papa listens to the BBC, which is from England and

41

tells quite a different story about how the war is going. I used to think the news was about reporting all the facts, but if you listen to those two different radio stations you soon learn otherwise.

There are French police and German Gestapo officers all over the city and if they catch you listening to the BBC you'll be in big trouble.

Tomorrow Maman is taking me and Annette to the cinema to see *Rebecca*. Annette says everyone at the tea dance was talking about it. I suppose she'll be trying to look like Joan Fontaine next. She's already mooning around over pictures of Laurence Olivier and sighing like a sick horse.

Josie's Journal – Friday 17th January, 1941

We almost didn't get to go to the cinema today because of what happened to Papa yesterday. I thought Maman might actually refuse to let any of us ever leave the house again, she was so angry and upset and shaken. To be honest, I wouldn't have blamed her if she had – it was a terrifying ordeal for all of us.

There was a knock at the door and Kenza went to answer it as usual. At first I thought it must be Papa back from his boring meeting in the mellah, having forgotten his key. But then Kenza appeared in the salon where Maman, Annette and I were sitting and she looked worried. She handed Maman a folded note and said a man had asked that it be delivered to Madame Duval immediately. When Maman read it, her face went completely white and she leapt to her feet, not even noticing when her book tumbled to the floor.

'Maman?' Annette said. 'What is it?'

'It's Papa,' she replied, and her mouth was trembling so much that the words came out as if she was crying. 'He's been arrested. I have to go to the police station immediately.'

Kenza hurried away and came back with Maman's bag and jacket. She told Maman not to worry, that she would stay with me and Annette. We're old enough to be left on our own, but it was very kind of her because I was feeling awfully scared and it was reassuring having her there, even though it meant she would be late getting home to her own family.

Kenza made some supper for me and Annette but we couldn't really eat anything because our stomachs were tied up in knots, waiting for Papa and Maman to come home. I remembered how Maman hadn't wanted him to spend time in the mellah and I wondered what that meeting had really been about. Anyway, after what felt like an eternity but was actually only about 2 hours, the front door opened and in they walked. Papa was trying to be cheerful and make out that there was nothing to worry about, but it must have been very frightening for him really. I could see from the way her mouth was set in a tight, thin line that Maman was pretty furious. I've noticed she gets like that when she's had a fright, like the time I wandered off in the Galeries Lafayette and got lost: when the store manager finally returned me to her (a shop assistant having taken me under her wing in the hat department when I asked to try on a broad-brimmed creation with a beautiful green feather), Maman didn't know whether to hug me or shout at me. So she did a bit of both, but the shouting didn't last very long and the hugging went on for some time, even when we'd retired to the *salon de thé* and I was trying to eat a chocolate éclair.

I wondered whether she had shouted at Papa or just hugged him, but Maman was in no mood to answer questions and so I kept quiet. Annette told me later that Papa had been arrested along with a whole load of other people at the meeting and that the Gestapo had taken them all in a van to the police station, where they were threatened with being put in prison. The Germans are obviously not at all keen on the idea of people having meetings. Maman had to pay the police quite a lot of money to get him released.

So our good fortune came to the rescue again this time, but I can see how anxious Maman is. It took a lot of courage to walk into the police station when she might have been arrested herself. I suppose if she'd been wearing the necklace with the little gold star, things might not have worked out as they did.

Papa, Annette and I finally managed to convince her that going to the cinema to see *Rebecca* would be a good way of taking all our minds off yesterday's unpleasantness. And thank goodness we did, because I absolutely loved the movie. It's taken from a book and I'm going to try to find out where the library is so I can get hold of it and some others too. I miss the books we left behind so very much. Sometimes I imagine them in our old home alongside the globe, all lined up on their shelves with no one to read them, just spiders creeping over them and nobody there to dust off the cobwebs. That makes me feel quite sad because I always think books have a life of their own and they'll be feeling pretty lonely without us. Perhaps when we get to America we can ask someone to pack them all up and send them to us in our new home.

Zoe – 2010

I'm feeling more and more nervous about meeting May and the other wives at the Club. Pathetic, really, I tell myself. It's not as if I'm having to face the Gestapo, like Madame Duval did.

I make sure I get there a bit early and sign in at the front desk, then quickly head to the ladies' loo. I wash my hands carefully, following the routine that helps me calm my nerves when I'm feeling particularly anxious, using a generous dollop of soap from the dispenser and water as hot as I can bear. Then I repeat the ritual twice over again for good measure – I don't have a nail brush here and you can't be too careful in a public place – and pat the skin dry with a paper towel. The harshness of the soap and hot water leave the scaly patches in the folds of my fingers red and burning, but at least the pain is a sign my hands are properly clean.

After I've combed my hair and touched up my lip gloss, a quick glance at my watch tells me I'm now a polite five minutes late for the lunch. Resisting the urge to wash my hands all over again, I swallow my nerves and head for the terrace overlooking the tennis courts, where May has reserved a table.

'Don't be so stupid,' I admonish the side of myself that baulks at every bit of social contact. 'It's just a friendly lunch.' May's been so kind arranging this gathering. Plus I need help getting started with making the quilt because I haven't a clue where to begin, so I have to do this.

The others are already sitting around the table and May gives me a hug, then makes the introductions. Anneke and Mila, from Rotterdam, have spent the morning having a tennis lesson and a swim. Claudine – from the south of France – looks as if she's just come from the beauty parlour, judging by her immaculate hair and nails, and Kate – the crafting queen bee – has been at a committee meeting that May's hosted at her house. I especially warm to Kate, who is about my age, I think, a few years younger than the others. We're a disparate group, bound together by our foreignness, somehow needing the reassurance of this club with its resemblance to the European countries we've left behind to give us a sense of belonging.

The women are friendly but, as the newcomer, there are the inevitable questions for me to field. Under cover of the white linen tablecloth, I tug nervously at a hangnail on my thumb. We soon begin to discover a few shreds of common ground, though: Kate went to university in Bristol so she knows the city well, and Claudine's husband works in Tom's office at the port. Once the waiter brings our starters, I begin to relax a little.

Kate seems particularly kind. May has told her that I'm interested in learning more about quilting, and she fishes a book from her shoulder bag to lend me.

'This is a good place to start,' she says, turning to a page that lists the equipment quilters use.

'I had no idea I'd be needing all this,' I confess. 'I thought it would just be a question of cutting up pieces of material and sewing them together.'

Kate laughs. 'A few of us make that mistake to start with and learn the hard way. But quilting has its roots in the beauty and precision of geometry. A little bit of planning goes a long way.

Don't worry, though,' she continues. 'You won't need everything on the list to begin with. I'll come with you to the mall – there's a shop there that's good for crafting supplies. I'll help you choose the basics you'll need to get started. There are some fabric stalls in the Habous, too, that I can show you sometime. Do you have anything particular in mind?'

'I've already got the material I want to use to make the main blocks,' I reply.

'Great,' she says. 'Then we can get you started. Later, once you've sewn the blocks, we can visit the fabric stall to get whatever else you need for setting them, and for the sashing and binding.'

I look at her, blankly. She must be able to tell I haven't got a clue what those terms mean because she pats the cover of the book she's lending me. 'Have a read of this before we meet up to go shopping – things will become clearer.'

By the time we've finished our coffees, May has arranged that we'll meet for lunch again at the same time next week, and Claudine says she'll organise a dinner party sometime as they all want to meet Tom too.

I stash Kate's book in my bag. 'See you next week at the mall then.'

She nods. 'And in the meantime, you could wash and starch the material you're planning to use. That will help you when it comes to cutting your pieces. Have a look at the block designs too and see which one you'd like to try. Just remember that simple is good, especially when you're starting out.'

Over supper that evening with Tom, I chat away about my crafting project and my new social life. And even though, to my ears, the tone of my voice sounds a little too artificially bright, I can see the relief in Tom's eyes. He watches me carefully, searching for any signs that the closeness we used to have might stand a chance of being rekindled. Then I ask him about his day and it's his turn to summon up some semblance of enthusiasm as he describes the meetings he's sat through and the challenges of keeping track of the company's fleet of container ships as they navigate the turbulent waters of the world's oceans. His tone seems as falsely upbeat as mine.

We get up from the table and Tom heads off to watch TV, stretched out on the sofa with the rest of the bottle of wine, surfing channels that offer international news and reruns of old American soap operas dubbed into French. I climb the stairs to the attic and pick up the quilting book that Kate lent me.

I think we both know our marriage feels as empty as ever. But at least tonight we've tried.

Josie's Journal – Friday 31st January, 1941

Very annoyingly, Papa and Maman have been discussing my education and they've decided I need an English tutor to come in two afternoons a week to help me prepare for school in America. They're not making me go to school here, thank heavens, although at one stage Annette told me they were considering whether or not to enrol me at the Lycée Jeanne d'Arc, which is a Catholic school near to the American consulate. Papa had met a lady who teaches there and he'd asked her all about it. In the end they've decided against the school, though, because hopefully we're not going to be here that much longer if our visas come through. So instead the lady Papa met is going to come to our house on Monday and Wednesday afternoons when she's finished teaching at the school. I'm quite cross that they think I need to practise my English more, but I can't tell them I'm writing my journal in English because then they'll want to see it to check my spelling and grammar and I'll get told off for putting down the truth about things.

At least I don't have to go to school every day, though. Nina doesn't go to school at all and it's a lot more fun spending time with her. She's teaching me some words in Arabic, so it's not like I'm not learning anything.

The lady teacher is called Miss Dorothy Ellis.

After I found the library and read the book of *Rebecca* (which is even better than the movie, in my opinion), the librarian, who is called Mademoiselle Dubois and who is very pretty and kind, suggested I might enjoy Dorothy L. Sayers books too. She was right. She's very good at knowing about the hundreds of books in the library and recommending things. I think being a librarian could be a very interesting job. You could read as much as you liked in between checking books in and out for people.

The library is a very fine-looking building on the other side of the *nouvelle ville* and even though it's a bit of a walk to get there it's worth it. I love wandering through its rows of tall bookshelves, feeling as if I can not only hide away from the world there but even escape into other worlds between the covers of all those lovely books. It's helped me to stop missing our home in Paris quite so much and to feel not quite so trapped here by the circumstances of the war. Mademoiselle Dubois kindly showed me where to find the books that are translated into French, so I can read those ones to Nina. She loved listening to *Lord Peter et le Bellona Club* and she was very good at guessing who the murderer might be.

We've been spending a lot of time in the courtyard and Nina can skip up to 200 times now without stopping. My record is 339. When we're not reading Dorothy L. Sayers books, Nina tells me about her family and life in Morocco. One day I confessed to her that I have a lot of nightmares and that there are many times when I don't sleep well and she said she has a very ancient auntie who might be able to help me. Apparently her auntie is a sort of storyteller who is very wise so people come to listen to her. Nina says she's very good at listening to people and in her turn diagnosing what they need and then she sells them better dreams if they are troubled. I didn't realise you could buy dreams but Nina says you can, but you can only get them from someone like her ancient auntie who has special powers. I think I would very much like to meet this 'dreamseller' to see if it's true, but when we asked Kenza if we could go she shook her head very firmly and said my maman wouldn't approve. I know she's right about that, but I'd still like to buy some new dreams.

I'm not looking forward to having lessons. They'll get in the way of being able to spend time with Nina in the courtyard. My only hope is that Miss Dorothy Ellis will be as nice as Mademoiselle Dubois and as entertaining as Dorothy L. Sayers, then it might not be so bad. She will be starting next week.

The other big news is that the British and Australian armies have been fighting the Italians in Libya and have captured an important port called Tobruk. Annette says if they manage to make more progress then maybe the war in North Africa will be over very soon and that should make it easier to get our visas for America. Things are bad in France, though, so we still can't go home. And Maman hasn't heard anything at all from Uncle Joseph.

Josie's Journal – Monday 3rd February, 1941

Miss Ellis came today and she is very nice. She makes her lessons fun and said we can read some Dorothy L. Sayers books sometimes. She also said my English is excellent, so take that, Annette! But she's going to help me with grammar a bit and things like commas and apostrophes, which can be quite tricky. Before we started our lesson, we had a cup of tea with Maman and Papa in the drawing room. Miss Ellis seems to know Papa pretty well and it turns out she was introduced to him by one of the vice-consuls at the American consulate. It's quite the social hub, Maman says.

Miss Ellis has a bicycle, which she calls her Steel Steed, which means a kind of horse. She left it in the hall. I was watching her from the stairs when she was leaving after my lesson. Papa came out of the drawing room to say goodbye to her and he handed her a brown envelope, which she put into her leather portfolio and then stashed that in the basket on the handlebars of the Steel Steed. I imagined at first it was payment for her teaching me, but when I thought about it afterwards it seemed a bit too big for that. It's probably some boring newspaper article about the war. When we were drinking our tea, the adults were talking about how the Germans are sending new troops called the Afrika Korps to help out the Italians. Papa said he read about it in the papers this morning. I don't think the British army is making so much progress after all.

At the weekend, Kenza asked Maman if she could take me and Nina to the medina, which is where they live. Maman wasn't too sure at first, but after I begged her and promised to stick close to Kenza at all times she gave in. What I didn't say is that Nina and I have hatched a plan to try to see the dreamseller. I won't be breaking my promise to Maman because the ancient auntie lives in the same riad as Kenza and Nina and other members of their family.

Actually Kenza's house isn't all that far from ours, but the medina feels like you've stepped into another world. You go through an arch shaped like a keyhole and suddenly you're in a maze of tiny streets. It would be very easy to get lost in there. Some of the walls are painted as blue as the sky and the buildings are crammed so close together that they make the streets shady, so it's not as hot as the boulevards of the *nouvelle ville*. As we walked around, all sorts of people came up to say hello to Kenza and Nina and to ask about me. I was very pleased when Nina told them I'm her best friend. They all commented on my green eyes as they're an oddity in the medina, where all the eyes seem to be dark brown.

There were so many extraordinary things to look at. A man was sitting cross-legged in front of a wicker basket and when we drew close he took the lid off to reveal a large snake. He played a tune on a strange-looking pipe and began to rock back and forth and the snake rose up to face him, swaying along in time to the music as it unfurled itself. The way the brown, scaly coils of its body slid over themselves so silently and effortlessly and its hood opened above eyes that were cold-looking and unblinking made my stomach twist with a feeling of sick fear. I was very relieved when the snake finally sank back down into its basket and the man put the lid back on, although my stomach still felt a bit queasy for quite a long time afterwards. When I put a few coins in the hat the man held out, I snatched my hand back quickly, thinking the snake might push its way out of that flimsy-looking basket at any moment and sink its fangs into me. After that, we moved on a bit and watched a juggler who could throw knives high in the air and catch them without cutting himself. My heart was in my mouth!

There was a storyteller too. Nina explained to me that in Moroccan culture they have special people who know all the old stories and it's quite a performance when they tell them. Her auntie, the dreamseller, is too old nowadays to tell stories in public, so we would visit her in the privacy of her own home, which is Nina's home too. But this storyteller was a very public one. First of all, a musician banged a drum to announce that the storyteller was there and the crowds started to gather. Then the story began to unfold, but the storyteller didn't just sit quietly and say the words, he acted it out and had the whole crowd laughing uproariously or trembling in fear or gasping in amazement. I didn't understand what he was saying as it was all in Darija, but that didn't really matter because he was so good at expressing each of the characters that I found I could still follow the gist of it. There was a little boy and a powerful sultan and an evil djinn who was threatening everybody. The sultan and his army tried to overthrow the djinn, but in the end it was the little boy's cunning that won the day. At the end of the story the crowd cheered and clapped and the musician came round with a hat for people to throw money into so I put in a couple of francs, which was most of the pocket money I had left, but the storyteller deserved it for his excellent and entertaining performance.

Then we went back to Kenza's house for some refreshments and she left us playing in the courtyard while she went to get on with some cooking. That was our chance. Nina put a finger to her lips and led me to a staircase in one corner of the building. My heart was in my mouth in case Kenza came back and caught us as we climbed to the floor above the courtyard and crept along the tiled passageway to the door to the ancient auntie's room. I felt a bit bad about disobeying her, but I really wanted to get some better dreams to help me sleep well. Nina knocked quietly on the door. I was excited and a bit nervous at the same time at the prospect of meeting the dreamseller. I only had a few *sous* left over from giving tips to the snake charmer and the juggler and the storyteller, but Nina said that should be enough to buy a good dream.

A soft voice called to us to come in and Nina pushed the door open. It was quite dark inside the room and it took a few moments for my eyes to adjust after the brightness of the whitewashed walls of the courtyard. The room smelled of incense and patchouli oil, and a small tin candle lantern cast the patterns of stars on to the walls. In the corner sat the dreamseller and Nina ushered me forward to sit on a pile of soft cushions at her feet. She drew back her shawl from over her hair, which was as white as snow, and peered at me with her bright eyes. Her face was very lined and also she had tattoos on her forehead and her chin. I asked Nina about the tattoos afterwards and she told me it was an old tribal custom but it's frowned on in Islam because altering the creation of Allah is *haram*, which means forbidden, so people don't really have it done so much any more.

The old lady reminded me a bit of a bird, putting her head on one side as she watched me. Her shawl was beautiful, covered with embroidered designs that Nina says tell the stories of her tribe. She lived in the desert before she came to be nearer her family in the medina. The dreamseller spoke in French and asked me to tell her who I was and why I'd come. I told her about the bad dreams and she nodded. All the time I was talking, her eyes never left my face. It was like she was listening to my words but taking in everything else about me too, hearing the things I wasn't saying out loud as well as the ones I was. I felt as if she was reading the secrets of my innermost soul, which was a bit disconcerting, but at the same time I sensed this was someone I could trust completely. When I'd finished telling her about my dreams and how I was too afraid to go back to sleep sometimes after them, she reached out and took my hand in hers, which was like the claw of a bird too and painted with henna in patterns and swirls like the tattoos on her face. She closed her eyes for a few moments. And then she started to talk, telling me my own story. As far as I can remember, this is what she said:

'The first part of your journey is over. The next part is only just beginning. You are going to find a new home in a land that is strange to you at first, but it will take you into its heart and you will be safe there. There are difficult times ahead, but your own heart is filled with courage and you are stronger and braver than you know.'

She stopped for a minute and looked at me again, with her head tipped to the other side. Then she smiled a very kind smile that softened the fierceness of her face, and said, 'When the moon shines on one hundred bowls of water, no matter where they are, each bowl is filled with moonlight. Remember that when you wake in the night. The moon that shines on you here is a reminder that love is like the moon in those bowls of water – it is everywhere. Your bad dreams come from the fear and the sadness you carry with you. It's now time to let them go. Love and courage are stronger than those things. It's only when you let go of fear and grief, though, that you will find the freedom to be brave and to love fully.'

Well, I thought, she could probably have guessed a lot of that from looking at me. I'm clearly a refugee from France and on my way to America like so many other people in Casablanca. But I was pleased to hear the bit about courage and freedom. And I liked the bit about the moon in the bowls of water – I'll definitely bear that in mind when I wake up in the middle of the night and maybe it will help a bit. It's quite reassuring to think of the moonlight shining on our old house in France as well as our new house here in Morocco.

Then she turned to Nina and said some things in Arabic that I couldn't understand but Nina nodded and thanked her. I tried to give the dreamseller my last few sous but she shook her head and smiled broadly at me. It was then that I saw her front teeth were missing. Her face was very wrinkled and as brown as the leather cover of this notebook, but it was one of the kindest and wisest faces I've ever seen. She absolutely refused to take my money and then she said something rather strange. She told me that she couldn't take money from a member of her own family. I suppose she was being extra kind because Kenza is her niece and I'm a friend of Nina's.

When we left the dreamseller's room, Nina told me the rest of what she'd said. 'She sees that your heart is filled with grief. You need to go to the ocean. Write the names of the things you've lost on stones you will find there and then cast them away into the waters. The ocean is big enough to take your grief and keep it safe for you, freeing up space in your heart for other things. The dreamseller says this is an important lesson for you to learn now and you must remember it. It will help you later in life.'

While we were having a cup of mint tea and some cookies back downstairs in the courtyard, Nina casually asked Kenza if she would take us to the ocean one day soon. She says she will, as long as Maman says it's okay.

Now it's time for me to go to sleep. I suppose writing things in my journal is a bit like writing things on stones and throwing them into the ocean, so Kenza didn't need to worry because in a way Papa and the dreamseller have given me the same advice.

I think I'll sleep a bit better tonight. Goodnight.

Zoe – 2010

The darkness feels as stifling as the bedcovers that I've shoved aside, creating a crumpled range of hills against the solid wall of Tom's back. He's lost, deep in sleep, each steady in-breath catching on a faint snore, each out-breath a quiet sigh. His exhalations are strangely expressionless, containing neither satisfaction nor sadness. Somehow, their neutrality – which makes him seem even more distant and unreachable – infuriates me. What a relief it is to be able to admit that in the silent darkness. Our day-to-day careful courtesy towards one another feels so very brittle and forced. I wonder what Tom really thinks about me, how much he, too, is leaving unsaid.

How is it possible to lie so close to someone and still to feel so alone? My wakefulness and his oblivion only serve to further emphasise how far apart we are these days. I know the statistics are not encouraging: few marriages survive what we've gone through.

The move to Morocco was supposed to have given us a fresh start, but somehow everything we'd tried to leave behind seems to have found its way here along with the few belongings we packed in our suitcases.

Sometimes we still can't bear to look at each other.

Every morning, he showers off the sweat and the dust from his early run through the city and emerges, transformed, ready to step out of the wreck of his marriage and into the calm, ordered world of his work, a place where he can be something other than a half of us. Dressed in his suit, he drives in his air-conditioned car to his air-conditioned office, where I imagine there are polite, smiling colleagues and coffee from a machine and an orderly pile of work to get through so he doesn't have to think about anything else. It's not surprising he's not exactly keen to come home in the evenings. I wonder what he sees when he stands in front of the mirror in the hall, tying his tie in a neat knot just before he leaves the house. Is that image real for him? The calm, tidy, controlled career man. Or, like me, does he see what lies beneath the surface – the wreckage, the pain, the tangled mess of emotions? When I catch sight of my own image in the mirror, I see what a bad job I do of trying to wear my own disguise. My hair is stringy, pulled back in an elastic band, the dark roots only emphasising the matching dark circles beneath my eyes, and I'm usually wearing an old T-shirt and sweat pants, the appropriately saggy uniform – given the sagging post-baby flesh it conceals – of the stay-at-home mum.

Yesterday evening he suggested we might go away for a weekend. The thought of packing bags and driving for hours to stay in a hotel filled me with panic. We can scarcely bear to be in this house together, where there's space for us each to escape into our own rooms so that we don't have to sit and bear witness to each other's guilt and hurt. I couldn't bear the thought of being trapped in a hotel room with him. And besides, as any young mum knows, going away for a weekend is more trouble than it's worth. By the time you've packed everything a baby needs so that you can haul them to an unfamiliar place where the routine you've tried so carefully to construct collapses, unsettling them so they can't sleep, the whole thing seems totally pointless. Tom was annoyed by my reaction and I could see he was hurt at my rejection of his idea. But he dropped the suggestion so quickly that I suspect he, too, was a little relieved: he'd done the right thing by making the offer and, as usual, I was the killjoy who'd refused it.

His steady breaths continue, oblivious as he is to the turmoil of my night-thoughts, and all of a sudden I can't bear to lie there beside him for another second. Very quietly, so as not to disturb him, I ease myself from the bed and tiptoe upstairs to Grace's room. The shutters are slightly ajar to allow any faint breath of a breeze up here among the rooftops to cool the heavy air. I can hear the soft shuffle of feathers as the roosting doves resettle themselves in the darkness.

I draw aside a swathe of the mosquito netting, just enough to slip beneath it and ease myself on to Grace's bed. I feel far less lonely here. Very gently, I gather my sleeping daughter into my arms. The torment of my raw, itching hands seems to lessen a little when I'm with her, soothing my troubled mind too.

A finger of moonlight slips between the gap in the shutters, pointing towards the pile of neatly folded fabric on the chest of drawers. Following Kate's advice, I've washed the old clothes that I'm going to use to make the blocks and then starched and ironed them, so it'll be easier to cut them into equal-sized squares. I've chosen a design called Tree of Life from the quilting book. Each block uses a geometrical pattern of simple triangles and squares, in what I've learned is called an on-point setting. Once I've sewn thirteen of the blocks, I'll arrange them in three rows, held in place by sashing strips, and then stitch them on to the backing, adding a binding around the edges of the quilt. But that'll come later. For the moment all I need to think about is sewing one triangle of fabric to the next, building up the branches of my first tree. I'm looking forward to getting started, once Kate shows me where to get a cutting mat, square-up rulers and a rotary cutter.

I stroke a wisp of Grace's hair, as soft and ethereal as a moonbeam.

It reminds me of the dreamseller's words to Josie about the moon being able to fill an infinite number of bowls of water. My love for my daughter is the same, I think: my heart overflows with it; as infinite as moonlight.

Reading Josie's journal feels like stepping through a door and finding myself in another world. Her life here in this house – in this very room – almost feels more real to me than my own. I imagine her lying in this same bed, watching the moonlight and listening to the murmuring of the doves. Did she feel safe up here, with her family asleep in their rooms downstairs? Or did the ever present threat of Nazi Germany, in a world turned upside down by war, keep her awake at night? Despite her papa's wealth, which certainly must have helped a great deal, it can't have been easy being Jewish refugees in a strange land, where dark threats lurked around every corner, whether or not they'd 'lapsed', as Josie puts it.

Casablanca in the 1940s seems to have been the sort of place where people could easily fall through the cracks and disappear.

Am I all that different from Josie and her family, though? I, too, am a refugee of sorts, running from something I can never escape.

It would be very easy to fall through the cracks in my marriage. And simply disappear.

Josie's Journal – Tuesday 11th February, 1941

The big excitement in Casablanca is the recent arrival of a very famous star called Josephine Baker. She is a singer and dancer and she used to put on shows in Paris. But now she's come to Morocco and she's going to be performing here at the Rialto Theatre. Papa has got tickets for him and Maman. Annette and I are not allowed to go because some of the dancing is a bit too exotic. I'd still be interested to see it, but Annette says 'exotic' means they don't wear very many clothes and so it's inappropriate for a child like me. I know she was only saying that because she's annoyed that she can't go either. She got even more annoyed when I said that must mean she's still a child too. Maman calmed things down by promising to take us both horse riding next week, which will be a lot more fun than sitting in a hot theatre. There's a place just outside the city where you can have lessons. I can't wait!

It says in the newspaper that Josephine Baker travelled from Marseille with 28 pieces of luggage. Annette said that would be all her costumes, but she got annoyed again when I pointed out she'd just told me that exotic dancers don't wear very many clothes. She's started calling me Little Miss Know-All, but I've chosen to take that as a compliment. It's certainly better than only ever thinking about boys and hairstyles.

The other very interesting thing that it says in the newspaper is that Josephine Baker travelled with her menagerie of animals. She has a Great Dane called Bonzo, several monkeys and two white mice. Nina agrees with me that seeing those animals would be much more interesting than seeing exotic dancing.

Kenza took Nina and me to the ocean at the weekend. Maman was a bit anxious about letting me go, but Papa paid for us to go in a taxi so it was fine. We drove along the coast a way, past the fishing boats in the harbour and one or two warships that were patrolling out at sea, until we came to a place where there was a peaceful stretch of beach with no one else on it. The driver parked up in a grove of olive trees and went off to lie in the shade. Kenza, Nina and I walked down to the beach and they took off their headscarves. We all let the wind blow over our faces and it was hot and cool at the same time. The ocean went on for ever. Its powerful waves were crashing on to the pebbles at the water's edge, making them roll and tumble. I thought about the dreamseller's instructions and I wondered if all those thousands of stones carried other people's grief. I could see what she meant: the ocean was vast enough to contain it all.

I'd brought a bottle of ink with me, which I'd borrowed from Papa's desk, and a paintbrush from my art box. We told Kenza what I was going to do – although we left out the fact that I was following the instructions of the dreamseller – and then Nina and Kenza helped me find some stones that were the right shape and size, big enough and flat enough to write on, but not too big for me to be able to throw them far out beyond where the waves break. After meeting the dreamseller, I'd thought about what she'd said and decided what I needed to put on the stones. I wrote four things. The first one was Home. The second one was France. The third one was Friends (the ones I've left behind). On the fourth one I didn't write any words, I just drew a six-pointed star like the one on my necklace in the sandalwood box.

While the sun and the wind helped the ink to dry, I washed my paintbrush in the salty water of the Atlantic Ocean. Then I took each stone in turn and held it in my hands for a moment before throwing it out as far as I could. The sea swallowed them all up hungrily. I felt a great wave of sadness, but it was different from the heavy lump – like a pile of rocks – that I've been carrying around for so long. Mixed in with it was a feeling of relief that I didn't have those rocks inside me any longer. And so the sadness seemed not to take up the whole of my heart any more and there was a bit of room for other things. Kenza gave me a big hug and wiped away my tears with a corner of her scarf and then the three of us walked along at the water's edge for a while, letting the wash of the waves foam over our bare feet and feeling the warm wind on our cheeks. We came to a stretch of wet sand, and suddenly I felt like running and then I did a cartwheel and Nina joined in. Then the three of us were all running and laughing and I realised the dreamseller had been absolutely right. It was a kind of freedom.

There have been three nights since then and I haven't had any bad dreams at all. Last night I dreamed I was dancing on the beach with Josephine Baker and her animals and we were all laughing, even the mice.

Zoe – 2010

Kate and I meet up at the mall and she shows me the way to the crafting shop, which is tucked away in a corner on the upper floor. It's a treasure trove of a place, crammed to the ceiling with shelves containing spools of thread and pieces of felt and sheets of card in all the colours of the rainbow. As well as the things I'll need for cutting my selection of old clothes into precise squares and triangles, I buy a large spool of ivory thread and a packet of pins with bright-coloured heads. Kate offers to lend me her sewing machine for piecing my blocks, but I politely decline. I want to sew them by hand. Each block will be a labour of love, as well as it being a way of keeping my hands busy – a welcome distraction from scratching at my inflamed skin. I want to immerse myself in this project, taking my time. I want to focus on every stitch and every scrap of fabric.

Once we've finished our shopping, we retreat to the coffee shop so that I can show Kate the design I've chosen and she can give me a few more tips for getting started. I turn to the bookmarked page.

'The Tree of Life.' She smiles. 'That's the perfect choice for a beginner. You'll be working with squares and quarter-square triangles to make the tree and you'll need some plain fabric for the setting squares and triangles you'll use to surround the patterned pieces – the book gives you the measurements here, see, depending on the size you want your finished quilt to be. I'd suggest you cut everything out for your first block and pin it, just to get an idea of how it all fits together. That way you won't make any mistakes. The hand-piecing will take some time, but it's a very good way to start to understand how the design works.'

She takes another look at the book and turns the pages. 'All the different block patterns tell a story. See here, for example, this log cabin design is hundreds of years old. The square in the centre is usually red, to represent the fire in the hearth, or sometimes yellow for a light shining from a window. And then the offset strips of fabric surrounding it are the logs of the cabin. You can just imagine how comforting that would be if you were a settler in the Wild West, longing to be safe inside a cosy home. By the time you'd sewn enough blocks for your quilt, you'd have created a whole settlement.'

'And the Tree of Life?' I ask. 'Does it tell its own story too?'

She sips her coffee and turns back to the page with the design I've chosen. 'Indeed – a Tree of Life is a powerful symbol of family and ancestors. Its branches map generation upon generation, each following on from the ones that have gone before. It reminds us that we're never alone, you see. Everything is interconnected. A tree may lose its leaves in wintertime but then, after a period of hibernation, there's a rebirth in the spring as new life unfurls. I love that idea of making a fresh start, of hope reawakening.' She unwraps one of the little almond biscuits that the waiter's delivered with our coffees and takes a bite, still considering the pattern. 'Then, too, it tells us we are rooted in the earth, which nourishes us and gives us strength. And even though a tree will age and die, it holds new life in its seeds – it represents the idea of life after death, of an ending also holding the promise of a new beginning.'

She raises her eyes to mine and I smile, then look away, hiding my sudden tears by raising my coffee cup to my lips.

'It can be a lonely business starting life in a new place, can't it, Zoe? But we soon begin to put down roots, just as a tree does.' She gives my arm a little pat of encouragement. 'I think you've chosen the perfect design for your quilt. As you sew each block, bringing your little forest to life, you will see how deeply satisfying it can be to create something so beautiful out of old scraps and cast-offs.'

Once we've finished our coffees, I gather my bags together and we go our separate ways. I'd spotted a bookseller on the way to the craft shop and I head back there now. Most of the books on the shelves are in French or Arabic, but they have a small selection in English, as well as a children's corner. I spend some time browsing and then carry the pile of books I've chosen for Grace over to the till. I've picked up three Miffy picture books, a book of African folk tales and a beautifully illustrated copy of *Tales from the Thousand and One Nights*. The last one is more for me to read, but I know she'll enjoy looking at the pictures with their vibrant colours and intricate patterns, as I tell her Scheherazade's stories about the adventures of Aladdin and Sinbad the Sailor, even if she doesn't understand the words yet. Then I head for the taxi rank and home to stash all my new purchases away in Grace's room.

Josie's Journal – Sunday 16th February, 1941

Papa and Maman have been to the American consulate today for their interview. When they came back they were both in high spirits. 'They loved your maman,' Papa told us. 'Of course they loved her, everyone does. But she charmed them completely and the vice-consul we saw said he's going to do all he can to get our application processed as quickly as possible.'

Annette was very pleased at this news, but I didn't feel quite as excited as I thought I should. I'll miss Nina and Kenza and Miss Ellis, and Mademoiselle Dubois at the library. I'm reading *Jane Eyre* at the moment and it's brilliant. Annette said, 'Beware of the mad woman in the attic,' and I said, 'That's no way to refer to your own sister,' which made her laugh a lot.

When he's not at the American consulate or meeting friends for a vermouth cassis at the Hotel Transatlantique, Papa still sometimes goes to meetings in the mellah. I asked him if I could come too one day because I'd like to see if I could bump into Felix again before we leave. Papa said it wouldn't be possible for me to come to any of the meetings and anyway I'd find them very boring. But he told me he'd ask around and pass on our address to a man who comes along to the meetings who seems to know everyone in the Jewish

Quarter. That way, the man can remind Felix where we are, if he comes across him, and maybe Felix can come and visit us one day soon. I'd like that. I can introduce him to Nina too.

Annette started teasing me, saying I'm pining for my boyfriend. I did my best to ignore her. She's going to a dance at the Hotel Excelsior tomorrow night with a group of friends, but it's very obvious that she mentions one called Olivier more than the others. So I wondered out loud whether Laurence Olivier is heartbroken that he's been replaced in her affections by a substitute who shares one of his names and that made her shut up.

Miss Ellis has been teaching me about how to use colons and semicolons in my writing. They are useful for complicated lists. E.g. The British army has captured the following cities in Libya: Bardia; Beda Fomm; Benghazi; and, with the help of the Australians, Tobruk and Derna.

We're also taking it in turns to read chapters of *Jane Eyre* out loud, which is much more fun than learning grammar. The other day while it was my turn to read, Papa popped his head round the door and handed Miss Ellis another one of those mysterious brown envelopes. She put it to one side without even looking at it. But later on, when she left me grappling with semicolons and went to powder her nose, I noticed it wasn't stuck down and snuck a quick look to see what was inside it. It was just some boring-looking lists of places and numbers. Not a semicolon in sight!

Maman has booked our riding lesson for Thursday morning.

70

Josie's Journal – Thursday 20th February, 1941

Today we went to the farm for our riding lesson. Papa decided we should make it a family day out and hired a car. He called it our chariot and told me it was a 1936 Dodge Sedan. Maman looked at it a bit doubtfully as it was quite dilapidated and had a few dents, but I was excited that it was ours for the whole day and we could go wherever we wanted. Kenza had made us a picnic and Papa loaded the baskets of food and crockery into the trunk. Then we all piled in and set off. At first the car made some crunching sounds and jumped and stalled a few times because Papa wasn't used to the controls. But then he got a bit better at driving it and things went more smoothly. We opened the windows as wide as they'd go so that the wind cooled us down as we sped through the streets of the city. Soon we had to shut them, though, because Annette complained it was messing up her hair. I pointed out that we were going to ride horses, not out dancing with Olivier and Co. But as we were now on a country road and there was a lot of dust coming in too, Maman said she thought we really did need the windows closed.

After about an hour we arrived at the farm. It had lots of silvery olive groves and also some rows of trees with glossy green leaves, which Papa said were orange orchards. It was a very beautiful place.

There was a neat white fence around a paddock of horses. In the distance was a backdrop of hazy blue mountains and it felt very peaceful. I said that I'd like to go and explore the mountains sometime and Papa said we might be able to go on an expedition further afield one day, now he's got the hang of the car.

Annette and I were to have our riding lesson straight away, before the sun got too hot, so we went to the stables where white doves were cooing softly to each other from little nesting boxes in the eaves. A very nice man called Hamid was saddling up our horses. Mine was a lovely chestnut mare with a white blaze on her forehead and her name was Najima, which means 'star'. Annette's was called Marguerite because she was as white as the wild daisies flowering around the edge of the pasture.

Hamid put us through our paces in the yard outside the stable block, to let us get to know Najima and Marguerite and give them a chance to get to know us. We'd had a few riding lessons in the Bois de Boulogne when we lived in Neuilly, so it didn't take too long to feel comfortable. Then he led out his own horse – a tall black stallion called Malik – and jumped into the saddle without needing to use the mounting block at all.

We waved to Maman and Papa, who were sitting in the shade holding hands and listening to the doves, and followed Hamid and Malik along a dirt road running parallel to the line of mountains in the distance. We had a lovely ride through the orange groves and Hamid let us canter when we got to a meadow on the other side. It was filled with a carpet of wildflowers – buttercups and daisies and pink mallow – which made me think of the colourful rugs hanging up in the Habous. We rode through it and the flowers rustled like the folds of Maman's best silk evening gown as we passed. Hamid told us that in a couple of weeks they'll disappear once the short spring is over, and there'll just be dry grass and dust. Marguerite lived up to her name and pulled up a bunch of daisies to eat. Even Annette forgot to be as moody as she is usually and laughed her head off at that. We took the horses down to a stream, lined with forget-me-nots and dark green watercress, that ran along the boundary of the farm, and gave them a good drink. Hamid told us the water is very pure as it comes from the snow on top of the highest mountains. It's hard to imagine there can be snow in such a hot place. He said that in the summer the stream dries up completely.

We rode back slowly and I took some deep breaths of the country air, which smelled so good – of the horses, and the leather of their tack, and the faint scent of blossom from a line of almond trees that we passed. Back at the stables we gave our horses a handful of corn and I stroked Najima's neck and promised I'd come and see her again soon. Then we went to join Maman and Papa, who had just got back from a walk.

We spread out a picnic rug beneath a huge old olive tree whose trunk was as gnarled as something from a Grimm's fairy tale. The midday heat was a lot more bearable there than it is in the city streets and the air was filled with the hum of the cicadas and the songs of the tiny birds that fluttered among the silver leaves above our heads. Kenza had made a delicious kind of pie, stuffed with spices and nuts and sultanas, and there was lemonade to drink. Afterwards we peeled little oranges, so sweet and tangy they made my mouth water, and ate the segments along with almond macarons. Papa declared it to be a feast fit for a sultan and we all agreed.

Maman rested her head on his shoulder and he kissed her hair very gently. It was nice to see her looking a lot happier and more relaxed out there in the countryside. She is usually pretty jumpy in the city, where she says the French police are bad enough but the Gestapo really give her the creeps. Perhaps when we go to America we could live in the countryside on a farm with horses. I'd like that.

After lunch, my stomach was so full of all that good food that I stretched out on the picnic rug and let the little drops of sunshine dazzle my eyes. The golden light and the silver leaves seemed to weave themselves together into a rich tapestry. It's possible that I dozed off for a moment or two. When I opened my eyes again, I sat up and leaned my back against a comfortable bit of tree trunk, watching the horses contentedly munching on hay in the paddock. High above them a bird of prey hovered against the blue sky, seeming to be frozen there. It reminded me of the dreamseller with her bright eyes and talon-like fingers with the henna designs, and for a moment I was tempted to tell Papa and Maman about my visit to see her. But I thought the better of it because Annette would probably just be scornful and make fun of me and Maman might not let me go to the medina with Kenza and Nina again if she thought I was listening to what I knew she'd refer to as superstitious nonsense. It wasn't nonsense, though, because it helped me sleep much better and stop having so many of those bad dreams.

Suddenly the bird spotted something and swooped down as fast as an arrow. As it rose into the air again, a snake was writhing in its talons. It made me feel a bit sick because the scene that had been so beautiful and peaceful just a second before had turned into something quite brutal. The others hadn't seen it. The bird flew off before I could point it out, and in a way I was glad because I didn't want to disturb their peace.

I had a nice bath when we got home, to wash off the dust and the sweat. My legs are quite sore from not being used to riding. I hope I'll sleep well again tonight after all that fresh country air. But I keep remembering the image of the bird with the snake in its claws and it makes my stomach feel quite queasy, the same way I felt when I saw the snake charmer in the medina.

Kenza has given me a tin lantern, which she brought from her home, to put by my bed. It's like the one in the dreamseller's room.

She says Nina has one too, to help keep the darkness at bay while she falls asleep. The top and sides of it are pierced with the shapes of moons and stars and I love to watch the light from them flicker on the wall. It's almost as if they are keeping me company.

I think I will stop writing now and read a bit of my next Dorothy L. Sayers book instead. It's called *Strong Poison* and it has a heroine in it called Harriet Vane, who is an expert in all kinds of poisons. Lord Peter Wimsey has to rescue her from prison when she is accused of using arsenic to murder her lover, and he falls in love with her too and proposes. But Harriet Vane says she never wants to get married. I don't know if I would ever want to be married, unless the man was very kind like my papa or Felix. I think I'd probably rather have animals instead, like Josephine Baker.

Zoe – 2010

Tom said he'd be working late this evening – something to do with having to call the company's Vancouver office – so not to keep supper for him as he'd grab something from one of the takeaway cafés next to the port.

After reading about the tin lantern that Josie used to have beside her bed, I take one of the ones that sit in a row on the sideboard in the sitting room and bring it upstairs with me to Grace's room. I'm a little anxious about having it too close to the swathes of mosquito netting, so I set it on the chest of drawers against the far wall, alongside my quilting things. I've cut the starched fabrics into neat squares now and selected the ones I'll use to piece my first block, subdividing some of the squares into quarter-triangles. I need fifty for each tree, plus some additional squares to form the trunk. As Kate suggested, for the first one I've begun pinning all the pieces together before I sew a single stitch, to get a feel for the pattern.

Grace sleeps soundly, arms flung wide. I light the candle in the lantern and take a seat in the brocade-covered armchair that I've set in the corner by the window. It'll be the perfect place to sit and sew in the daytime with the sunlight streaming in, accompanied by the preoccupied murmuring of the doves on the roof.

This evening, though, I sit and watch the stars from the lantern as they flicker across the wall and then reach for one of the books I bought the other day.

I turn the pages, flipping through Scheherazade's tales of princes and princesses and djinns until my attention is caught by the title of a short fable tucked away towards the end. It's called 'The Dream'.

'Listen well,' it begins, 'it is told that long ago and in a far-off land a wealthy merchant lived in a fine house with a courtyard of white marble and a fountain carved with peacocks. He was foolish, though, and squandered his riches until one day he found himself to be penniless. He lay down to sleep with the heaviest of hearts, not knowing what to do. That night, a man appeared to him in a dream and said, "Your fortune lies in the city beyond the mountains. Go and seek it there."

'And so the next day the merchant packed his few remaining rags and set off. After several weeks of travelling, and having encountered many hardships along the way, he finally arrived at the city beyond the mountains. It was late and he had no money, so he lay down in a garden and fell asleep. In the night, a band of thieves came to the garden and from there they broke into a neighbouring house. Hearing the noise, the owners raised the alarm and the police arrived. They arrested the merchant, whom they found lying in the garden, and beat him soundly with their sticks before throwing him into jail.

'After he'd lain in his cell for several days, the head of the police had the man brought before him, at last, and demanded where he'd come from and what had brought him to the city.

'The merchant told the policeman about his dream and how a man had appeared telling him to seek his fortune in the city beyond the mountains. "But when I got here, the only things I received were the blows you and your men bestowed upon me with such generosity."

'The head of the police burst out laughing. "What a fool you are! I, too, have been told things in my dreams. In fact, three times a man has appeared to me and said that I must travel to a town on the other side of the mountains, where I will find a fine house with a white marble courtyard. In the centre of the courtyard I will find a fountain carved with peacocks and, if I dig beneath that fountain, I will find a casket filled with gold that has been buried there. But am I as great a fool as you? Would I go all the way across the mountains because of words that came to me in a dream? Of course not! What an idiot you have been."

'The merchant said nothing, but as soon as he was released from jail he hurried home to his town on the other side of the mountains. In the white marble courtyard, beneath the peacock-carved fountain, he discovered the buried treasure that had lain there all along. Thus were the words of his dream fulfilled.'

I lower the book and watch the stars flicker on the wall by Grace's bed, mulling over what I've just read. It's a story that's been told and retold time and time again down the ages in various different forms, the saga of the search for something that turns out to have been hidden within all along. Is that what Tom and I are doing here? Are we searching for answers when really, all this time, we've held the key to them within ourselves? I think about our relationship and wonder, fleetingly, where Tom is right now. Is he really still at his desk, making calls beneath the stark fluorescent strip lights of the shipping office? Or is he somewhere else? A restaurant or a bar, maybe, with some of his colleagues, unable to face another silent and awkward dinner here with me. Or with just one of his colleagues, perhaps. When I go through his jacket pockets before I take his suit to the cleaner's, will I find a receipt for a dinner for two, printed with tonight's date? It wouldn't be the first time. We were still living in Bristol and he'd said he'd be working late, just like he had today. The following day I found the receipt. That evening, when he came home, I handed him the slip of paper – a bill for two steaks and an expensive bottle of red wine. I scanned his face carefully, watching for any sign of guilt, but he just thanked me and said he'd be needing it to claim against expenses as it was from a rather tedious business dinner with an insurance broker. I didn't say anything. I don't know whether he was telling the truth or not, but either way the seeds of doubt had lodged themselves in my mind, taking root there and beginning to grow, fed by his coldness and the distance that was building between us, their tendrils silently twining their way into my thoughts.

I watch the candlelight cast its stars across the walls of Grace's room, then glance back down at the book on my lap.

Do I already know the answers to the questions I've travelled so far to find? Perhaps they've been there all along, in my dreams.

Josie's Journal – Friday 28th February, 1941

It's the last day of February and there's still no sign of our visas for America, despite Papa spending several more mornings queuing at the consulate to try to see where they've got to. There are so many refugees in Casablanca now and everyone wants a visa. Maman is getting quite anxious, especially since there seem to be a lot more German soldiers around these days. The Afrika Korps is helping the Italian army to fight the British in Libya and they come to Casablanca for a rest sometimes. They career through the city in their grey trucks with the black and white crosses painted on the sides, making pedestrians scatter as they carve their way through the streets, and you see them sitting in groups at the cafés, ordering glasses of beer and guffawing raucously. Somehow you get the sense they are always laughing at you, not with you. Maman is careful to lower her eyes as we hurry past on our way to the shops or the hairdresser, not making eye contact. They've completely taken over some of the bars, where they get drunk and behave badly, so Papa tends to stick to the Hotel Transatlantique when he wants a cigar and an aperitif. He says he's having to ration his cigars now as well, because it's harder to buy them and the price has gone up a lot.

Maman says that's a good thing. She doesn't like him smoking them in the house, which is one of the reasons he goes out so much.

Gasoline is another thing that's rationed and is now a lot more expensive. Papa says we can go to the farm to go riding again sometimes but not every week. He said we'll still go on an expedition to the mountains one day but we need to save up for it. I got a bit worried then and asked him if we were running out of money, but he just ruffled my hair and told me not to concern myself about that, we're still very fortunate not to have those sorts of worries. He did buy Maman a beautiful gold bracelet for their 20th wedding anniversary last weekend and she still goes to the salon to get her hair and nails done every week, so I guess we must be okay.

One excellent piece of news is that Papa bumped into Felix in the mellah the other day. He and his family are doing okay, living in a room in a house belonging to a baker. Papa reminded him to come and visit us one day and he says he will. Apparently he's quite busy helping the baker deliver his bread. Felix has the use of a bicycle – another Steel Steed like Miss Ellis's – so he promised Papa that he'll cycle to the *nouvelle ville* one afternoon when he's free. I'll ask Kenza to make some of her special *ghoribas* for us – I think he'll like them.

Speaking of Kenza's baking, at lunchtime she mentioned she was going to make *ma'amoul* this afternoon, so I think I'll go and see how she's getting on. I like the ones with dates in best. If Nina's here, we can read a bit more of *The Nine Tailors* by Dorothy L. Sayers, which Mademoiselle Dubois managed to find in French for me at the library.

Josie's Journal – Thursday 13th March, 1941

Quite a lot has happened since I last had time to write in my journal.

As he had promised, Felix came to see us last week. It felt a bit awkward at first, when Maman and Papa made us come and sit in the drawing room with them. Annette came in and sat down too, even though she really didn't need to be there. Felix is my friend, not hers, and she wasn't the slightest bit interested in talking to him when we were all in the camp together. But she sat down opposite me and kept grinning to try to embarrass me. I glared at her a couple of times but that just made her grin all the more, so I decided to ignore her instead. It's not like I'm silly around boys the way she is. She was really bugging me, though. Then Kenza brought in mint tea and the *ghoribas* I'd asked her to make and gave me a smile, which made me feel a bit better. We also had bottles of Coca-Cola as a treat and Felix said it was his very favourite thing. It's quite hard to get them these days too, like Papa's cigars, so we only have them on special occasions. I was glad everyone was making an effort to make Felix feel welcome (except for Annette, who was still being a pain). It felt a bit like we were celebrating no longer all being in the camp and being one step closer to America, fingers crossed.

Maman asked Felix how his parents were doing. He said they were okay, although his mother's health hasn't been too good. They were just hoping to get the paperwork for their visas all lined up soon, like everyone else. The baker gives them bread in return for help in the bakery and Felix doing the deliveries, and the baker and his wife are very kind and share their meals so they have enough to live on. When Felix said that, it made Annette stop grinning. I suppose it made her realise just how lucky we are with Papa's good fortune so she can still have riding lessons and have her hair waved and go to dances.

Papa chatted to Felix about his delivery rounds. He cycles all over the city and loves having his bike. He even goes to the ocean sometimes. I wondered to myself if he might want to write some words on stones one day and throw them into the waves. I decided to tell him about the dreamseller when we were on our own. I think he might quite like the idea. What made me think about that was the fact that he looked a bit changed since I'd seen him last. He definitely looked older and taller – but then so do I, I suppose, because it's been nearly 4 months since we moved into the house on the Boulevard des Oiseaux. He also has a bit of a moustache growing on his top lip and with his broken tooth it makes him look a little like a pirate. But it wasn't only those things, something in his expression had changed too. I thought his eyes didn't smile the way they used to. He was a bit more serious and that made him seem more grown-up too. Maybe he just felt a bit awkward, though, like I did, sitting on the stuffy chaise and being interrogated by Papa and Maman, because once we'd finished our drinks and cookies we went out to join Nina in the courtyard and then he relaxed a lot more and his lopsided smile was as bright as ever.

Nina liked him too and the three of us got on very well, even though we come from such different backgrounds. It seems strange that there's so much fighting going on in the world when it's perfectly possible for a Jewish boy to be friends with a Muslim girl and a lapsed Catholic-Jewish girl. He didn't mind turning one end of the skipping rope while Nina and I took turns in the middle, although he refused to have a go himself because he said skipping is for girls only. He's taught himself to juggle and he showed us how, with three oranges that I borrowed from Kenza. Nina and I had a go, but we can only do it with two so far.

When it was time for him to leave, Papa came down to say goodbye while I was returning the oranges to the kitchen because Kenza needed them for the tajine for dinner that night. When I came back, Papa asked me if I'd like to go for an outing to the Parc Murdoch with Felix the following week. I suppose Felix must have proposed that to Papa. Anyway, it was nice to be asked and I said I would, even though I knew Annette would tease me about it when she found out.

-x-

Today Felix turned up for tea and cakes again (no Coca-Cola this time, but there was a jug of lemonade) and when the air began to cool a little Papa glanced at his watch and said we could go to the park. The MOST exciting thing happened there, so I'm writing it down straight away so that I don't forget any of the details.

Parc Murdoch is a wonderful place, an oasis of green in the middle of the white city, with grass and palm trees and many beautiful flowers. Felix says it's one of his favourite places to be. There are no nice gardens in the mellah. Anyway, we were sitting by the drinking fountain, chatting about what we are going to do when we get to America, when suddenly a huge dog came up to us. It was a very fine creature indeed, with a glossy coat, and it was wearing a very smart leather collar so I knew it wasn't a stray. I was so busy petting it that at first I didn't notice its owner, who was standing alongside it. But when I did notice her, my jaw nearly hit the ground in amazement. I recognised her from the photos in Papa's newspaper. It was Miss Josephine Baker, the famous exotic dancer and singer! She is so beautiful with her very short and very glossy black hair and her enormous eyes. I would have expected her to be taller but she's actually quite petite, especially alongside her Great Dane, who I now realised was none other than Bonzo. As you would expect from an exotic dancer, her movements are very graceful.

Even more amazingly, instead of just walking on she stopped and spoke to us! I was thinking that I couldn't wait to tell Papa, Maman and Annette. Josephine Baker asked us if we liked the park and she told us that, like Felix, it's one of her favourite places to come when she's in Casablanca. She lives in Marrakesh now, but likes coming to the ocean sometimes. I plucked up the courage to ask her about the rest of her animals. She said that two of the monkeys – who are called Glug-Glug and Gugusse – were quite bad-tempered and they'd been fighting quite a lot so she had to make sure they stayed apart at all times or else the fur would start to fly. The mice are well. Their names are Curler and Question Marker because of their tails. She asked me whether I like animals and I told her that it's my dream to have a farm when we get to America, with horses and turtle doves and maybe a Great Dane like Bonzo. She was very nice and listened carefully, not like most grown-ups. She said it's important to have dreams in life.

Then she asked whether we would like her autograph, but she realised she didn't have a piece of paper to write it on. Surprisingly, Felix reached into his pocket and pulled out two folded sheets of notepaper. It was the exact same shade of pale blue as the writing paper Papa has on his desk at home. Miss Josephine Baker took out a pen from the beautiful embroidered handbag she was carrying and she signed one of the sheets and handed it to me. I was very pleased to have her autograph and couldn't wait to show it to Nina.

I was also thinking that now Annette wouldn't be able to say I was making the whole thing up.

I thought Josephine Baker would sign the second sheet for Felix, but instead she popped it back into her handbag with her pen. I think she must be a bit absent-minded. Then she said goodbye and she and Bonzo carried on with their walk.

I felt awful that Felix didn't get an autograph, so I offered him the one she'd given me. But he said I should keep it and he would look at it sometimes when he came to visit. That was very generous of him and typical of his kind character.

Sure enough, Maman and Annette were very impressed when I got home and showed them Josephine Baker's autograph. I'm keeping it in the sandalwood box, along with my necklace.

Zoe – 2010

I open the sandalwood box and take out the folded square of blue paper. I imagine a block of such sheets sitting on Monsieur Duval's desk, and this one being folded up and put into Felix's pocket. The autograph is faded, but still legible, the handwriting elegant and flowing.

The internet connection in the house is painfully slow at the best of times, and frequently drops altogether, especially if there's been a thunderstorm, as there was last night. Every now and then the Atlantic brews up a mass of lowering storm clouds and unleashes a furious display of sound and light on the city. These African storms are of a terrifying scale I've never witnessed in England, but there's something magnificent about the power and the fury of them too and they clear the air and leave the streets washed clean the next morning.

I want to find out more about Josephine Baker, so I pack my laptop and the folded sheet of paper in Grace's changing bag, strap on the baby carrier and head out to try and find the library. There are cafés with Wi-Fi closer to home, but I don't feel comfortable there and I certainly don't want to expose Grace to any danger. I've searched online and found there are several libraries in Casa, but there's only one within easy walking distance of the Boulevard des Oiseaux. I hope it may be the one Josie used to frequent, although of course the city has changed beyond all recognition in the intervening seventy years and she doesn't mention the exact location in her journal, so I have no guarantee that it still exists.

When I find it, however, I'm encouraged by the appearance of the building. The library's in one of the original districts of the *nouvelle ville*. Its art deco façade and the slightly musty smell of old books that hangs faintly in the air make me believe it could be the same one. I nod to the librarian sitting at her desk, typing rapidly at the keyboard of her computer, and tiptoe across the polished tiles, the soles of my trainers squeaking faintly in the silence.

I head for the bathroom first and give my hands a thorough wash, then make my way to a vacant desk at the end of one of the rows of books. The air is cool and the Wi-Fi efficient as I sign in and access the internet. Grace has fallen asleep, soothed by the peace and quiet of the high-ceilinged room with its air of studious concentration, and I spend an hour browsing.

I hadn't heard of Josephine Baker before, but she was certainly famous in her day. Born in America, she moved to France in the 1920s, where she made her name performing at the Folies Bergères. When the war broke out and France was occupied by the Nazis, she left Paris and spent her time travelling in North Africa and other parts of Europe. Her image smiles at me from my screen, huge dark eyes and a sleek crop of shining hair, just as Josie had described.

I search for a picture of her autograph and compare it with the signature on the folded sheet of blue notepaper. It's identical. I shiver as I sit there, holding the autograph in my hand, feeling a sense of awe at this tangible thread of connection to Josie's extraordinary life. It must have been a strange mixture of glamour and fear, of liberation at having escaped occupied France and frustration at being trapped here on the edge of the African continent, waiting for the chance to leave. Josephine Baker's handwriting on this slip of ordinary writing paper seems to encapsulate an existence that was at once bizarre and mundane.

With each day that passes, I find myself more and more drawn into Josie's world, captivated by her storytelling. I can hear her voice so clearly as I read. But now a sense of unease dawns on me. The fear she felt, the danger that lurked just beneath the surface of her privileged lifestyle in the *nouvelle ville*, have wormed their way under my skin too. Sometimes I'm tempted to turn to the end of her journal to see if there are any clues as to how she and her family finally escaped. But I still resist that urge, not wanting to miss a single word of her story as it unfolds.

As if picking up on my uneasiness, Grace begins to stir, opening her eyes and smiling up at me, so I pack away my laptop and gather up my things. I wander with her among the rows of shelves, idly browsing. The vast majority of the books are modern paperbacks, but here and there older editions with faded cloth-bound covers are sandwiched between the bright spines. A thought occurs to me and I find the English fiction section, tracing authors' names until I reach 'S'. And there it is, a copy of *Strong Poison*, by Dorothy L. Sayers. My hands tremble a little with excitement as I take it down from the shelf. It's clearly not been a very popular title – I imagine her books are a little dated nowadays, superseded by more up-to-date crime novels and thrillers. There are only a few date stamps on the lending record sheet stuck inside the front cover. And one of the first stamps, in faded ink, is a return date of March the 5th, 1941. It could have been Josie. No, I decide, it *was* Josie who pulled this very book from the shelves all those years ago and carried it to the front desk for the librarian – the kind and pretty Mademoiselle Dubois – to stamp. She would have read this book in her bed beneath the mosquito net in the room under the eaves, her tin candle lantern casting its stars around her as she lost herself in the world of 1920s England.

I walk back to the front desk and ask the librarian whether it's possible for me to register to borrow books. 'Certainly,' she says with a smile, handing me the forms to fill in. Once she's taken a photocopy of my passport, she enters my details into her computer and checks out the book. Then she stamps the sheet on the inside cover and hands it back to me.

It feels like I've made another direct line of communication to Josie. My date stamp now sits below hers. I run my hands over the yellow cover, with its black printed title. Josie's hands held this book. Maybe she read it to Nina, sitting in the courtyard beside the pomegranate tree, transporting herself and her friend to another world.

And at last it will sit beside the bed in the same attic room once again, as a candle lantern casts its stars on to the walls.

Josie's Journal – Sunday 30th March, 1941

Yesterday was a pretty interesting day. Mama and Papa had decided to hold a Dinner Party. You could tell by the way they talked about it for two weeks beforehand that it was definitely not just going to be a dinner party, but a Dinner Party: capital D; capital P.

Over the breakfast table they discussed all the details: who would be invited; what food would be served; whether Papa would be able to lay his hands on enough bottles of good wine; whether the men might like to smoke a cigar afterwards (which Maman said would be allowed in the drawing room, just this once); whether Papa would, in any case, be able to lay his hands on any cigars. Most of it was pretty boring, actually, but I did prick up my ears when I learned who was coming: Mr Stafford Reid, who is a vice-consul at the American consulate; Miss Dorothy Ellis, my English teacher; Madame Hélène Bénatar, the kind lady who had helped us in the refugee camp, who is a widow; and Olivier, Annette's beau (it's official now) and his parents. That meant Annette was going to be allowed to be at the Dinner Party too. Maman has decided she's old enough now and it's high time she learned how to hold her own in polite society. Annette gave me a very superior look at that point in the discussions, but I was actually relieved that I'm still not old enough to be included. Polite society can be extremely boring if you ask me. I stuck my tongue out at Annette and unfortunately Maman saw me do it and said I needed to start to learn how to behave in a more ladylike manner. She told me I would have to put on my silk dress and be there at the start to pass round the nuts with the pre-dinner drinks and it would be a good opportunity for me to practise making polite conversation with grown-ups. Annette stuck her tongue out back at me then, but unfortunately Maman did <u>not</u> see that. Typical.

I didn't really mind, though. I thought it would be nice to see Miss Ellis and that I'd like to meet Madame Bénatar and thank her for helping us and Felix's family to get our *Permis de Séjour* so we could get out of Aïn Chok and come to live in nicer places. Mr Stafford Reid is American, so I was looking forward to asking him where the best place might be to buy a farm over there. Olivier is a drip, so I wasn't going to bother talking to him.

Anyway, all the plans finally came together and the Dinner Party was last night.

Handing round the little bowls of roasted almonds and a tray of tiny *bakoula* pies made by Kenza (which everyone loved) gave me the chance to say hello to everyone and make up my mind who I'd like to talk to. As I'd suspected, Olivier's parents are just as dull as him, so after I'd handed them their snacks I moved on pretty quickly, leaving them to Annette. Madame Bénatar was lovely, with an extremely kind smile. Her teeth are a little crooked and that made me think of Felix. She studied in France and was the very first woman in Morocco to become a lawyer. She spends her time helping refugees like us, especially people who are having a very difficult time because of the war and the way the Nazis are treating Jews. I think I might be a lawyer in America, although I'll probably only be able to do it some of the time as I'll still need to look after the animals on the farm.

Then I moved on to chat to Miss Ellis and Mr Stafford Reid. Miss Ellis introduced me as her protégée and explained that we share a passion for the books of Dorothy L. Sayers. It turns out Mr Reid (who is very handsome) is a fan of Lord Peter Wimsey too, so we had a very good chat about *The Five Red Herrings*, which we are reading in my English lessons at the moment. There are six suspects in the case of the murder of a Scottish artist: one is the culprit and the others are the five red herrings. Mr Stafford Reid asked who I thought the murderer might turn out to be and why, and he listened very carefully to my reasoning – although he didn't give away whodunnit of course.

After that, Maman said that dinner would be ready and I could go off to my room to read my book.

I decided I'd sit on the stairs for a while, just where they curve so you can't be seen from below, and listen to the conversation in the dining room a bit more as some of it was turning out to be pretty interesting after all.

And then two very interesting things happened while I was sitting there.

The first was that Annette came out to powder her nose and Olivier followed her. He grabbed her in the hallway and I was about to shout at him to let her go when I realised she was actually grabbing him right back. They had quite a long kiss, a bit like Deanna Durbin and Robert Stack in *First Love*, and then Annette smoothed her hair down and went back into the dining room. Olivier waited a minute or two and had a good look at himself in the hall mirror, then he went back in too.

The conversation in the dining room carried on and a lot of it was about the war, of course. It always is these days. The Afrika Korps have brought very powerful tanks called Panzers to fight the British in the desert and have pretty much managed to drive them back out of Libya to Egypt. Judging by the excited tone of the Radio Maroc news reporters and the more serious tone of the BBC ones, this probably really has been happening. It's quite frightening to think about the Germans becoming more powerful and taking over everywhere, so I decided to stop thinking about that and imagined how I would tease Annette about kissing Olivier instead. I was just thinking I might go up to bed and read another chapter of *The Five Red Herrings*, when the second very interesting thing happened.

Miss Ellis emerged from the dining room to powder her nose. Just after that, Mr Stafford Reid appeared too. This in itself was an interesting development and for a moment I wondered if they were going to kiss each other as well. But instead they just stood quite close together and talked quietly. I had to very carefully lean my head against the banisters to be able to hear what they were saying.

First of all, Mr Reid said, 'You're right, Dorothy, Guillaume is the perfect man for the trip.' I listened even harder at that because Guillaume is Papa. Then Miss Ellis said, 'Yes, but travelling on his own might create suspicion.' And Mr Reid nodded and said, 'But not if it's a family holiday to the mountains.' Miss Ellis replied, 'Do you think Delphine would agree to such an undertaking?' (Delphine is Maman's name). And Mr Reid said, 'She wouldn't need to know it's anything other than a family trip. Guillaume will be able to persuade her, I'm sure.'

Then Miss Ellis said, 'Do you think it will be safe for the girls?' and Mr Reid said, 'I think it will be safe <u>because</u> of the girls. They'll be the perfect camouflage. A family outing to explore a little more of Morocco – what could be more innocent?'

I had my forehead pressed so hard against the banisters by that point that they left red dents in my skin. But then Mr Reid and Miss Ellis went back into the dining room, where the conversation seemed to become a bit more boring again. I suppose people had drunk a great deal of the good wine by that stage of the proceedings. They were all laughing a lot. I stayed sitting on the stairs for a while longer but no one else came out and so in the end I went quietly up to my room. I hung my dress up carefully in the wardrobe, as Maman had instructed me to do, and then I lay on my bed for quite a long time just thinking about everything. I didn't even read my book. I wondered about those brown envelopes that Papa had been passing to Miss Ellis and the list of places and numbers I'd seen and I had a feeling that somehow this plan for a trip to the mountains was linked to them, although I couldn't work out how exactly.

I've decided not to say anything to Papa or Maman about the conversation between Mr Reid and Miss Ellis. It will be interesting to see what happens about the proposal of a family trip to the mountains.

But I'm definitely going to say something to Annette about kissing Olivier, that's for sure.

Zoe – 2010

Next time I go to the library, I find a book on the American presence in Morocco during the war. Searching through the index, my eye is caught by a familiar name: Stafford Reid. I leaf through to the pages on which he is referenced. He was one of a number of vice-consuls appointed to serve in Morocco in the 1940s, I read. Officially, they were here to help deal with the flood of refugees from across Europe seeking visas for the United States. But then I come across a paragraph that tells of a very different reality. Several of the vice-consuls had another, more clandestine remit. They were appointed to gather intelligence, as well as to help establish and co-ordinate a resistance network in North Africa. It was a group that would come to play a key role in the course of the war.

Among other undercover activities, I learn that Stafford Reid's role had been to establish a radio network with its base in a hidden room in the basement of the American consulate attached to an antenna concealed in the roof. Known as Station Lincoln, it provided a crucial communications hub, with Reid responsible for the coding and decoding of messages.

As I read this, my hands begin to itch and burn. I fish a tube of cream out of Grace's changing bag and massage some into the red welts. The relief it provides is only temporary, though, and a few minutes later I'm unable to resist scratching at them again, worrying at the skin the same way my anxiety troubles my brain. Did Josie's father know what he was getting involved in when he began going to those 'meetings'? Was he becoming a pawn in the very dangerous game of chess that was being played out on the plains of North Africa? Did he realise the danger he was exposing himself to? And did he know his girls were being used as a cover, as Josie suspected when she overheard the conversation on the stairs?

The burning of my skin becomes unbearable and I can't concentrate on the words on the page in front of me any more. I think Grace must sense my anxiety because she gives a little whimper in her sleep and angrily punches the air with one chubby fist. I put my laptop away and gather everything together, checking out the book on the American campaign in North Africa at the front desk.

I don't want to go home just yet, so I decide to walk back via the Habous. Other than walking to the library and back, I haven't dared attempt any longer walks since the time I got lost in the medina. My confidence in being able to navigate my way around the city is still a little shaken. But Kate's told me it's much easier to find your way around the Habous than the twisting alleyways of the old medina and it's the best place to look for quilting fabrics, so I push down the anxiety that rises in my chest and take a deep breath to steady myself. Grace seems quiet and contented, lulled in the baby sling by the closeness of my body, as I walk beneath a Moorish arch into the shady streets.

Arcades of smaller Mauresque arches accommodate rows of tiny shops crammed with burnished copper and brassware, which gleams in the dark interiors alongside silver-framed mirrors. There are bright-coloured rugs hanging on tall frames, and shelf after shelf of painted pottery. One shop sells pretty wooden boxes inlaid with mother-of-pearl and I wonder whether this could have been the one where Josie bought hers. 'Best quality, best quality,' the man assures me, and I nod and smile and continue on my way.

I stop outside one shop that is crammed from floor to ceiling with antiques, fascinated by some bundles of pearl-handled fish knives and cut-crystal champagne coupes that probably date from the 1920s or 30s, I guess, and might well have graced an elegant home like the Duvals' on the Boulevard des Oiseaux. In one corner sits an old valve radio set, next to a vintage telephone and a gilded samovar. I almost expect the clipped tones of a Second World War BBC reporter to announce the latest news from the front.

'*As-Salaam-Alaikum*,' I greet the man sitting on a stool sorting through a bundle of old postcards.

'*Wa-Alaikum-Salaam*,' he replies, getting to his feet. 'You are searching for something in particular, perhaps, Madame?'

A box full of tin-plate toys has caught my attention. 'May I look at these?' I ask him and he gestures to me to be his guest.

The toys look as if they've been much loved and well played with over the years. There's a fleet of battered cars and a little aeroplane, a tin whistle, a balancing acrobat, and a clockwork cat, which has lost its key. At the bottom of the box I spot the curve of a crescent moon. As I pull it out, I realise it's attached by fine chains to a cascade of stars. I carefully untangle them, revealing a mobile to hang above a baby's bed. The tin is dull and tarnished but I rub one of the points of the moon with a corner of my shawl and it gleams softly.

'How much?' I ask the man. He names his price – a few dirhams – and then reaches a small round box down from the shelf behind him, its filigree metal aged by verdigris. 'Maybe this would interest you too?' he asks. He winds the key in the base and then raises the hinged lid. The delicate notes of a lullaby chime softly, entrancing Grace. 'I can give you a good price for both if you like.' He and I both know he's already made the sale, it's just a question of bartering a little for the sake of good form. He wraps the tin wares in newspaper and I add them to my bag.

I thank him, but am in no hurry to leave. There's so much to look at, so many items that are relics of the days when Josie and her family were here. The shopkeeper busies himself polishing the samovar and I imagine a genie emerging from its elegant spout. Who did it belong to, I wonder, and how did they come to transport it to Casa in the first place? How did it get left behind?

The man notices my reluctance to leave his shop. 'I think you are interested in the past?' he asks. 'It is indeed fascinating to find these connections to history, *n'est-ce pas*, Madame?'

I nod, picking up a pearl-handled button hook and picturing how a woman like Madame Duval might have used it to fasten a pair of long gloves in preparation for attending one of the tea dances at the Hotel Excelsior.

'Please take my card.' He hands me the rectangle of cream paper, embossed with the name *Monsieur A. M. Habib, Propriétaire*, and the address of the shop. 'Do you live in Casablanca, or are you just passing through?'

I smile at his use of the term that Josie had used in her journal. 'I live here.'

'Ah, you are a *Casawi* like me then,' he says, making a small bow. I know he's just being polite – *Casawi* is a term the natives of Casablanca proudly use to refer to themselves – but I've warmed to this courteous fellow history-lover. 'In that case, please do return any time, Madame . . . ?'

'Harris,' I reply.

'You are most welcome any time, Madame Harris. I often find new items. But there is no need to buy, of course. It is simply a pleasure to share these things with a fellow history fan.'

'*Merci*, Monsieur Habib.'

'*Je vous en prie*. God be with you.'

'And also with you.'

I pick up the heavy changing bag, bulging now with my laptop, library books and my purchases, and readjust my shawl. Grace peeps out, wide eyed with wonder as we walk through the narrow streets lined with their heaps of colourful wares. I pause here and there to examine embroidered scarves and shawls that I might be able to use for the quilt. I like the idea of adapting older items for the sashing strips that will hold my blocks in place and for the border of the finished quilt and so I make a mental note of the location of the places that stock second-hand fabrics.

Stepping back through another arch into the wider, palm-lined avenues of the *nouvelle ville* feels a little like stepping from one world to another and I blink in the sunlight, getting my bearings. We're not far from home now. I pat the mobile and music box for Grace's room through the plastic coating of the bag, reassuring myself that buying them wasn't a dream. I glance back through the archway. It felt like going back in time. I almost expected to bump into Josie and Nina, looking for things to spend their pocket money on, each shop an Aladdin's cave of treasures.

Back home, I clean the mobile until the moon and stars shine with a gentle silver light and then I hang it beneath the mosquito netting over Grace's bed. I place the music box on the nightstand and carefully wind the key. Then I lie next to my baby daughter, listening to the lilting notes of the lullaby, as she watches the moon and stars above her and waves her hands, cooing her approval.

But I can't settle. I rub at the scaly skin on the underside of my wrist with the nubs of my bitten fingernails, trying to scratch away the irritation. Now that I've discovered Monsieur Duval was becoming involved with the embryonic resistance network in Casablanca, a lump of fear has lodged itself in my stomach. It's a visceral sense of anxiety that I can't shake off.

I imagine Josie watching the snake charmer in the medina and know now that she felt exactly this same sense of foreboding.

Josie's Journal – Tuesday 1ˢᵗ April, 1941

Surprise, surprise! Over breakfast this morning, Papa asked us how we'd all like to go on that expedition to the mountains that we'd talked about the first time we went to the farm. I pretended to busy myself in extracting the stone from the juicy date I was eating so that I wouldn't have to look him in the eye, which might have given away the fact that I'd been expecting this turn of events all along.

Maman wasn't so sure. 'But Guillaume, mightn't it be dangerous to travel, when there's so much more military activity now?' she said.

I glanced up then, to see what his response would be. He reached over and took Maman's hand and said, '*Chérie*, I wouldn't dream of exposing my wife and daughters to danger, you know that. You are the most precious things in the whole wide world. Don't worry, I've spoken to Stafford about it and he says it's still safe to travel in Morocco. The fighting is far away in Libya and Egypt. We have two whole countries between it and us.'

I found that very interesting because, of course, Papa was telling the truth in a way. I was sure he <u>had</u> spoken to Mr Reid and Mr Reid would have said it was safe (as long as Maman, Annette and I were there to provide camouflage). But he wasn't telling the whole of the truth. In the background, the Radio Maroc newsreader was describing the latest tremendous victories the Nazis had won by sinking convoys of ships in the Atlantic and pushing the British back in the desert of North Africa. I felt a bit sick then, not just because it made me think of all the dead bodies sinking into the ocean to join my stones but also because when people don't tell the whole truth it makes me wonder whether they can really be trusted at all. I realised that Papa was becoming a bit like the radio broadcasts: it wasn't exactly lying, but there was an important bit of the truth that was being held back. I know Papa would never want to do anything to hurt us, unlike the Nazis, but it still made my stomach tie itself into a tight knot to think he wasn't telling the whole of the truth and so I pushed my plate away with my breakfast unfinished.

We're going next week, if Papa can hire the car and lay his hands on a canister of gasoline. I imagine Mr Reid will probably help make sure that happens.

I know I should have been feeling excited and happy to be going on such a trip and I tried to remind myself how beautiful and mysterious the mountains looked when we went horse riding on the farm. But instead of their hazy blue layers being filled with the promise of new places to explore, now when I picture them in my imagination they seem a little sinister, hiding secrets and lies.

I went to find Nina after breakfast. I told her about the exciting surprise of the planned trip (and now I realised I was doing the same thing as Papa and the radio newsreaders, leaving out some of the important bits of the truth, so that made me feel even worse). Nina really was very happy and excited for me, though. She said I'd love the mountains and seeing the huge expanse of the desert on the other side of them, which is like an ocean of sand. That didn't make me feel better either. In fact, I began to see our situation here a bit more clearly. Morocco is a country bounded by a vast desert on one side, where Panzer tanks lurk like hyenas waiting for a kill, and a vast ocean on the other, where U-boats wait to prey on other ships like sharks. And we are caught in the middle, like little white mice.

But then Nina told me that her very old auntie, the dream-seller, originally came from the mountains. The tribes there are known as the Amazigh – which are what we know as the Berbers – and they have lots of very interesting traditions and customs. Maybe Nina could see I was feeling a bit subdued and needed cheering up because she told me a story, which the dreamseller had told her, and it did make me feel a lot better:

Three children, a brother and two sisters, were left abandoned in the desert by their wicked stepmother. They wandered for days and were getting very hungry and thirsty when they arrived at a magic well. Whoever drank from it changed into a dove. First the brother drank from it and turned into a turtle dove and then one of the sisters had a drink and she did too. The remaining sister realised what had happened and so she didn't take a drink. She carried on, wandering lost and alone in the desert. Eventually she arrived at the palace of a king. The king saw her and fell in love immediately because she was very beautiful. He said, 'Will you marry me?' But the girl said, 'I will not marry you unless you can bring back my brother and sister to me.' The king said, 'Where are your brother and sister?' and the girl said, 'They have become doves.' Then she heard a sound of cooing from the roof and she looked up, saying, 'There they are, on top of your palace.' The king said, 'I will bring them back to you.' He went off and caught the pair of doves and then he asked the girl, 'Where did these doves drink?' The girl said, 'From a well in the desert,' and the king said, 'I must bring them back to the well to let them become human again.' The king rode off on his fine black horse. When he came to the well, he threw the two doves in. They came out as humans and the king said, 'Come, we must go to your sister.' When they arrived back at the palace, the king said to the brother and sister who had been doves, 'Will you let me marry your sister?' They agreed. The marriage celebrations lasted seven days and they all lived happily in the palace from that day on.

Nina said that when I am away on my travels, wherever I am, when I hear doves calling from the roof I will know that they are my Moroccan brother and sister, Felix and Nina, who have drunk from the magic well and are travelling with me.

Zoe – 2010

I sit by the window sewing my first Tree of Life quilt block. My fingertips are sore from gripping the needle, but the task stops me from biting at my nails and the skin surrounding them. At first my stitches were clumsy and annoyingly irregular, but I'm making progress – the seams are straighter now and once the pieces are pressed they look quite neat. The starch irritates the skin of my hands, making it even rougher, but I don't want to use too much cream for fear of staining the fabric.

There's a breath of wind up here among the rooftops today and I've opened the shutters to let the light flood the attic room. The faint breeze stirs the mobile above Grace's bed, the moon and stars rotating slowly in their separate orbits. On the roof, the doves mutter beneath their breath as they ruffle their feathers and search for windborne seeds that have become caught along the line of guttering.

I think of the story Nina told Josie and I smile as I imagine the birds have drunk from the magic well. Perhaps they're really the three friends who used to play in the courtyard and read their library books in the shade of the pomegranate tree.

But those children are long gone. I wonder where they are these days. They'll be in their eighties by now. I picture Josie living in America, a grandmother probably. She'll still have her farm and be surrounded by her animals and her many grandchildren. It's comforting to think of her that way.

I reach for another triangle and lay it against the one I've just finished stitching into position, right sides together, making sure it lines up perfectly with its neighbour before I begin on the next row of backstitch.

The house is quiet. Alia has finished for the day and let herself out, softly closing the door behind her. I don't expect Tom will be back for hours. He'll work late again, I'm certain of that, still angry after the argument we had last night.

By the time he arrived home, I'd given up waiting and had eaten another solitary supper, alone at the dining table, which Alia had laid for the two of us as usual. When Tom walked in, swaying slightly as he pulled off his tie and threw it over the back of his chair, I got up without a word and carried my empty plate to the kitchen. I was intending to fetch him his own plate of the chicken, which was keeping warm in the oven, but he misinterpreted my actions and must have thought I was judging him, deliberately walking away so we wouldn't be in the same room together. He strode through to the kitchen behind me and grabbed my wrist, making me gasp as his fingers closed around the tender skin. His breath was sour with the smell of beer. He let go of me immediately, shamefaced and apologetic, though still clearly frustrated at my silence.

'Talk to me, Zoe,' he said, and I heard the sharp edge of anger in his voice. 'We can't go on like this. You always seem to be avoiding me.'

'I could say the same to you,' I retorted. Instead of anger, my own voice held nothing but cold detachment. 'You're the one who's out all day, leaving before I'm even awake and not coming home until after dark. Another long day at the office, was it? Or another evening at a bar? Did you go out drinking with someone or were you on your own?'

He dragged his fingers through his hair, exasperated. 'Don't do this, Zoe, please. I feel as if I can't reach you any more. We need to talk.'

I noticed he'd avoided answering my question and a flash of anger flushed my cheeks. I hated being put into the position of having to ask in the first place, feeling suspicious and needy. I could hear how bitter my words sounded. I wasn't going to ask again. His avoidance was answer enough. I was certain he'd been out with someone.

I put his supper on to a plate and pushed it across the counter towards him. 'Not really possible to talk if you're never here, is it, Tom?' I said, as evenly as possible.

He looked at me tiredly. 'You know what I mean. We need to try counselling again. I know it was a disaster last time, but neither of us was ready for it then. If I can find someone we can talk to, would you give it another go?'

I stared at him blankly. 'I thought we *were* giving it another go by moving here. I thought it was going to be different, like you promised. But it's the same old pattern, isn't it? You caught up in your work, when you're not in some bar or other looking for more amenable company. Me stuck here at home. What's the point of going over it all again? It's not going to change what's happened.'

He shook his head, helplessly, and when he raised his eyes to meet mine they were full of the emotion that he tries so hard never to show, red-rimmed with the tiredness and the hurt. That unexpectedly guileless glimpse of his pain felt like a physical blow and I had to look away, flinching involuntarily.

'Please, Zoe. We have to try again. For the sake of the people we once were. I don't know where the woman I married has gone, but I do know I want to find her again.'

His plate of congealing food sat between us, as cold and unappealing as the conversation. Automatically, my hand came up to my mouth and my teeth tore at the skin alongside my thumbnail. I only registered the action when I tasted blood and felt the new pain I'd inflicted on the raw skin. It's about the only thing I'm capable of feeling these days. And it stops me from speaking the truth, from saying things I'll only regret afterwards. The woman he married is dead and gone, I wanted to tell him. She's been replaced by a hollowed-out shell of a wife, only able to find solace in the company of her baby daughter. She sits in the attic room and sews one triangle of fabric to the next in the hope that it'll keep her torn and bleeding fingers busy long enough for the pain to stop.

'Eat your supper,' I said wearily. 'It's late. I'm going to bed.' My words instantly doused the heat of our exchange, the storm subsiding as quickly as it had blown up. As I climbed the stairs, I felt the frosty silence fall once more behind me.

One of the doves suddenly flaps its wings, the sound causing a flurry of soft admonishments from its roof-mates. I glance across at Grace, but she's sleeping soundly and the birds settle again without waking her.

Once I've finished sewing the seam, I reach for the little music box that sits on the windowsill. I open its lid, tracing the filigree, which the years have covered with a coating of soft green verdigris. The notes float on the evening air, chasing away the silence and the sadness, and I hope they fill Grace's dreams with a tune from long ago.

Josie's Journal – Thursday 3rd April, 1941

I'm not going to write much tonight because we're heading off on our trip tomorrow and that means getting up early. If you ask me, there's been an awful lot of preparation for a so-called relaxed family holiday. Papa has arranged the car and the extra gasoline we'll need and Maman has been trying to think of everything else we might want for any eventuality that may occur. She's been worrying about whether we will need mosquito nets, whether we'll have enough warm clothes for the cold nights and whether we might run out of water or starve to death. I think the time we spent in the refugee camp has had a lasting effect on her. But Papa has assured her that we will actually be staying in very nice hotels.

He spread the map out on the table and showed me exactly where we're going. First we'll visit Meknes to see Bab Mansour, which is a huge and ancient arched gate covered with beautiful mosaic tiles. Then we'll go to Fez, where we're going to stay the night in a traditional riad that is now a guest house, recommended by two English friends of Miss Ellis's who have been staying there too. That will be very interesting to see and should reassure Maman that we really are staying in comfortable places if they are suitable for English ladies. After that, we'll head into the mountains, driving up through a long valley that leads to Taza, a city at the head of the pass. Beyond that is the desert. Papa showed me some pictures in a guidebook. Taza is very ancient and began as a fortress because it was used to defend one of the very few passes through the mountains. The town is surrounded by ramparts to protect it from marauders. When I saw the photos of those high walls, I hoped that they would help protect us, just in case the camouflage provided by me and Annette being along for the trip needs a bit of reinforcement.

Beneath the town there are caves in which people live. They are called 'troglodytes'. I think it would be very interesting to be a cave dweller. You probably wouldn't have to worry about being polite and brushing your hair and having dinner parties. Maybe it wouldn't be so much fun in the winter, though, because there can be snow in the mountains then, even in Africa.

We will spend two nights in Taza, giving us time to explore the town and the mountains and perhaps venture into the desert, although that'll depend on how the gasoline supplies are holding out. According to the map, it is approximately 330 kilometres from Casablanca to Taza.

After that we'll drive all the way home in one day, which will be a lot of driving for Papa. I hope the Dodge Sedan will be up to it, and that we can have the windows open sometimes because it's certain to be very warm in the middle of the day. Papa says we'll mostly try and travel earlier and that it'll be cooler in the mountains in any case.

I'm not going to take my journal with me on the trip because Annette and I will be sharing a room when we stay at the hotels so I won't be able to write in it without her poking her nose in and demanding to read what I've said in case I'm writing anything about her. I'll just take some notes so I don't forget things and then I can write up everything about the trip when we come home again.

In the meantime I've found the perfect hiding place for it under the floorboards in my room. I think my sandalwood box will just fit in there too, for safekeeping while we're away.

I hope I sleep well tonight, although I'm feeling a mixture of excited and anxious about the trip. But I'm determined to be the best possible camouflage for Papa so I will be acting the perfect tourist.

Goodnight.

Josie's Journal – Wednesday 9th April, 1941

We got back late last night. Even though the trip was very interesting, I was pleased to be home again and have my own bed to sleep in. Annette snores, and in Taza we had to share a bed. She took up most of it, even though it would have been quite large enough for two people if she had kept to her own side. I think she must have had a few bad dreams of her own, because she was very restless and kept kicking me. I'd take her to see the dreamseller if I thought it'd do her any good, but I know if I suggested it she'd make that face like she did when we went past the leather tannery in Fez.

But I'm jumping ahead again. Here's what happened on our trip to the mountains . . .

We set off early and first of all we followed the road alongside the ocean. I looked out of the window and thought about the words I'd thrown into it. I felt a bit sad, but mostly it was a quiet sadness, one that didn't feel as painful as before.

Then Annette said, 'Josie is biting her fingernails again,' and Maman turned around in her seat and told me to stop. She asked me what I was thinking about that was making me anxious and I said, 'Having to share a room with Annette tonight', just to teach that sister of mine a lesson for telling tales.

We turned inland on to the road to Meknes. There was a police roadblock on the outskirts of Rabat. They were members of the French police, not the Gestapo, but even so it made Maman go very quiet and her shoulders went all stiff and crept up towards her ears. But Papa had all our papers in order and, after they'd peered at me and Annette sitting in the back of the car, they waved us on. The camouflage appeared to be working.

Maman's shoulders relaxed again as we picked up speed. It was a bit like the road to the farm, very dusty, and we passed through quite a few settlements of various sizes where stray dogs came and barked at us as we passed in the car. All there was to look at were the scrubby trees and spiky bushes and the occasional donkey. In the distance, though, were the foothills of the mountains, like the humped backs of whales rolling along the horizon. They were faint at first, covered in a blue haze, but as the hours went by they became a bit clearer and you could start to pick out the shadows of valleys and the dark smudges of cedar forests.

The town of Meknes clamps itself on to a solitary hill that rises from the plain, looking a bit like a barnacle on a rock, and we reached it as the midday sun was beginning to make the car feel like being in the oven in our kitchen when Kenza is making bread. So we were very thankful to reach our first hotel and be able to stretch our legs.

In the room that Annette and I were to share there were two narrow beds and a washstand with a basin and a jug of water so we could splash our faces and wash our hands. It was almost lunchtime and so we went and sat at a table in the courtyard beneath some trailing vines that made it a nice cool spot. The waiter brought us our lunch, which was lots of little snacks like olives, and tapenade with *khobz* to spread it on to, and fried *brionats*, and slices of stuffed *m'semmen* pancakes. It was all quite delicious.

Afterwards Papa said we should all go and have a rest on our beds until the day cooled off a little and then we'd go out and explore the town. Annette fell asleep and snored a bit, while I read *Lord Peter Views the Body*, my next Dorothy L. Sayers book, which I got from the library before we left. Mademoiselle Dubois has now met Nina, as she comes with me to choose books sometimes, and she kindly lets us take out extra books on my ticket since she knows there are two of us reading them.

The town of Meknes felt a lot more peaceful than Casablanca. We wandered through the streets, where there were stalls with baskets of fruit and olives and some with leatherwork and Berber rugs. I stopped beside a man who was sitting in front of an easel, painting a picture of the turquoise minaret that rose like Rapunzel's tower behind a wall covered in scrambling vines. He stopped painting and smiled at me, then asked me in French what I thought of his artwork. I told him I liked it very much, although I was mostly being polite as it just looked like a lot of rough blobs of paint really.

Then Papa, Maman and Annette arrived and he smiled even more and they got talking. His name is Gustave Reynier and he told us he likes painting scenes in Morocco because the light is so good. I looked at his painting again, which was a bit of a muddle close up, but then I stood back a little and suddenly I saw what he meant – the blobs of paint transformed themselves into the rug stall alongside the wall, a door with green shutters, and the trailing leaves of the vines. He'd managed to get the light and the shadows just right so that you could feel the heat and see the way the sunshine slanted along the pavement. I actually did like it very much then. He and Papa were getting on very well and Monsieur Reynier asked us if we'd care to join him for an aperitif at a local café. So we did and he told us stories of his painting adventures in Morocco and Algeria. He asked us where we were headed and when he heard our destination was Taza he nodded his head in approval.

'You'll enjoy seeing the mountains and the desert. It's a fascinating landscape, far starker than the one around here, but beautiful in its way. Altogether a different light again.'

I wondered whether our bumping into Monsieur Reynier was part of Mr Reid's secret plan for our trip, so I was watching carefully to see whether any brown envelopes were exchanged, but Papa just sipped his glass of pastis and chatted about Paris, which was another city that Monsieur Reynier loved. And then I remembered that I was the one who had struck up the conversation with him in the first place so I guess he was just a bit like one of Lord Peter Wimsey's red herrings.

The next day we drove to Fez, which wasn't nearly as long a journey as the day before, so we had more time for relaxing over breakfast under the vines in Meknes before we set off. The morning air was fresh and a pair of turtle doves were murmuring to one another in the branches of a fig tree in one corner of the courtyard, which reminded me of the ones at home in Casablanca, and of Nina and Felix of course. It made me very happy to imagine they'd drunk from the magic well and were accompanying me on this trip. I didn't feel quite so anxious about having to be camouflage for Papa when I thought my friends were there to support me.

Then we set off again in the Dodge Sedan and the road began to climb a little, bringing the mountains even closer.

We arrived in the ancient city of Fez at midday and the metal of the car was so hot by the time we managed to find the riad we were going to be staying in that Papa said you could fry eggs on it. I would have liked to have tried that but sadly we didn't have any eggs to hand.

I was especially interested to see Fez for two reasons: one was that I had read that it had the oldest library in the world; the other was that we were going to be staying in the guesthouse where two of Miss Ellis's friends lived so I was on high alert to see what might happen. Maybe there would be some more clues as to the real purpose of the trip. I was determined to be on the lookout for brown envelopes or any other suspiciously furtive exchanges.

Miss Bertha Smith and Miss Gertrude Evans were sitting in the courtyard of the riad when we arrived. 'Welcome, welcome,' Miss Smith said, striding towards us with her arms spread wide. In her flowing kaftan she looked a bit like a ship in full sail. 'Dorothy has told us so much about you. We've been looking forward to meeting you and to showing you Fez.'

Then she told us to call her Bert and said that Miss Evans went by the name of Gert. They are two ladies who have come from a university in Cambridge, England, to study at the famous library in the Al Qarawiyyin university at Fez since it has only recently been opened up to non-Muslims. This is because you used to only be able to enter the library from the mosque so non-believers were forbidden to enter, but a new separate entrance was created just last year, which allowed it to be open to others as long as they were scholars. Women are allowed in and in fact Bert told us that the whole university was founded by a woman called Fatima Al-Fihri in the 9th century, more than 1,100 years ago! Bert told us more very fascinating facts about the university and the city as we sat and sipped cups of mint tea in the beautiful tiled courtyard with a fountain bubbling away quietly to itself in the centre. Bert and Gert are staying in the riad while they study some of the very ancient documents in the library. Maman asked them if they hadn't thought of going back to England because of the war but they said it made it all the more important to see the documents in case the war destroyed things. Gert is one of the first female professors at Cambridge, and Bert has studied architecture so she finds the buildings of the ancient medina in Fez very interesting. I liked them both very much and thought I might like to study at an ancient university somewhere one day. In the Dorothy L. Sayers books, Lord Peter Wimsey studied at Oxford University. I asked Gert about it and she said she was biased but she thought I should go to Cambridge. There's a college called Girton that women can go to, although when I told her we were going to be living in America she said that in that case I should apply to Vassar College, which is entirely for women and has a very good library too.

By the time we'd had lunch we all felt that Bert and Gert were firm friends. Gert said she would take us to visit the library the next morning, if she could square it with the guards, because we would find it very interesting and there was a very good view of the city from the roof. But first, Bert took us on a tour of the medina that afternoon. It was much, much bigger than the medina in Casablanca and some of the streets were so narrow you couldn't really say they were streets at all. Sometimes Papa had to turn sideways on because otherwise his shoulders touched the walls on either side.

We looked at the arrays of stalls with their baskets of olives, dates, spices and fish, and we saw a butcher's shop with camel meat hanging from a hook on the ceiling. There were rug sellers and leather workers too. Then Bert bought some sprigs of mint from a stall and said we should hold them to our noses because we were about to go and see the famous and very ancient traditional leather tanneries and the smell was really pretty dreadful. She was right. The tannery looks a bit like a giant honeycomb of stone vats although it certainly doesn't smell as pleasant as a real honeycomb would. The tanners use bird droppings and urine to treat the hides while they are being dyed different colours and the stench of sulphur and ammonia makes your eyes water. The sprigs of mint helped a bit and Bert showed us how to crush them a little between our fingers to release more of their sweetness. First the hides are rubbed with salt to remove the hair and then they are put into one of the very stinky vats and men get in there with them and stamp on them until they become soft. I dread to think what their feet must smell like when they go home at the end of the day. Perhaps their wives make them wash before they come into the house. At the end of the process, the hides are rinsed with mimosa flowers to get rid of the bad smell. (Maybe that works on the men's feet too.) It was very interesting to see how the different colours were made, using plants like indigo, poppies and saffron, but I must admit it was quite a relief to move on from the tannery and be able to breathe some fresher air at last.

After a very tasty supper (the cook at the riad is almost as good as Kenza), we retired to our beds.

True to her word, Gert took us to visit the library at the university the next morning. The guard wasn't keen to let us in at first, but Gert was very persuasive, and he obviously knew that she was a very intelligent scholar who treated the library with deep respect, and so in the end he let us pass. Gert showed us shelves of leather-bound books, some over a thousand years old and written on camel skin. She also showed us a very old wooden plaque, which she explained was the university degree certificate awarded to its founder, Fatima Al-Fihri, all those centuries ago. She smiled at me and said, 'Ironic, isn't it, that my own university still doesn't award proper degrees to women.'

There was a reading room, which we tiptoed through, feeling a great sense of awe at the thought of all those scholars who had studied here down the years. Even Annette was impressed. And then Gert led us along a narrow corridor and up a winding stone staircase, which grew narrower and narrower until at last we emerged, blinking, into the bright daylight on the roof of the library. Beyond the concertina-like folds of the green-tiled roofs of the university buildings, the huddled jumble of the medina's streets stretched for miles. Far in the distance, in a haze of heat and dust, the mountains of the Middle Atlas rose from the surrounding plain. Papa pointed towards them. 'Taza must be somewhere in that direction,' he said. And judging by the preoccupied expression in his eyes, I surmised that Gert and Bert were most probably just two more red herrings and that the real reason for our trip lay in those mountains.

I liked Fez very much. If we weren't going to America, I think I might even have liked to have lived there and been a scholar, reading ancient books in that quiet library.

I've written a lot so I think I'll stop for a bit now and finish writing down the rest of the story of our trip another day.

Josie's Journal – Friday 11th April, 1941

I didn't have time to write anything in my journal yesterday as Maman insisted that Annette and I accompany her to the hairdresser – in my case for a trim and in Annette's case for a far more fancy wave and set, which she'd wanted to try out ever since she saw Katharine Hepburn in *The Philadelphia Story* at the cinema a couple of weeks ago. Then I had an English lesson with Miss Ellis in the afternoon to make up for the ones I'd missed with us being away. She asked me to tell her all about our lovely family outing to the mountains. Ha! I was quite tempted to say that now I knew why we'd gone on that trip, just as she and Mr Reid did, but I realised I was probably still going to be needed as a decoy to protect Papa in the future and that if I blew my cover then they might ask him to go on other trips without me, which would put him more at risk. So, for the sake of protecting him, I just imagined I was a radio newsreader and told the story while leaving out some of the important bits of the truth. Perhaps I'll get a job as a radio presenter in America instead of a lawyer, except my programme will tell the whole truth about things. I bet a lot of people would be very interested to listen to that.

The chergui is blowing today, whipping up the dust and filling my eyes with grit when I tried to go and do some skipping in the courtyard, so we are staying inside with all the doors and windows tight shut and that gives me time to finish writing the true story of what took place on our trip . . .

We said a fond farewell to Bert and Gert, and they promised to visit us in Casablanca sometime, if they ever got the chance to come and see their friend Dorothy Ellis.

From Fez the road began to rise more steeply as we climbed into the mountains. The scenery was completely different on the way to Taza, much greener, and there were shady forests and pastures where sheep grazed contentedly. We drove along a deep valley and Papa said we were between two mountain ranges – the Middle Atlas and the Rif. The air smelled different, of woodsmoke and wild thyme, and it felt much fresher than down on the plain.

Then the road got really steep and we had to stop the Dodge Sedan and put water in the radiator because steam was coming out. Before he could put the water in, we had to wait a bit for the radiator cap to cool down enough for Papa to open it, so I went for a little wander along the side of the road. Perched on the rocky slopes above us, I spotted a herd of black goats balancing on the pinnacles and shards of the sheer mountainside. It was hard to imagine how they'd managed to get themselves up there. They seem to leap around the rocks like acrobats. A man came past us herding a flock of sheep down the road. His head was swathed in a turban, which he'd wrapped around his nose and mouth too to keep out the dust kicked up by the trotting hooves. All you could see were his deeply hooded eyes. He didn't stop, just kept on following the river of sheep as they flowed downhill to the greener pastures. Apart from that it was very peaceful and we didn't see another soul. A large bird with a white head and vast black wings circled overhead, as if it was watching us. When I pointed it out to Papa he said it was a kind of vulture called a lammergeier and it was keeping an eye out for food. That made me shiver a bit because it seemed like it might be considering us for its next meal. Thankfully we managed to get going again soon after that, so the lammergeier had to swoop off to search elsewhere.

The road climbed and climbed some more, and the landscape changed again, the green fading to grey. The mountains were bleaker, made of blocks of bare rock, and I imagined the vulture would find all sorts of tasty snacks of carrion here as it seemed to be a place where nothing would survive for long. I hoped the car wouldn't run out of water or gasoline and tried not to bite my nails. And then, around a couple of hairpin bends in the road, we got our first sight of Taza. The town is perched, like one of those black goats, on top of a mountain pass, and its high, forbidding walls tell anyone who approaches it that this is a serious fortress. The walls are made of ancient stones and seem almost to be part of the earth itself, as if the ground has grown upwards to protect the buildings within. We entered through a huge gateway and drove through narrow streets until we reached a square where our hotel stood in one corner. I was pretty glad to have got there safely. The Dodge Sedan seemed to be thankful too and it hissed and clicked a bit as we drew to a stop, as if it was breathing a sigh of relief.

The good thing about the hotel was that each of the bedrooms had its own small balcony where you could watch the comings and goings in the square. There were two bad things, though: the first was that Annette and I had to share a bed. Neither of us was very pleased about that, but one of us decided to make the best of it while the other one moaned for about an hour. No prizes for guessing which was which. The second was that a scorpion scuttled out from under the bed, which made us both shriek. I think Annette's complaining probably disturbed it. It curled its evil-looking black stinger over its back and crept towards Annette, who just stood there, petrified. Almost without thinking, I grabbed a water glass from the bedside cabinet and put it right over the scorpion. It didn't like that at all and kept jabbing crossly at the glass with its stinger, making tiny, cross, pinging sounds. Then Annette ran to fetch Papa and he disposed of it for us. It wasn't a very big scorpion, but Papa said that the smaller ones can still be very poisonous. He then checked our room in case there were any more. But luckily there weren't.

In the late afternoon we went for a walk around the ramparts. I thought about the day when I stood on the beach with Kenza and Nina, because here, too, it felt as if you could see for ever, and the mountains were like the waves of another vast ocean stretching away to the horizon. To the east was the beginning of the desert, which I imagined to be a different kind of ocean altogether – a sea of nothingness, although the war had even managed to make its presence felt there, as it had throughout the rest of the world.

We walked back to our hotel through the medina, which is at the very top of the town. It was very interesting to see that the women here – the Amazigh, as Nina had informed me – didn't wear veils like they do in Casablanca and the other cities we'd visited on the way to Taza. Instead, their faces were covered with tattoos like the ones the dreamseller had. It made their eyes look very fierce somehow and at the same time very beautiful, a bit like the scenery of the mountains.

The call to prayer began from the minaret of the mosque. It looked very different to the pretty turquoise one in Meknes and the beautiful white ones in Fez as it was made of bare bricks. It was nestled in a corner of the ramparts, solid and businesslike, as if it was a stronghold built to defend the faith. I remembered what Gustave Reynier the artist had said about the light here and I saw that he was right – it's somehow clearer and softer all at the same time and even though the town and the surrounding lands are very bleak and stern-looking, the light transforms them into something magical.

I kept a sharp eye out for people who might approach Papa, but no one did that evening, not even a red herring.

-x-

Next day we were back in the car, following a tourist circuit that was described in Papa's guidebook. Papa reassured Maman that he'd refilled the canisters of water and gasoline so we wouldn't run out and become stranded and turn into food for the vultures. Actually, Papa didn't say that last bit, I just thought it.

We drove along a ridge to start with and admired the views of the mountain ranges. There were even still traces of snow on some of the highest peaks. Then we descended into a forest of cedar trees, which stretched their long branches towards us like arms, reaching out to embrace us and to pull us into the darkness beneath them. We were in a steep gorge and the rocky walls here were a deep red colour, quite different to the grey blocks on the road to Taza. Maman read from the guidebook that we were approaching the Caves of Chikker and Papa pulled off the road so that we could go and explore. Out of nowhere, it seemed, a man appeared and beckoned us to come to the mouth of a chasm in the rocks. I wondered if he might be a troglodyte and actually live in the cave, but Papa asked him and he said he actually lived in a house nearby and herded sheep in the hills. He wore white robes and had a big stick tucked into a belt around his waist. Papa asked him about the caves and the man said he would take Papa in to see them. He looked at Maman and Annette a bit doubtfully and they looked back at him equally doubtfully. Then Papa looked at me and raised his eyebrows, as if challenging me, to see if I was brave enough to venture inside. The gaping black entrance, surrounded by sharp stalactites like long, thin teeth, was a bit frightening. But the jagged fangs then made me think of Felix, who is not frightening at all. And I thought what if this man was the reason we'd come on this trip, and what if Papa needed me for camouflage at this point? So I nodded my head firmly, accepting the challenge.

The man lit two tin candle lanterns and handed one to Papa. Then he led the way into the blackness. The first cave was quite small, but the man took us to a narrow opening in the rock at the back of it and we found ourselves in a twisting tunnel, scrambling up and down over its rocky floor. Papa shone his lantern so that I could see where it was safe to put my feet and I was thankful for the light it cast. I was very aware of the vast weight of the mountain pressing down above our heads and the blackness beyond the small circle of lantern light, which seemed even darker than the darkest night.

At last we came to a huge cavern, which opened up all around us. The sight was quite extraordinary. Strange stalagmites, sculpted by water and time into shapes like beehives and giant bathtubs and weird statues, rose from the floor, where an underground river flowed between them. The man held his lantern high above his head but in places the light still didn't reach the roof of the cavern, which was so high, somewhere far above us. The pierced patterns in the tin cast stars of light on to the walls and it felt like we were standing in the middle of the universe itself. Then the man led us to another strange stalagmite, which must have been about five times as tall as Papa, and he showed us that we could climb it using a series of natural steps that had formed on one side. When we reached the top of the mound there were hollows containing little pools of perfectly clear water, which Papa said had filtered through the rocks over thousands of years. Above us, hanging from the roof of the cavern, were what looked like velvet curtains in shades of pink and cream. Then I realised they were swathes of stalactites, but I could hardly believe they were made of stone because they seemed to drape themselves in such soft folds from the ceiling. The man took the stick from his belt and tapped them gently. I was already finding it hard to believe my eyes, but then I couldn't believe my ears. A strange, other-worldly music filled the cave, like chiming bells, reverberating and echoing from the walls. I could almost feel the waves of sound passing through me and I closed my eyes for a moment. I imagined I was in a vast cathedral or mosque or synagogue and suddenly I saw that it didn't matter which it was or which particular version of God you believed in because faith was something deeper and stronger, something like that music drawn from the rocks pulsing through my body, more powerful than any words written down by mankind. Papa and I stood in silence listening as the last notes slowly died away and then he smiled at me in the candlelight and his face was so full of love that for a few seconds I couldn't breathe. I thought, 'I will always remember this moment, as long as I live.'

The man said the tunnels continued even deeper into the earth but to go any further would need ropes and special equipment. Some scientific expeditions had begun to explore further but the war had put a stop to all that for the time being. I thought it would be very interesting to be a scientist exploring those mysterious tunnels and perhaps being the very first person on earth to see what lay in their depths. But it was time to go, so we went back out the way we'd come and it was quite a relief to be back in the fresh air and the glare of the sunlight once again. Maman and Annette were sitting on some rocks at the side of the stream and I realised it must be the same water that had flowed in that underground river in the great chamber. It felt like Papa and I had glimpsed another world entirely.

We ate a picnic lunch beneath a cedar tree whose spreading branches made it look as if it was curtseying, and we drank some of the water from the stream, which was as fresh and cold as newly melted snow. Then it was time to carry on. The tourist circuit climbed up to a place where there were still a few traces of actual snow by the side of the road and we stopped to make snowballs. Even Annette forgot to mind about her hair getting messed up and joined in. Papa said that in winter the snow was so deep here that you could ski on it. None of us said it, but I know we all hoped we wouldn't still be around for the next ski season.

When we got back to the hotel, after I'd checked under the bed for scorpions, I went and stood on the balcony for a while, watching the traffic in the square, which, very interestingly, included a man leading a camel. Then I realised someone was watching me. A scruffy-looking man was sitting at a table at the café opposite and he was openly staring up at the window where I was standing. Even from that distance I could see he wasn't a local. With his pale, close-shaven head and black robes, he reminded me a little bit of the vulture we'd seen the day before. When he saw that I'd noticed him, he picked up his cup of coffee and raised it in a tiny salute. Covered in confusion, I turned away, pretending to pay attention to a passing truck filled with crates of chickens, and when I looked back he'd gone.

-x-

By the time Maman tapped at the door to let Annette and me know it was time to go down for dinner, we'd washed off the dust from our day's outing and changed into our good dresses. This was the last night of our family holiday and it felt like a special occasion. It also felt like the final opportunity for the real purpose of our trip to reveal itself, unless any of the red herrings we'd encountered turned out to be a cunning double bluff, which, as I know from Dorothy L. Sayers, can sometimes happen. So I was determined to remain on high alert for anything out of the ordinary happening or for the appearance of any of those brown envelopes.

In the end I didn't need to be on high alert for very long at all, though, because when we walked into the restaurant there was Papa sitting at a table in the corner and seated alongside him was the vulture man from the café across the way.

Papa looked a little uncomfortable and Maman looked distinctly unimpressed as the man was even more rough-looking when you saw him close up. His hair was shaved close to his head but what there was of it was very pale, as if the sun had bleached it the colour of desert sand. His hooked nose added to his vulture-like appearance and his eyes were the cold, hard blue of ice. He grinned at us as we approached and his teeth were yellow and pointed, reminding me a bit of the wolf in the fable of The Wolf and the Lamb. Papa introduced us and the man grinned even more. His name was Monsieur Guigner, which sounded a bit suspicious to me, meaning as it does to wink an eye. As Lord Peter Wimsey would have observed, winking often indicates that someone is either telling a joke or being a bit sly.

We stood by the table, waiting for the man to get up and leave, but he just stretched out his long legs and settled himself even more comfortably in his seat, taking a leisurely sip from the glass of pastis in front of him, so Papa had to be polite and ask him if he would care to join us for supper. He said yes, of course, and I got the impression he was quite enjoying the obvious discomfort that his presence was causing. I noticed that his eyes slid sideways towards Annette every now and then when he was pretending to be listening to what Papa and Maman were saying about all the fun we'd been having on our family holiday and how interesting it was to see a bit more of Morocco. He told us he himself was just back from a long trip to the desert, actually, and so Taza was the first bit of civilisation he'd seen for a while. He pricked up his ears (just like the Wolf) when Maman mentioned Casablanca. 'And where exactly do you live in that fair city, Madame Duval?' he enquired. I felt very uneasy again when she told him rather reluctantly and he said that by an amazing coincidence he had friends who lived on the Boulevard des Oiseaux and what number was our house? He didn't look like the sort of person who would have any friends at all really.

When our supper was served, his table manners left a good deal to be desired. He talked with his mouth full and waved his fork around while he was chewing, which are things we'd been taught not to do when we were very young. I saw Maman shoot another very annoyed look at Papa, who just shrugged very slightly as if to say, 'Well, what can I do?' I don't think Monsieur Guigner noticed as he was busy reaching past Annette to help himself to more of the lamb tajine, as if it was the first proper meal he'd eaten in days.

At last, he wiped his mouth on the back of his hand and stretched out in his chair again. The rest of us had already finished our meal and Annette and I politely declined Papa's offer of dessert. The grown-ups ordered coffee and then Annette set aside her napkin and asked to be excused as she said she felt a little tired after our day of exploring. Maman nodded at her, and at me too, but I'd decided to stay put if Monsieur Guigner was going to, just in case anything interesting happened. After Annette left, he stood up suddenly and said he had very much enjoyed the meal and our company but if Papa and Maman would excuse him he thought it was time he got back to his lodgings too. They looked very relieved and relaxed a lot more as the waiter arrived with their coffee. But I was watching Monsieur Guigner leave and I noticed that, instead of turning right out of the restaurant door towards the exit, he turned left into the corridor leading to the hotel bedrooms. Something in the way he moved reminded me of the way the scorpion had scuttled across the floor of our bedroom towards Annette with its evil intent. I quickly put my own napkin on the table and excused myself, saying, 'I think I will go up to the room, after all, and read my book for a while.'

Papa and Maman nodded, scarcely glancing at me, and I hurried off in the wake of the vulture man.

It turned out my instinct was right. When I reached the third floor, where the bedroom Annette and I were sharing was located, I caught sight of Monsieur Guigner at the end of the long corridor, disappearing into our room. After a second's silence, I heard a faint scream so I ran along the hall as fast as I could and flung open the door. That awful man had grabbed Annette and was trying to kiss her while she was twisting and struggling to get out of his grip. His hands were on the buttons of her dress. I realised he was far too strong for the two of us to wrestle to the floor (knowing that I couldn't count on Annette to be of much help in that department), so I decided to try the element of surprise. I said loudly, 'Why, good evening again, Monsieur. Are you staying in the hotel too?' He spun around and behind him I caught a glimpse of Annette's pale, shocked face. She looked terrified, and fear is something my big sister rarely seems to show. She wiped at her mouth with the back of her hand and then fumbled with the buttons of her dress, trying to do them up where he'd torn at them, even though several were now missing.

'Papa and Maman are on their way,' I said, as if I was talking to Annette. 'They said they'd come and give us a hand getting everything packed up tonight to save having to do it in the morning.'

Vulture Man backed away from Annette, closer to the door, and I quickly slipped into the room, putting myself between him and my sister. She reached her hand out and grabbed my arm and I noticed she was shaking quite badly.

'Ah well,' said Monsieur Guigner, smiling and showing those yellow teeth again, 'I too have an early start tomorrow, so I'll say goodnight to you two charming young ladies. It has been a very great pleasure meeting you.'

'Goodnight,' I said, and I shut the door very firmly in his face. Annette reached past me with her trembling fingers and turned the key in the lock.

'Are you all right?' I asked her. She was still looking awfully pale.

She nodded. 'I . . . he just appeared. I thought it was you coming in but . . . oh, thank goodness you appeared when you did!'

She hugged me so tightly I could hardly breathe. And, for once, I really felt like hugging her back. We agreed that we wouldn't say anything to Papa and Maman. That would only have meant getting the police involved and we knew how much that would upset Maman. She'd never let any of us go anywhere ever again. So we kept it to ourselves and just hoped we wouldn't be seeing anything more of Monsieur Guigner.

On the long drive home the next day, I heard Maman say to Papa, 'What on earth was that dreadful man doing in Taza anyway? I know he said he'd been in the Foreign Legion, but do you think he could have been a deserter? He didn't seem to have the slightest bit of military bearing about him. It was very annoying, him latching on to you like that in the restaurant.'

Papa just sort of grunted and changed the subject pretty smartly and then he seemed to be concentrating very hard on the road ahead. I didn't know whether any brown envelopes were exchanged with Monsieur Guigner. But I did know that I never wanted to see him again.

So that was the end of our family trip to the mountains. And then, sure enough, I just happened to look over the banisters as Miss Ellis was leaving after my English lesson the day after we got back and saw Papa handing over some folded-up papers, which he withdrew from the pocket inside his jacket. 'Well done, Guillaume,' she said quietly. 'I'll get them to Stafford straight away.'

Of course, it could have been Bert and Gert in Fez, or even the artist Gustave Reynier in Meknes, who had given Papa those papers but, using my powers of deduction, I decided that the most likely real contact was Monsieur Guigner. Whatever the information was that vulture had gathered during his lengthy trip to the desert, it was clearly of importance to our friends in the American consulate.

Zoe – 2010

When I need to take a break from sewing, I spend my time either at the library or walking through the Habous. I feel close to Josie and her family there, not wanting to break the spell of her story as it unfolds on the pages of her journal. I've become a regular visitor to the shop beneath the arches where I bought the tin mobile and the music box for Grace's room. I may only have spent a few dirhams, but the owner – Monsieur Habib – always greets me like one of his very best customers, with great courtesy and the usual exchange of formalities. We speak a mixture of English and French, peppered here and there with phrases in Darija.

'*Bonjour*, Madame Harris.'

'*As-Salaam-Alaikum*, Monsieur Habib.'

'How are you today?'

'I'm fine, thank you. How are you?'

'I am fine also, thanks be to God. And how is your family?'

'They are well. And your family?'

'All good, *Alhamdulillah*.'

'*Alhamdulillah*,' I reply, echoing his thanks to God.

'Please, take a seat. By fortunate coincidence, I have just made some tea. You will take a cup, please?'

'I should like that very much. *Merci bien*.'

'*Je vous en prie, Madame.*'

Once the mint tea has been poured into a vintage tea glass decorated with gold filigree, and handed over with the customary toast to good health of '*Bisaha*', Monsieur Habib shows me his latest finds. He knows I'm fascinated by anything from the first half of the twentieth century and seems to take pleasure in unearthing items he thinks will interest me.

'Look at this ice bucket,' he says. 'See, it's engraved with the name of the Hotel Transatlantique?' He pulls out a duster and begins to polish it.

'When does it date from?' I ask.

'Around the 1930s or 40s, I imagine,' he replies. 'You can just picture a glamorous couple there for an evening of dancing, being served a bottle of Perrier-Jouët in this, can't you? Such elegance.' I tuck my less-than-elegant trainers beneath my chair and rearrange the folds of my shawl to cover them. He sighs wistfully for those long-gone stylish days, raising an eyebrow at the sight of a couple of tourists dressed in skimpy T-shirts and shorts who pass his shop without a second glance. The Senegalese man who sells leather handbags approaches them, displaying the wares strung over his long arms, but they shake their heads at him and cross the road to browse in the souvenir shop over the way.

The Senegalese trader smiles and lifts a hand in greeting to Monsieur Habib, then continues on his circuit of the street, which he's carved out as his territory. There's stiff competition among the street traders for the prime spots in the Habous, although they have to be on the lookout for the police, who'll move them on if they catch them.

I watch him as he goes. He's immensely tall – over six and a half feet, I'd guess – and has the proud bearing of a warrior. And yet he's reduced to flogging cheap handbags to tourists, walking miles every day through the streets. He must get very tired of the refusals. It's hard, thankless work for a few dirhams a day.

'Monsieur Habib,' I say, 'what do you think happened to all the refugees that passed through Casablanca in the war years?' While I don't imagine he's old enough to remember it himself, that time must have been very fresh in the minds of his parents.

My question catches him by surprise and he slowly puts down his duster and raises his eyes to mine. He seems to be appraising me, and something shifts between us as he gauges my genuine interest in his answer before he replies.

'Most of them managed to travel on to other destinations – to America mainly. And even though America took in more refugees fleeing the Nazis than any other country in the world, they still had strict quotas on the number of immigrants they would receive and there were hundreds of thousands of people on the waiting lists. Certainly some didn't make it. There were anti-Semitic round-ups here, just as there were in France once the Germans invaded. A few, I imagine, might have stayed on.' He takes a meditative sip of tea and wipes his moustache with a paper napkin before continuing. 'Things changed pretty quickly in Morocco, too, at that time, as the nationalists began to campaign for independence. It was only achieved, finally, in the 1950s, but those were turbulent times, speaking in terms of our internal politics as well as the external forces of the war, so plenty of people would have fallen through the cracks in the system. The numbers of refugees here would have been overwhelming.'

He follows my gaze towards the Senegalese man. 'Not that things are all that much better today.'

I take a polite sip from my own glass and place it carefully back on the silver tray between us. 'I've read in the newspaper about the refugee problem in Europe,' I agree. 'But is it particularly bad here?'

Monsieur Habib looks at me pityingly and I feel horribly igno-rant. 'Where do you think those migrants who cause the problems in Europe come from? They are from Africa, mostly. From the war-torn countries in the north and the south alike. From places where life is very cheap and very hard. Take Ismael, for example.' He nods towards the Senegalese trader who has reached the end of his trajectory down the street and begun to trudge back towards us. 'How bad do you think it must have been in his country for him to find this life a better option? He told me he saw members of his family tortured and killed in ways I would never repeat to a lady such as yourself. He is one of the many who are passing through, waiting for an opportunity to move on when he has managed to earn enough money to pay the men who traffic people like him across the Mediterranean. Can we really imagine how it must feel to be so afraid of what lies behind you that you are prepared to throw yourself headlong into an unknown that is going to be filled with danger and loneliness? Leaving behind your family and your culture and seeking something better in a land where you are not welcome and you are not understood? It's no different for him and the thousands of others like him than it was for those who fled here in the war.' He sighs again, picking up a painted tin biplane and then replacing it carefully on the shelf. 'We like to think we learned lessons from those wars and yet history continues to repeat itself, year after year.'

I sip my glass of tea again, thinking about his words and feeling pretty awful. The life I'm leading is so very privileged. I'm growing more and more aware of that every day I spend here. I have my own problems, that's for sure, but that still shouldn't stop me from trying to help those whose problems are even greater than mine.

'Does Ismael have any family here in Casablanca?' I ask. 'A wife and children?'

Monsieur Habib shakes his head. 'No. He's on his own, as far as I know. But that's probably a good thing. It's far worse for women and children to be refugees. They become so vulnerable. They are in a minority, *Alhamdulillah*, because when you do come across them their stories are the worst of all.'

'How do you know this?' I ask him. 'Did you read about it somewhere?'

'There is no need to read about it, Madame Harris,' he replies, and his expression is filled with sadness. 'Such refugees are all around us. But we don't usually open our eyes and ears wide enough to see and hear them. It doesn't take much to seek them out, though. My wife volunteers at a project offering support to women and children who have fled their homes in other countries and become stranded in Morocco. If you wanted to, I could take you there one day to see for yourself what life is like for them.'

'I should like that very much indeed. Perhaps there'll be something I can do to help?' I fish out an old till receipt from Grace's changing bag and write down my phone number on the back. 'Please would you arrange it with your wife and let me know?'

He takes the slip of paper from me and looks at it a little doubtfully. Then he raises his eyes to mine again. 'I will do this for you, Madame Harris. But only if you are sure you want to. Once you have heard their stories, it is hard to see the world in the same way ever again. I'm afraid it can be a rude awakening, hearing what mankind is capable of doing to our own.'

I think of something Josie wrote in her journal. And I say to him, 'But if we leave out some of the important bits of the truth – or choose to ignore them – then surely we are living a lie? And that is no way to live at all, is it?'

He nods, still a little reluctant, and puts the folded slip of paper in his pocket. Then I stand, thanking him for the tea, and take my leave.

'*Au revoir*, Monsieur Habib.'

'*Adhhab bisalam*. Go in peace, Madame Harris,' he replies.

But there is no peace in my soul whatsoever as I walk home, mulling over the hypocrisy of the words I've just said to him, and wondering what Josie would have to say to me about the lie I am living every day if she were here with me now.

Josie's Journal – Saturday 12th April, 1941

Nina and I were on our way home from the library yesterday when who should come cycling by but Felix. We shouted and waved, having not seen him for a few weeks. He stopped for a chat and we showed him the books we'd taken out – two Agatha Christies translated into French (she is Nina's latest favourite author), and *Gaudy Night* by Dorothy L. Sayers, which Mademoiselle Dubois has had on order for us for ages and which had finally miraculously arrived despite everything being in such turmoil in France.

Felix said he liked the look of *Death on the Nile* as it seemed to be about the desert and he'd like to go to Egypt one day when the war is over to see the Pyramids and the Sphinx. I invited him to come back with us for tea and we could all start to read it together. But he said regretfully that he had something to do, so could he come another time? Of course, I said, or maybe we could come and visit you one day because Nina and I both agreed that we'd like to see the bakery and maybe try some of the traditional Jewish *challah* that I'd told her about from Paris days. He didn't seem too keen for us to do that, though, and said it was nicer coming to my house, where there was the courtyard and Kenza's cooking.

I asked him quite nonchalantly if he was going to the Parc Murdoch and whether he'd seen anything more of Miss Josephine Baker recently, but he just laughed and said he'd heard she was keeping company with the Pasha of Marrakesh these days.

Then he cycled off with an air of some importance.

I've heard on the radio that the Germans have driven the English back in Libya, although they haven't been able to recapture the port of Tobruk, which the English have been defending fiercely. Both Radio Maroc and the BBC seem to agree on that point, so it probably really is true.

Maman has joined a committee run by Madame Bénatar to help refugees. More camps have been set up and they need things like medicines and help with organising their *Permis de Séjour* like we did when we first got here. Maman says it's good to give something back, even if we probably won't be here much longer. She's getting a bit annoyed with how long it's taking to get our American visas sorted out, given how much time Papa spends at the consulate. I was tempted to say that she should ask Mr Stafford Reid why that might be, because I'm beginning to suspect that Papa is proving to be quite a useful link in some sort of secret communication system and so it probably suits Mr Reid that our visas are taking such a long time to come through. But perhaps Papa hopes that by helping them he is ensuring that we can get out when the time is right, and also that his secret work will ensure a warm welcome awaits us in America. I'd like to be able to ask Papa whether my deductions are correct, but I know he wouldn't tell me. A secret is a secret.

I'm going to ask Kenza if she can show me how to make *ghoribas* and then we can take them to one of the refugee camps. That should help cheer people up a bit.

-x-

Kenza's Recipe for Ghoribas:

(Makes about 50 small cookies)

2 eggs plus 1 separated egg

½ a tea glass of sugar

½ a tea glass of melted butter

3 large spoonfuls of honey

4 tea glasses of flour

(Sift the flour with 1 teaspoon of bicarbonate of soda and 1 teaspoon of cream of tartar)

A pinch of salt

Zest of an orange

In a big mixing bowl beat together the 2 eggs plus the white of the separated egg (keep the yolk aside for later) and the sugar. Add the butter, honey and orange zest and beat some more. Then carefully mix in the sifted flour until the cookie dough comes together, soft enough to be rolled into little balls between your hands. Put the balls of dough on to a buttered tray and brush with the beaten egg yolk. Bake in the oven for 10–15 minutes.

Josie's Journal – Tuesday 29th April, 1941

Maman had organised a meeting at our house this morning for ladies who were interested in supporting the work of the Committee for Assistance of Foreign Refugees. As its director, Madame Bénatar was coming to address them and I'd been looking forward to seeing her again. There was also going to be a representative of the Jewish community, who had been invited to come along and speak about some of the challenges people are facing, stranded in Casablanca trying to escape from the Nazis. Maman asked Annette and me to be on door-opening duty and welcome the guests as they arrived because Kenza would be busy with the refreshments.

Madame Bénatar arrived early and she was just as kind and intelligent as I'd remembered her to be from the evening of the dinner party. Then the other ladies began to arrive and Annette and I were kept busy answering the door and showing them upstairs to the drawing room. It was almost time for the meeting to begin, and all the ladies were sipping mint tea and eating Kenza's honey cakes, when there was one more knock on the door.

Annette answered it and I heard her say, 'Oh! I'm very sorry but my mother is busy at the moment so she can't give you any money. Please could you come back tomorrow, perhaps?' I looked to see who she was talking to and there on the doorstep stood a very poor-looking woman with a black headscarf pulled low over her face. At Annette's words, she lifted her head and the shawl slipped back a bit. I think Annette and I both winced when we caught sight of her eyes, which were completely swollen and sore-looking, almost shut tight apart from a sticky ooze, which was attracting the flies. It looked so painful it made my own eyes prickle in sympathy. The lady started to say something, when I heard my own name being spoken by someone standing in the street behind her. I was surprised to see it was Felix. And then I realised that the poor woman with the terribly sore eyes was his mother, whom I remembered from the refugee camp.

'Hello, Josie,' Felix said, catching sight of me over Annette's shoulder. 'My mother has been invited to come and speak at the meeting.' He looked quite ashamed and embarrassed because he'd heard what Annette had said.

I felt so terrible then that we'd tried to turn her away, assuming she was a beggar going door-to-door to ask for help. I reached out and took her hand in both of mine and said, 'Madame Adler, it is such a pleasure to see you again. Please come in and Annette will show you upstairs. In the meantime, Felix, I hope you'll join me and Nina in the courtyard for some lemonade?'

That gave Annette time to realise her mistake and I could see that the penny dropped because she also shook Madame Adler's hand and apologised for not having recognised her straight away, then led her away to the meeting.

Felix, Nina and I sat by the pomegranate tree and had our own tray of refreshments. It felt a bit awkward at first. We chatted about the weather (getting hotter) and the war (getting worse). On Radio Maroc there'd been reports of a German victory at Halfaya Pass, close to the Egyptian border, and the bombing of Saint Paul's Cathedral in London; on the BBC there'd been reports of more unsuccessful German attacks on Tobruk and the news that Saint Paul's Cathedral

143

had been damaged in German bombing raids but was still standing, which was a symbol of British defiance against the Blitz.

Sitting there in the courtyard discussing these things, it occurred to me that we were getting as bad as the grown-ups, talking about the war and avoiding other things that really mattered. But then we ran out of things to say, so I plucked up my courage and asked Felix what was wrong with his mother's eyes.

He swallowed a gulp of lemonade and then said, 'It's called trachoma. Our living conditions are pretty bad in the mellah and lots of people get ill. My mother is ashamed because she feels she caught trachoma on account of where we live being so poor and dirty. But it's hard to keep things clean when it's so crowded and we don't have a proper bathroom.'

Nina asked, 'What is trachoma?' And Felix told us it's a very unpleasant infection where germs get into the eyelids, causing scars. When they are badly scarred, the lids turn inwards so that the lashes scratch the surface of the eyes. Felix's mother was in so much agony that, in desperation, she'd pulled out her eyelashes with a pair of tweezers, but as they're now growing back it's even more painful. Slowly this torment is making her go blind. Felix said this is just one of the conditions that the people living in the mellah are having to suffer. There are many other diseases too and several people have died as they wait for their visas.

I understood, then, why he didn't want me and Nina to visit his home at the bakery.

He looked very sad and a bit frightened – not at all like his usual cheerful self – and I realised how brave he must be. Then I said, 'Well, it's a very good thing your mother has come to tell the meeting today about these problems. I'm sure Madame Bénatar and my maman and all the other ladies will want to do everything they can to help.'

I passed Felix the plate of honey cakes and he took another one. Then Nina asked him to teach us some more juggling (we still can't manage three oranges at once) and things went back to being a bit more normal between us all again.

I asked Nina to tell Felix the story about the brother and sister who turned into turtle doves and the sister who saved them and married the king. She really is an excellent storyteller, much better than I am, a bit like Scheherazade herself, who told stories for one thousand and one nights to save herself from being killed by the king who'd married her. Felix agreed that it was a good one and for a few moments we all looked up at the doves on the roof and listened to them talking softly to one another. Then Felix showed us how he's trying to learn to juggle four oranges at once and by then he looked a lot happier.

When we heard sounds of the meeting ending, we went back inside and said goodbye to Madame Bénatar and Felix's mother. It was nice to see she looked a bit happier too and she even managed a smile, although her poor eyes still looked so sore.

After they'd left, I asked Maman what could be done to cure Madame Adler's trachoma and she sighed and said there was some medication that could help but it was very hard to get supplies because of the war. The ladies who had attended the meeting were deeply moved by what Madame Adler had told them about the terrible conditions in the mellah, though, and they were going to try to help as much as they could. I felt very glad then that there are still people in this world like Madame Bénatar and my maman who are kind and caring. I think maybe I would like to find out more about becoming a doctor when we get to America and then I could come back to Africa to help people who are suffering from horrible things like trachoma.

We are so lucky to be able to live in this nice house with proper bathrooms. I just hope our good fortune doesn't run out. I'm not sure I'd be able to be as brave as Felix if I had to live in the mellah.

Annette has said to Maman that she'd like to do something to help the committee ladies too, so that's what I believe Lord Peter Wimsey would call a jolly good turn up for the books.

Zoe – 2010

In the peace and quiet of the library, I read up about the progress of the war. By the end of April 1941, the simmering struggle for territory in North Africa was reaching boiling point. Rommel's Panzer divisions had pushed back the British and Australians, forcing them to retreat into Egypt and leaving the troops holding the port of Tobruk, in Libya, surrounded by the enemy. But they continued to hold out, stubbornly refusing to surrender; it was a siege that would last more than a year until the Afrika Korps finally managed to overrun the city in June 1942.

How much of that would people like the Duvals have been aware of, I wonder. The radio broadcasts they listened to would have been filled with propaganda on both sides. It must have been very tempting to try to believe the messages put out by the BBC, but the reports on Radio Maroc of German victories and the edicts issued by the pro-Nazi Vichy government in France must have been a constant, terrifying threat for the refugees in Morocco, whose options were rapidly running out.

I hug Grace a little tighter as I read, needing the reassurance of her warmth in the hushed, air-conditioned atmosphere of the library.

It's not only the thought of that ominous menace from so many years ago that's unsettling me today. There's something else that I've tried to push to the back of my mind, but it keeps intruding, distracting me from my reading. In the end I give in and decide to go for a walk instead. I replace the books on their shelves and whisper a quiet 'thank you' to the librarian as she smiles at me on my way out.

The streets are as noisy as usual, filled with the cacophony of motorbikes and taxi horns, and the intrusive – if mostly well meant – comments of the street vendors and hustlers. I've learned that if I keep my shawl drawn over my face as much as possible, they tend to leave me be, though, as I head for the Parc Murdoch.

It's an oasis of greenery and relative peace in the middle of the dirt and decrepitude of the city, a place where I can wander with Grace beneath shady trees and hear the songs of the birds. I suppose the fragile melody of that birdsong must always be there beneath the clamour and din in the city streets but, as happens so often in life, some voices get drowned out and we have to listen all the harder to be able to hear them. I think of what Monsieur Habib said about the refugees – they are all around, but we don't usually open our eyes and ears wide enough to perceive them.

I find an empty bench and sit down, allowing myself a few moments to think about what happened yesterday.

I still don't really know what prompted me to look at Tom's phone. He left it on the counter in the kitchen when he went out to buy Sunday morning croissants from the bakery. I suppose the urge to check up on him was my insecurity getting the better of me. The fact that he never changes his passcode should surely tell me all I need to know – a sure sign that he has nothing to hide. But I still couldn't resist a quick check of his messages. There was nothing there, apart from some texts from a couple of male colleagues he's mentioned before, arranging a time for a game of tennis at the Club later that day. Just before I set the phone back down on the counter, I scrolled to the folder of photos. And it was what I found there that has been so strangely unsettling.

There were no incriminating pictures of him with other women, it wasn't anything like that. Just one photo after another of what looked like a sunrise over the city skyline. When I examined them more closely, I discovered that it wasn't only one sunrise, but dozens of them, all taken from roughly the same place on his early morning runs. Day after day, he'd been out there alone and he'd paused to watch the sun coming up over the roofs and towers of this dirty city. It had meant so much to him that he'd captured each of those sunrises on his phone. Somehow, the thought of him doing that made me want to cry. It seemed to me an act of intense loneliness. He wasn't taking those pictures to share them with anyone else. He was just looking for a glimmer of hope, holding on to the promise of a new start that each day brings. It was a rare glimpse of his secret heartache. It made my heart break too.

Guiltily, feeling I'd intruded on something intensely private, I put the phone down and busied myself preparing a pot of coffee. And when Tom arrived back with the paper bag containing our breakfast, I didn't mention the photos to him. But I did try to be better company as we sat and ate, telling him about a lunch I'd had with May, Kate and Claudine last week and asking him more about his work.

For an hour or so it felt as if we'd managed to find a little piece of flotsam to cling on to in our ocean of hurt, keeping our marriage afloat. But then he'd gone off to play his game of tennis and I'd retreated to Grace's room, as usual, to sew and read, and we'd drifted apart once more as the silence and sadness descended on the house again.

Josie's Journal – Thursday 8th May, 1941

The threat of me being sent to school has been rearing its ugly head once again because Maman says she's sick and tired of waiting for our visas and it's taking so long that I'm in danger of falling behind and she's afraid I'll find it hard to catch up when we finally get to America. But Miss Ellis told her that there is a problem with finding places for students at the Lycée right now, especially for my age group, due to the numbers of refugees living in Casablanca these days. She gave me a good report, though, and said my English is really quite remarkably good, thanks to all the reading I do. (I'm not meaning to be big-headed, just repeating what she said.) She has reassured Maman that I'm keeping up with where I should be at this stage, but she's also suggested that she can come four afternoons a week now so that we can do a bit more maths, history and geography.

I was a bit worried that we might not be able to afford the extra lessons (although the private school would be even more expensive) but today I overheard a conversation between Maman and Papa that made me have some very mixed feelings:-

Maman said, 'Guillaume, how on earth are we going to continue to afford the rent on this place? We never expected to be here this long and there's still no end in sight.'

Papa said, 'My darling, don't you worry about it. I'm already planning ahead. I've written to Armand and told him we're happy to proceed with the sale of the Paris house.' (Armand is Monsieur Albert, who took over from Papa at the bank.) Papa went on, 'He'll be delighted – you know how much his wife loved it – and he's offering a reasonable price given how uncertain things are in France right now. Really, it's too good an opportunity to turn down. He'll be able to transfer the funds quite swiftly, so we'll be fine.'

I felt very sad to think of some other family living in our old home with all our things – and especially my books, which I knew I'd never get back now – but at the same time it was a relief to know we could stay in the *nouvelle ville* and not have to move to the mellah, where we might get trachoma like Felix's mother.

I think Maman felt the same way too, because she said, 'Oh, Guillaume, our wedding china and all the paintings and books . . .' and it sounded to me as if she was crying.

But then Papa reassured her and I think he must have put his arms around her because her sobs became muffled. He said, 'Delphine, I promise you we will replace it all when we get to America. This is only temporary. We just have to hold on a bit longer. Our life here really isn't so bad, is it? I promise you we'll be all right.'

She gave a big sniff and it sounded like she was blowing her nose. Then she said, 'I'm scared, Guillaume. I know you've become involved with . . . things. I know you're helping Stafford. But it's dangerous. What if they arrest you again? Do you understand what you're risking?'

Papa's voice grew very low and very serious then and he said, 'Delphine, you and I have spoken about how horrifying this war is. I can't just sit here and let it happen around us. If we don't take a stand then who will? But I promise you, *ma chérie*, I'm being careful. I wouldn't do anything that would put you and the girls at risk.'

I was quite surprised that Papa was making all those promises, especially the one about not putting us at risk because he already had done that when he got arrested and when we went on the trip to the mountains (except Annette and I still haven't said anything to anybody about Monsieur Guigner coming to the bedroom and grabbing Annette). But I understood that Papa just wanted to make Maman feel better and that sometimes that sort of kindness is more important than telling the absolute truth.

Despite him trying to reassure her, I heard Maman begin to cry again and this time she was sobbing quite loudly, which pretty much broke my heart. Then I heard her say, 'I'm so sorry, Guillaume. This is all my fault. It's because of me that it's come to this. You and the girls would be better off without me.' I nearly ran down the stairs to throw my arms around her then and tell her that wasn't true at all, but Papa said it instead before I could do so:

'Don't ever say that, Delphine,' he said, very loudly, and it sounded like he was nearly crying too. 'Don't ever apologise for who you are. You know we love you and we'd be nothing without you.'

Then he said, a bit more calmly, 'Stafford has a plan. I can't say any more, but it is part of something much bigger. I can play a part in it and in return we will get our visas for America when the time is right. Can you trust me, Delphine, just for a bit longer? I'm only trying to do what I think is best for all of us.'

After that there was silence for a while. They were probably hugging and kissing, I imagine. So I crept back upstairs to my room to write all of this down in my journal.

It's awful that Maman feels that way – I'm guessing it's because of her being Jewish. But at the same time it's very interesting to know that Maman has guessed what Papa is up to. And also to have confirmation that my deductions so far have been correct. Lord Peter Wimsey would be proud of me.

151

Zoe – 2010

Somewhat reluctantly, I think, Monsieur Habib has finally arranged to take me to the centre for refugees where his wife works. He shuts his shop at midday every Friday to go to the mosque for prayers and doesn't reopen afterwards, so we agree that he and his wife will come and pick me up from home in the afternoon. I decide I won't bring Grace with me on this occasion, until I've seen what the centre is like.

Madame Habib is a little shy at first – and surely she must wonder who this pushy expat woman is who has intruded in their lives this way – but she thaws a little as I ask her more questions, gradually becoming less reticent as she talks about the centre and the work she does there. Thankfully, I discover, her English is even more fluent than her husband's.

'It was set up to try to protect the women and children who get stranded in Morocco. They come from countries like Nigeria and Mali and Senegal, following the old salt routes across the desert – an unimaginable journey in itself. Some are migrants, deciding to leave their homes to try and find a better life for themselves. But many are refugees, fleeing from persecution, starvation and war. Mostly they enter Morocco through Algeria, in the north, trying to get as close to the Spanish territory of Melilla as they can. It's a little corner of Morocco that's still owned by Spain, and the neighbouring towns of Oujda and Nador are swamped. But it's hard to get into Melilla, which is surrounded by a triple barrier of high fences topped with barbed wire, and it's dangerous too. They either have to try to jump the fences or to swim round. Those who fail become trapped here in Morocco and eventually make their way to the big cities like Rabat and Casablanca in the hope of making a living here until they can pay to be trafficked into Europe.'

'Do they not try to go home again, once they realise they can't get through?' Even as I say it, I realise how naïve the question is and I feel myself blushing.

Madame Habib shakes her head, her eyes filled with sadness. 'There is nothing for them to go back to, only the danger and deprivation that they were running from in the first place. The journey itself is dangerous, too. They become so vulnerable when they are homeless. They lose their family, their friends, their culture and their language. Pretty much all the main things that make up someone's identity. Can you imagine how isolating that is? What it means to lose every landmark that has helped you find your way in this world?'

We're driving towards the lighthouse on the furthest outskirts of the city, past the breakwater that protects the port from the ocean's currents, through clusters of shanties and cramped slums.

Monsieur Habib swerves to avoid a goat tugging at the brittle leaves of a bush that's been uprooted by the side of the road. 'They become like that.' Madame Habib points at the dead shrub. 'When their roots are torn from the ground of their home, there is nothing to nourish and protect them. They fall prey to all kinds of abuse and hardship. It's worst of all for the women and children, they are the most vulnerable.'

We pull up outside a makeshift building, with walls of bare breeze blocks and a corrugated tin roof. On one of the walls, someone has painted a mural of sunflowers. They look determinedly cheerful in the midst of so much bleakness, where the real thing would struggle to survive in the dust.

'Please,' says Madame Habib. 'Follow me.'

I stand back to allow Monsieur Habib to go first but he shakes his head. 'I don't go in. This centre is run by women for women and children.'

His wife stands holding the door open for me. 'Many of the people here have been traumatised at the hands of men,' she says quietly. 'We feel it's better that they know this is a completely safe place, where they won't be exploited or abused, where there is nothing that could retrigger their trauma. No men are allowed in.'

Inside, the large space has been subdivided by makeshift screens into different areas. There's a canteen where they are just finishing clearing and wiping the trestle tables, having served bowls of thick soup for lunch. In another corner is an area where medical examinations can take place, Madame Habib explains. Many of the women are pregnant, but a large proportion of those pregnancies are the result of rape. 'The counselling and mental health services we try to provide are as important as the physical care on offer. And then there are the extra complications of HIV, hepatitis B and syphilis. These women have been through hell and there are still many challenges ahead of them. We can only do so much here. They start off pursuing a dream – the "Dream of Europe", they call it. But it rapidly turns into a nightmare from which there is no escape.'

Madame Habib introduces me to another of the volunteers, sitting behind a makeshift desk. A long queue of women are waiting to speak to her. 'Latifa is trying to help sort out applications for replacement papers. If the women manage to make it as far as Melilla and try to get across the fences, very often they are caught by the Spanish Guardia Civil and handed back to the Moroccan security forces. They do not fare well at their hands, I'm ashamed to say. They are usually taken at night and dumped back on the Algerian side of the border. There are gangs there, waiting to prey on the vulnerable. That is where some of the worst things happen.'

Having their passports, money and phones stolen is often the final act of abuse after a long and traumatic ordeal. And then so many of these children also get lost along the way.'

The space is busy, filled with movement and activity, but there's something missing. As I watch, I realise what it is. There's very little noise. In a community centre like this back in Britain, filled with so many women and children, the sounds of chatter and laughter and kids at play would echo from the rafters. But here the atmosphere is oddly subdued. Children sit on the floor with paper and crayons, silently drawing pictures, each contained within their own bubble of wariness. They glance up at regular intervals, watching the room with big, dark eyes. I catch the attention of one little girl and smile encouragingly at her but she avoids my gaze and there is no answering smile in response, just a carefully blank look that renders her thoughts inscrutable. I guess it's a form of self-preservation, but it's one no child should have to learn to cultivate.

The women huddle in small groups, talking softly together or simply sitting and staring into space.

'Where do they all live?'

Madame Habib shrugs. 'The lucky ones share rooms in the *bidonville* that we passed on our way here.' It's not a word I'm familiar with and she notices my look of bewilderment.

'A *bidonville* is the word for a slum – you saw those shacks? Well, they are made of scraps of rubbish, bits and pieces of whatever can be found. A *bidon* is a tin can or an oil drum, so it literally means a tin-can-town. But not all the women and children here are fortunate enough to have the shelter of a shack to sleep in. Some camp out on the beach or in the sand dunes. Some are working in brothels and will sleep there. We can only provide a safe place and a meal for them during the daytime here. Their nights are filled with dangers.'

When I squat down alongside some of the children, the sour, stale smell of the fear that they wear on their skin is pungent in my nostrils. I look at their pictures. At first glance, they look like the kind of thing any child in my primary school classes back home would draw – stick families standing in front of houses with a scribble of blue sky overhead and a big yellow sun in one corner. But then I look more closely and the blood freezes in my veins, despite the stuffy heat of the room. The houses are burning. The people are bleeding and broken. There are soldiers with guns and knives. The colours the children have used are brutal – violent red, a blaze of orange, the black of despair, muddy brown. The pastel pink and pale blue crayons have scarcely been touched, their points still neat, whereas the darker shades are worn to stubs.

The little girl who'd looked up at me before reaches out and hands me her piece of paper. She still doesn't smile, but she does meet my eyes at last and I sense that she's offering me a gift, the only thing she has to give. I take it carefully and try not to flinch at the image of a body in pieces beneath a tree. She's drawn herself, too, a smaller figure with close-cropped hair, running away, her mouth open in a scream. She watches me carefully again, those big dark eyes taking everything in. And then, very gently, she reaches out a finger and touches my hand where the skin has cracked open in the crevices between my fingers. She looks at me enquiringly for a moment and then pulls back the sleeve of the dirt-smeared T-shirt she wears. At the top of her arm, near her shoulder, is a ragged scar, pink and raw-looking against the dark mahogany of her own flesh.

I reach out my own hand and touch it very gently too, wishing I could heal it, as well as the invisible wounds that scar her mind. She seems to know what I'm thinking because, at last, her solemn little face relaxes into a smile, as if she's accepted that we have a common bond. And then she slips her hand into mine and pulls me to my feet, leading me over to a cardboard box of picture books. She lets go long enough to pull a battered copy of French fables from the pile and gives it to me so that I understand I am to read to her, even though she's still not uttered a single word. We sit, cross-legged, on the cement floor, and I begin to turn the pages. My accent is terrible and I stumble over many of the words, but the little girl doesn't seem to mind. One by one, some of the other children draw closer until I'm surrounded. When I glance up, they are still watching me carefully, but here and there there's a flicker of amusement in their eyes. Whether it's at my attempts to read in French or at something in the story, I'm not sure. But I don't care. That tiny glimpse of an emotion – of any sort of positive feeling – means the world to me. So I carry on and hold up the dog-eared pages every now and then to show them the pictures. They nod politely, sagely considering the cautionary tale of the lazy grasshopper and the hard-working ant, and when I reach the end of that story the little girl reaches over and turns the page for me to begin the next one.

In the car on the way back into the city, I sit quietly, scarcely speaking.

'So, Madame Harris,' Monsieur Habib says. 'What did you make of our centre?'

Madame Habib turns in the passenger seat and says, 'My husband may not be allowed inside, but he and many of the other shopkeepers help raise money to keep the centre open. The men support us in this way.'

'I think it's a terrible place, and at the same time a wonderful place,' I reply. 'It's terrible that it's needed, and horrendous to see those women and children so traumatised. But it's wonderful to know there are kind people like you who give them a safe place to be and try to help them.'

Monsieur Habib nods. 'You're right. We shouldn't live in a world where a place like that centre is needed. It's a dreadful indictment on the human race, isn't it? But to solve the problem entirely would take something unimaginable: it would take governments working together, an end to war and famine, political stability throughout the whole region. It's not in our power to make that happen, not in our lifetime. And so, although it's not a solution to the underlying problem, we have to do what we can. It's impossible to stand by and allow that suffering to go on in our country. After all, we wouldn't be human if we didn't try to do what we can, would we?' He's impassioned, his English flowing more confidently than usual.

Madame Habib smiles at me. 'Madame Harris, would you come back another day and read to the children again? It was a big help to the other volunteers today as it allowed us to spend more time with the women.'

'Certainly,' I reply. It seems pitifully little, but it's all I can offer at the moment. And as Monsieur Habib said, we wouldn't be human if we didn't at least try to do what we can, no matter how insignificant it may seem in the face of all that those women and children are dealing with. I decide I'll go back to the bookshop in the mall and see if I can find some more reading materials that the children might enjoy, perhaps something simpler in French that I'll be able to read a little more easily.

Back at home, I head straight upstairs to wash my hands thoroughly before going into Grace's room. I sit among her books and toys and watch the late afternoon light play across the faded Berber rug, bringing its colours to life, and illuminating the silver moon and stars hanging above the bed. I breathe in Grace's familiar scent – a mixture of freshly laundered sheets and baby lotion. Then I wind up the music box and lift the lid.

The notes of the long-ago lullaby fill the air as I hold my baby daughter to my heart and begin to weep, hot tears of despair and compassion running down my face as I cry my heart out. For all the children who have got lost along the way.

Josie's Journal – Friday 30th May, 1941

I've not been sleeping very well, ever since I overheard that conversation between Papa and Maman. Now that she knows he is helping Mr Reid, but she doesn't know that I know she knows, it feels as if we are all keeping secrets from each other. The only person who remains blissfully unaware of what's going on right under her dainty nose is Annette. That's because she spends so much time going to the cinema and the hairdresser and out dancing with Olivier.

I know Papa and Maman want us both to have a happy time even though we are refugees from the war. I suppose they think I'm just getting on with my studies with Miss Ellis and having fun with Nina and Felix, like any other nearly-13-year-old girl. But I feel as if I'm carrying a heavy weight around with me. Pretending to be carefree is quite hard work.

Maybe if I write down the nightmare I keep having, it will help get it out of my brain and I'll be able to sleep better . . .

In my dream, everything starts off fine. Papa and I are in the caves near Taza, exploring the tunnels that lead off from the main cavern. We hold our lanterns up and they cast stars on to the rocks around us, lighting up the darkness. The stars look like the one on my gold necklace and there are thousands of them, just like in the night sky. This part of the dream makes me feel happy. But then I notice something strange is happening. The stars start to disappear, one by one at first but then more and more fade and die. It's very strange because the lanterns still seem to be casting enough light for me to see by, but something is extinguishing the stars. This is when I start to feel very uneasy and the ground beneath my feet seems to shift and shake. The tunnel begins to grow narrower, as if it's closing in around us, and the ceiling presses down from above. The rocks begin to make a ringing sound, softly at first, but it grows stronger and stronger. I notice that Papa has to turn himself sideways because the walls of the tunnel are as narrow as the alleyways of the medina in Fez. But they keep on getting narrower and narrower and, as I watch, Papa begins to be crushed. I'm filled with panic. He looks back at me with that look of love in his eyes and smiles, saying, 'I will always remember you, Josie, I will always love you.' Even as he says the words, though, the walls close in completely. Our lanterns are extinguished and then he is gone too and I am left all alone in the darkness. The only sound is the singing of the rocks, which seems to fill the air around me so I can't breathe. I fight against the fear and the panic and the terrible, terrible feeling of pain at losing Papa and being left alone in the darkness, and even though I struggle against it, I feel as if I'm drowning in a deep black ocean.

I always wake up at that point, just as I'm being pulled under. Sometimes I think I can still hear the sound of the rocks singing even though I know I'm now awake – it turns out to be the song of the muezzin calling the faithful to early prayers.

Whenever I have that dream, it takes a while for my heart to stop pounding and for the panic to subside. I remind myself that I'm in my bedroom, not a cave, and that Papa, Maman and Annette are safely asleep in their own beds downstairs. Then, if it's still dark, I light the pierced tin candle lantern that sits beside my bed and I lie watching the stars flicker on the walls of my room. As day breaks, the stars and the darkness fade away and the candle burns itself out. But even when the morning arrives, I'm left with the residue of all those awful feelings inside me.

It's no wonder I'm so tired. And I still keep biting my fingernails, despite my New Year's resolution.

Now that I've written down my dream, I'm going to try to think about nicer things instead, like how it's going to be my birthday in 12 days' time, on the 11th of June, and I will be turning 13. There's something quite satisfying about those numbers, although I'm not sure how much I'm looking forward to becoming a teenager. Annette isn't exactly a great example of what it's like. I hope I don't start being as silly as she is. Nina is 2 months and 3 days younger than me and she agrees. She's going to come to my party and Kenza has promised to make me a special birthday cake, with *amlou* for the filling because she knows how much Nina and I love that paste, which is made of almonds, argan oil and honey. It's going to be very delicious!

Josie's Journal – Wednesday 11th June, 1941

My 13th birthday has been a very good one, in spite of my concerns about officially becoming a teenager on top of all the other worries lurking in the background.

For breakfast we had my favourite Moroccan doughnuts called *sfenj* with bowls of *chocolat chaud*, which is about the closest you can get to heaven on earth in my opinion. Then Annette passed me a little box and in it was a pretty pearl on a gold chain. 'You may be my annoying little sister, but you are also a bit of a pearl yourself sometimes,' she said as I hugged her. 'I thought you might like to wear it now that you can't wear the star one these days.' I was quite surprised that she'd thought about that, since usually her head is too full to fit in many thoughts other than her own concerns: of Olivier and where to find a new powder compact, or whatever the next thing is that she urgently needs to perfect her latest look. She helped me fasten it round my neck straight away and I like it very much. It's sort of like the ocean has given me back a token in exchange for the words I gave it.

Papa and Maman then also passed me a little box. I have to admit, ungrateful as I know it seems, that a tiny bit of me thought, 'Oh no, not more jewellery.' It is possible to have too much of a good thing. But they were both smiling at me in anticipation, so I smiled back and opened the lid. To my surprise, there wasn't anything inside the box except for a little folded-up slip of blue writing paper. On it was written: *Dear Josie, your present is far too big to fit in here. Go and look in the courtyard. Happy birthday, love from Maman and Papa xx*

I ran downstairs and there beside the pomegranate tree stood a very fine bicycle with a basket on the handlebars, decorated with a bright red bow. My very own Steel Steed! Then I really did smile because that was the best present imaginable, even better than jewellery.

I hugged everyone and Papa helped me have a little practice to make sure I could still remember how to ride a bike from Paris days. After a few wobbles, I felt confident enough to try it out on the pavement of the Boulevard des Oiseaux and then Papa said I was good enough to ride it on the streets as long as I was very careful and didn't go on the main roads. There's not much traffic these days anyway because gasoline is in such short supply and pretty much everyone cycles or walks.

Nina was very excited to see the bike. She and Kenza gave me a pair of leather slippers, which I'd admired in the medina on one of the occasions when we went to their house. I put them on straight away and then gave Nina a ride on the back of the new bike. We'll be able to use it for going to the library and can put our books in the basket.

I still had to have my lesson with Miss Ellis in the afternoon because Maman said birthday or no birthday everyone has to be educated. But we just did some reading (no maths, for a birthday treat) and then Miss Ellis presented me with a gift too. It's a large book called a thesaurus and it is full of interesting suggestions for alternative, different, unconventional, unorthodox, out of the ordinary, substitute vocabulary. As you can see, I'm already putting it to good use.

Inside the front cover, Miss Ellis has written *For Josie, who loves words. Best wishes on your thirteenth birthday from Dorothy Ellis. 11th June 1941.*

And then it was time for my party in the courtyard. I'd invited Nina and Kenza and Felix and I did also tell him he could bring his parents. He said they sent their thanks, but they were busy. Out of his pocket, he drew two small lengths of stick and he presented one each to me and Nina. I didn't know what they were at first, but Nina did. She blew into one end and the stick made the sound of a turtle dove's coo. It was so realistic that the doves on the roof cooed back, which made everyone laugh. Felix explained that the baker had taught him how to make them, and he had a third one that he'd made for himself. It was another perfect present because it showed that he was thinking about Nina's story of the brother and sisters. Also, it will always help me remember the happy times I've spent in the courtyard with my friends. That made me feel a little bit sad at the same time, because it reminded me that the day will come when we will leave Nina and Kenza behind and who knows if we will see Felix and his parents in America as it's such a huge country. Also, I doubt I'll be able to take the bike with me when we go, but then I decided that when we do I will give it to Nina so she will always remember me and that thought cheered me up again.

Kenza had made the most delicious birthday tea, with little cinnamon and almond pastries called gazelle horns, plus the promised cake with the lovely *amlou* filling. Papa had even managed to lay his hands on some bottles of Coca-Cola for me and Nina and Felix, and the grown-ups drank mint tea. A very good time was had by all.

So I've had an amazing day and now feel very tired and happy. My pearl necklace from Annette is on my nightstand next to the turtle dove whistle from Felix, and my leather slippers from Nina and Kenza are beside my bed ready for me to put on in the morning. My bike is downstairs in the hall.

Thinking about it, I'm guessing that the money from the sale of our old house in Paris must have come through, judging by the very generous gifts from my family and the bottle of champagne that Maman and Papa opened at dinner this evening, which they said was to toast both their teenage girls. Annette had a glass too and I had a few sips.

But even though I'm now 13, I have to admit I still prefer lemonade.

Goodnight.

Zoe – 2010

We've been invited to Claudine's for dinner. As I put on my make-up, applying the mask that gives me the confidence to face these kinds of social situations, I smile a little, thinking that Josie would say this was going to be a Dinner Party, capital D, capital P. I've become so absorbed in her journal that she feels like a constant companion to me here in the house, keeping me company, a lively presence whose voice can be heard if you listen carefully enough to what lies beneath the silence. In some ways, her world seems more vivid, more real, than mine. Although she's long gone, she remains a life force, while I am the ghost in this house, drifting through its empty rooms.

I pull the black dress over my head and zip it up, then push my feet into a pair of high-heeled court shoes. It's the uniform I wear for any formal events to do with Tom's work: safe, careful, suitable clothes. The dress hangs a little more loosely than it used to, but the shoes pinch more. I suppose my feet must have spread from wearing nothing but my trainers for so long. They're far more comfortable in the heat when I walk to the library or Monsieur Habib's shop in the Habous.

Claudine's house isn't far from ours, but Tom drives us there anyway in the company car that comes with his job.

Tonight, everything is a reminder of that corporate world, which is the epicentre of our expat universe here in Morocco. The door is answered by a housekeeper, who takes my wrap and then shows us upstairs to the drawing room. The layout of the house is very similar to ours, just on a grander scale and furnished with far more elegance. We step into the room, lit by the diffused glow of a chandelier, and Claudine – the perfect hostess – sweeps us into the gathering, making introductions as she goes. Her husband, Théo, who's one of the company executives, has the greatest gravitational pull, drawing in Tom and his colleagues as they stand talking business, drinks in hand. The others are dotted in smaller groups, minor satellites in outer orbits. May calls me over to the sofa where she and Kate sit, and I join them, thankful to see their friendly faces. I tuck my feet beneath the couch and surreptitiously slip off my shoes, relieving my pinched toes for a few moments. May introduces me to Suzette, a woman with hair so stiffly lacquered it looks as if it wouldn't shift even if the full force of the chergui was blowing. She flashes me a brief smile (if Josie were here she would point out that it didn't quite reach her eyes, though), and I see her glance taking in my too-loose dress and my too-tight shoes, assessing me and deciding in an instant that I don't warrant much attention. She turns back to May and Kate, continuing a conversation about where to get the best manicure in the *nouvelle ville*. I curl my fingers around the stem of my glass, all too aware how ugly my own hands are with their chewed nails and patches of inflammation where the cracks in my skin have become infected.

I quickly glance across the room to where Tom is laughing loudly at something Théo has said. His glass is almost empty and he holds it out with alacrity for a refill when a bottle of whisky is handed round. Looks like I'll be driving us home again tonight, since he'll be in no fit state by the end of the evening. I bite my lip, praying that dinner will be served soon.

Kate notices my anxiety and gives my arm a little pat as she includes me in the conversation, asking how I've been since we last met for lunch. 'It's a bit of a shock to the system after England, isn't it? Do you feel like you're starting to find your feet? I reckon it took me about a year before I began feeling a bit less out of my depth in Casa.'

Grateful for her kindness, I tell her I've been doing a bit of volunteering at the centre for refugees and she turns towards me, giving me her full attention. 'That's not a place I've heard of,' she says. 'How did you get involved with it?'

I tell her about meeting Monsieur and Madame Habib and how they have made me more aware of the humanitarian crisis that's happening all around us. 'I don't do much, though – just a bit of reading to the kids. It's the other volunteers who really do the work of trying to support the women there.'

May begins to listen in to our conversation too. 'That's an interesting project,' she says. 'Kate, do you remember Anneke was telling us she'd heard about it at our last meeting?' She turns away from Suzette slightly and asks me, 'Do you know how they fund the centre?'

'Private donations mostly, I think,' I reply. 'They've been try-ing to get a government grant, but their applications keep getting turned down. There's so much pressure for that kind of thing, I suppose. I know they're grateful for anything they receive.' The picture books I bought to supplement the tattered collection were accepted as if they were priceless treasures, and one of the women had hurried away to find a new box to keep them in.

Suzette taps her long red fingernails impatiently against the side of her glass. 'Initiatives like that are well meaning, I'm sure, but really do you think we should be encouraging these people? Surely they'd be better off back in their own countries instead of putting a burden on others when they can't support themselves.'

Very carefully, so that I won't spill my drink because my hands are suddenly shaking with anger, I place my glass on a coaster on the side table next to me and then turn to face her. Rein it in, I tell myself silently, and when I speak I try to keep my voice level.

'It's impossible for them to stay in their own countries. They've lost what family they once had there – often having witnessed them being brutalised and murdered. Can you imagine how terrified you'd have to be to risk a journey of thousands of miles, on the run with nothing and no one to help you and knowing the dangers?'

She raises one over-plucked eyebrow, clearly annoyed that the new girl has had the temerity to voice an opinion that runs contrary to hers. 'What happens in those countries isn't our business though, is it, Zoe? We can't be responsible for the messes other people get themselves into. They're illegal aliens in Morocco. They know they're breaking the law by coming here.'

There's something condescending in the way she deliberately uses my name, putting me in my place. I realise my hands are now clenched into tight fists, the half-healed creases of my fingers cracking open again with the tension.

'I think we all know the problems the refugee crisis brings with it, Suzette,' I reply. Two can play the name-game, after all. 'But when we're faced with the immediate consequences, day in, day out, surely we who have so much can afford to give something to those who have lost everything. Even if it's simply a few books and a little kindness, it can help take their minds off the terrible things they've seen and experienced for a while. Maybe even help to give them back a little faith in humanity.'

Her smile is as tight as my clenched fists and for a moment I picture the mask of her face cracking open too with her own anger. 'It just seems such a futile gesture when you put it like that, doesn't it? A drop in the ocean. Perhaps our efforts could be put to better use elsewhere.'

'Surely even a drop in the ocean is better than none at all, though?' Monsieur Habib's words come back to me. 'It might not be a solution to the underlying problem, but we wouldn't be human if we didn't try to do what we can, would we?'

Suzette's smile fades and her eyes narrow for a moment. But then she turns away, having had enough of this fruitless conversation, and animatedly greets two men who have come to top up their drinks from the array of bottles set out on an elegant oval table on the other side of the sofa.

May puts a reassuring hand on my arm and says quietly, 'Don't be minding her now. It takes all sorts, you know.' Then, more loudly, she continues, 'Well, I'd like to meet your Madame Habib sometime. Kate and I do a bit of fundraising, one way and another, and it sounds like a project we could maybe help support.'

I smile at her gratefully and pick up my glass again, now that the risk of either spilling it down myself or chucking it at Suzette's smug face has receded. 'Thank you. The centre's a good place – you should see how much help they give to the women and children there, even with such limited resources.'

'Now,' she says, 'tell us how you're getting on with that quilt you're making. Kate says it's going to be a real work of art . . .'

Thankfully – and I'm sure the feeling is mutual – Suzette and I are seated at opposite ends of Claudine's mahogany dining table, although Tom sits immediately to her right. He's attentive, filling her wine glass and then topping up his own. I notice how she repeatedly touches his arm with her manicured fingertips, deep in conversation, inclining her blonde head towards his, drinking in his every word. Her eyes never leave his face and yet I somehow know she's aware of the effect this must be having on me. From where I'm sitting, it looks like an act. But it's one Tom seems to find very convincing. Kate sits on the other side of him and she catches my eye at one point and smiles. I wonder if she's enjoying the evening or whether she finds it as much of an ordeal as I do. As I watch, Tom turns away from Suzette and fixes his attention on Kate. She reaches for the salt but he leans over and passes it to her with mock chivalry, making her laugh. For a moment, it looks as if his fingers brush hers as he hands it over, but it's so fleeting that I think I must have imagined it. I shake myself, mentally, and silently tell myself to stop being so paranoid every time he even so much as talks to another woman. Kate's my friend, after all.

With an effort, I turn my attention to the lamb cutlets on the plate in front of me and attempt to listen to Théo's description of the latest attack on one of the company's ships by Somali pirates. I feel guilty at my lack of gratitude for the evening. I know it means a lot to Tom to have been invited, but I feel like a fish out of water. The whole thing just seems to emphasise how ill-suited I am to being a corporate wife, as I force myself to swallow the food and wine, which sit in my stomach like lumps of lead.

I watch the hands of the long-case clock in the corner of the dining room inch round painfully slowly, and wish I was back at home. There, where I can kick off my ill-fitting shoes and tiptoe up to the attic room to kiss the forehead of my daughter where she sleeps beneath the tent of mosquito netting, safe from all the unkindness and injustice in this world.

Josie's Journal – Monday 30th June, 1941

Papa announced today that he is planning another lovely family excursion for us all. I saw Maman shoot him an anxious glance and she looked as if she was about to say something. He reached over and took her hand reassuringly, though, and said, 'Don't worry, *ma chérie*, this will be a very pleasant and relaxing trip, I promise you.' I raised my eyebrows a little at that, thinking, *more promises?* He went on, 'We're going down the coast to stay in a nice hotel at the seaside. It's getting so hot in the city now and the incessant blowing of the chergui is wearing us all out. Won't it be wonderful to be on a beach where we can enjoy the sea breezes instead?'

Apparently the nice hotel is in a town called Mogador. It also has another strange name – Essaouira – which has all of the vowels and almost no consonants, but as Miss Ellis says, that's the Arabic language for you.

We have been studying the Portuguese empire a bit in my history lessons. Portugal started trying to invade Morocco about 500 years ago and occupied various places, building forts to defend them. There's not much left now except a few place names here and there, and some of the forts including La Sqala in the medina here in Casablanca with its cannons pointing out to sea to defend the old port. Miss Ellis took me to see it one afternoon. Those are the kind of lessons I enjoy the most. She teaches me about history and geography at the same time. She had given me a question sheet with various things I had to do, like sketching a map of the fort and the harbour, noting down the approximate size and number of ships the port could accommodate, and thinking about why the harbour is here in the first place. The Portuguese built forts in strategic places along the coast so they could defend their colony, but in the end the Berbers were too fierce and the Portuguese left again.

That's a bit of a shame because now we want to get to Portugal ourselves since it's a neutral country and there are boats from there to England and America. If Morocco was a Portuguese colony instead of a French protectorate it might be easier, but then I suppose if it wasn't a French protectorate we might not have been able to get in in the first place but have been stuck in Algeria instead, which definitely wouldn't have been a good thing.

Morocco's history is quite complicated with all these invasions. I asked Miss Ellis why the Moroccans don't just keep their country for themselves and she said, 'Their day will come.'

Once we have our American visas then Papa will have to go to the Portuguese consulate and join more queues to get our papers for passing through there too. I hope we won't be passing through Portugal for quite such a long time as we've been passing through Morocco.

Actually, a holiday by the sea will be very nice (or agreeable, pleasant, lovely and wonderful, as my thesaurus suggests). It really is getting very hot in the city and the beaches around Casablanca are not as good for sea bathing as those further down the coast. Papa thinks it would be a good opportunity to follow the road that runs along the coastline and explore the towns there along the way. He says we will see some more of those old Portuguese fortresses, which will be good for my education. I noticed that he squeezed

Maman's hand after he said that, and that gave me a suspicion as to what this trip is really about. I shall be on high alert again in case any more Monsieur Guigners creep out of the woodwork. I won't bring my journal with me but will leave it safely in its hiding place. However, Miss Ellis was delighted to hear we will be doing a tour of those old coastal fortifications and has given me quite a lot of work to take with me – so much for it being a holiday! I'll have to bring my schoolbooks and she has written out questionnaires for me to fill in at each place we visit. It's becoming quite a project. My books will be useful for taking notes, though, and then I can write everything in my journal properly later.

We leave on Saturday. Annette is already wondering whether she can persuade Maman to let her buy a new two-piece swimming costume. She's wanted one ever since she saw a picture of Ava Gardner wearing one in *Movie Life* magazine. They are all the rage in America apparently, although as I pointed out to her, it may be a different kettle of fish entirely on the beaches in Morocco.

I wish there was more room in the Dodge Sedan so that Nina could come. That would make the trip a lot more fun. But by the time Annette's suitcases (containing several changes of clothes for every possible social eventuality), plus her vanity case, (aptly named!), full of all her cosmetics and hair-styling things, have been accommodated, I shall count myself lucky if there's enough space for me.

Josie's Journal – Sunday 20th July, 1941

As Lord Peter Wimsey so wisely says in *Gaudy Night*, 'The great advantage about telling the truth is that nobody ever believes it.' This turned out to be a piece of very good advice and one that helped me to save Papa's bacon on our trip down the coast. But I'm getting ahead of myself again and had better start at the beginning as I write up everything that happened so that I don't miss out any important details . . .

Our first port of call was El Jadida. The Portuguese were there for 200 years and built walls to enclose the streets of the town beside the harbour. We climbed up on to the ramparts and walked around them, admiring the views and the fortifications. At the Bab el Bahr (which means the Sea Gate) there was a very good view-point from which I was able to sketch the harbour and fill in some of the answers to the questions Miss Ellis has set me. The fortress is very impressive and solid looking, and the Bab el Bahr forms a narrow entrance from the harbour to the town. You could see how easy it would be to defend El Jadida from an invasion: those Portuguese knew what they were doing.

As I was taking my notes and counting the boats in the little harbour, I happened to glance across at Papa. He, too, was admiring the views and then he drew a little notebook out of his inner jacket pocket and jotted something down in it, just as I was doing in my schoolbook. I said nothing and he quickly tucked the notebook away again. Then he smiled at me and suggested we go and look for a café in the town where one might be able to lay one's hands on an ice cream.

We did so and had a pleasant mid-morning pause in our journey, with coffee for Maman, Papa and Annette and a delicious lemon water ice for me. Annette has decided quite recently that she's too grown-up nowadays to eat ice creams and so she pretends to like coffee instead. I could tell by the way she kept looking at my lemon ice, though, that she was secretly regretting being so grown-up. I scraped the last drops out of the glass dish and licked my spoon clean, even though Maman says it's vulgar to do so, and then I gave her a big smile and said I hoped she was enjoying her lovely cup of coffee. She did not smile back.

Then we got back in the Dodge Sedan, which Papa had parked in the shade beside the town walls so it wasn't too much of an oven inside, and we carried on down the coast.

-x-

Our next stop was Oualidia and we reached it by lunchtime. Papa had planned that we were going to stay the night there in order to break our journey and also to visit the lagoons, which are famous for their bird life. Our small hotel was nice and comfortable and Annette and I had our own beds, so that was a relief.

There wasn't much homework for me to do at Oualidia. There had once been a harbour there but because of the currents in the ocean it silted up quite a long time ago. That was quite an interesting fact to write down in my geography book, but there wasn't much more to say about the town and its old port.

The next morning, we left our hotel early so that we could visit the lagoons. It was a spectacular sight. The morning sun slanted on the calm surface of the water, protected from the ocean by a line of sand dunes, where about a million birds were starting their day. Elegant flamingos stood in the shallows, ruffling feathers the colour of the sunrise and arching their long necks. Their graceful movements made me think of Josephine Baker: they were just as exotic as she is too. Occasionally a group of them would start all walking in the same direction at once and the way they carefully placed their feet at the end of their long legs reminded me of the ballet dancers we watched performing in *Swan Lake* at L'Opéra when Papa booked a private box for us as a Christmas treat in Paris last year. That feels like another lifetime ago now.

Larger, duller storks stood around here and there, enviously watching their more flamboyant neighbours with baleful eyes. And everywhere else you looked there were smaller birds, busily going about the business of searching for their breakfast in among the green stems of the papyrus plants – all sorts of different kinds of ducks and gulls and a bird with an interesting upwardly curved beak, which Maman says is called an avocet. It's hard to describe the memorable sight of all those birds who have made their home on that peaceful lagoon, but here are a few words from the thesaurus: a remarkably magnificent multitude; a splendidly spectacular extravaganza; an astonishingly marvellous throng; an impressively resplendent horde. All in all, I would say it was utterly superlative.

I picked up a flamingo feather that was floating on the water as a souvenir and collected one for Nina too. Maman explained that the feathers of flamingos are really white, but they turn their beautiful coral colour as a result of the tiny creatures the birds eat, sifted from the water with their bills. She warned me that the colour might not last on the feathers I'd found, but I didn't mind that, as long as it lasts until I can give Nina hers so that she can get an idea of what a sight it had been. It was the middle of the morning by the time we tore ourselves away from the lagoon and set off on our way again.

We stopped for lunch at Cap Beddouza and admired the light-house there, but there was no port and the beaches looked wild and inhospitable, with powerful waves. Once again, I jotted down the answers to the questions on the sheet Miss Ellis had given me and drew a sketch of the lighthouse. And once again I noticed Papa writing in his own little notebook and then tucking it safely back inside the pocket of his jacket.

We had to open all the doors of the Dodge Sedan to let the seats cool down a bit so they wouldn't burn our legs, and then we carried on to our next overnight stop, which was to be at Safi.

-x-

Three very interesting things about Safi are:

It is one of the main centres for the weaving of Moroccan carpets;

There are many argan trees growing along the road to the town and goats like to climb into them to eat the tasty and nutritious nuts;

It is the main fishing port in Morocco for sardines.

Apparently the Portuguese like sardines very much, which may be why they settled in the town in 1488 and built another of their fortresses to defend it. The fishing fleet in the harbour was so big that I had to make a rough estimate of the number of boats as there were too many to count precisely. Some of them were bigger than the boats we'd seen in the other ports so far on our journey, which led me to deduce that the channel leading into the harbour and the port itself must be deeper than in those other places. I sketched the fort and the harbour and answered the questions on the sheet, and then we went to look at the weavers at work in the medina. Their carpets are beautiful, made from yarns that have been dyed in vivid shades of pink, purple, red, blue and orange. They reminded me of the wildflowers on the farm where the horses live. I wished we could buy one to replace the rather dull rug beside my bed at home in the Boulevard des Oiseaux – it would be like stepping on to a cloud dyed with the colours of the sunrise every morning. But I knew it would be a waste of money as we'd have to leave it behind when we go to America. Watching the weavers at work, I could see why some of Nina's stories involve magic carpets that can fly. Women work at the frames, tying thousands of tiny knots in the different coloured yarns, and I was fascinated as the complicated patterns began to take shape beneath their deft fingers. I have no idea how the women keep the designs in their heads. I asked one of them and she explained that it's a tradition that has been handed down from generation to generation. She'd learned the patterns from her mother and would teach them to her own daughter when she was old enough. She let me try my hand at tying a few knots, but my attempts were pretty clumsy and she had to redo them. The women all laughed, but in a friendly way, their fingers still flying even as they watched my efforts and chatted to each other.

Later on, we had supper at our hotel and, even though I don't usually like sardines much, when they are freshly caught and cooked on a hot grill they are pretty perfect served with couscous and a sauce of fragrant herbs.

-x-

At last we reached our holiday destination of Mogador after our days of travelling and visiting all those interesting places along the way. It was quite a relief not to be spending hours in the hot car and to be able to unpack properly, knowing we'd be staying at our nice hotel for the next ten days. I was pleased to discover that the bed-room Annette and I were sharing had two beds and zero scorpions.

The thing Mogador is very famous for is its fresh air. There's a wind called the *alizé* which blows constantly on to the broad, sandy bay that forms the main beach. It makes the temperature here very pleasant and refreshing, not like the chergui. Luckily, too, there's a handful of little islands just offshore, which provide shelter from the ocean currents so the waves are smaller than those on the wilder beaches at Casablanca, making Mogador a perfect resort for sea bathing.

It was also nice not to have to do any schoolwork for a while as there would be plenty of time later on to sketch the Portuguese fortress and write my notes. But little did we know, as we enjoyed our seaside holiday, just how important my schoolwork was about to become.

We'd spent several days relaxing under a big umbrella on the beach, swimming in the sea and watching the other holidaymakers enjoying themselves too. It was easy to forget there was still a war on, apart from spotting one or two German army trucks on the streets. I imagine life will be like this all the time when we get to America – carefree days filled with pleasant views, ice creams and Coca-Cola. I was pleased to see Maman looking happier and more relaxed than she's been since we left Paris. I think the sea air and sunshine did us all good. There were dances at one of the bigger hotels every night, which Annette enjoyed, even if I found them a bit boring. I wished Nina and Felix had been there. We would have laughed at the serious young men with their oiled-back hair and stiff shirt collars who came over to ask Annette to dance. At least it stopped her pining for Olivier for a few hours. She made friends with a girl called Géraldine, who had scarlet fingernails that matched the equally scarlet lipstick she wore. Later on, Géraldine joined us under our umbrella on the beach a few times and she talked non-stop about her beau, Cédric, who had departed for America a few weeks ago. I glared at her a couple of times from beneath the brim of my sunhat as I was trying to read my book (*Murder Must Advertise*, by Dorothy L. Sayers, which is one of her very best, in my opinion), but she and Annette were too busy comparing the merits of their respective boyfriends to notice. I think Papa was getting a bit bored of the beach by that time (or maybe he, too, was finding all the talk of the wonderful Olivier and Cédric rather tedious), because he went for a long walk along the sand and when he came back he suggested to me that we should go and visit the Portuguese fortress later on in the afternoon once he and Maman had had their siesta at the hotel, so that I could complete my schoolwork. The girls wanted to go shopping for souvenirs and Maman said she'd accompany them, so I was looking forward to having a peaceful hour or two with just Papa.

Down by the harbour, the salty air and constant scouring of the wind had eaten away at the stones of the fortifications over the years, softening the edges a little, but they still looked good and solid, with cannons sitting in the crenellations all the way along their length, pointing out to sea. It was an impressive sight. Those Portuguese invaders knew a thing or two about defending themselves, so it shows how fierce the Berbers must have been if they still managed to drive them out in the end.

Papa and I strolled along the ramparts, enjoying the breeze and the seagulls swooping above our heads. We didn't talk much – I think we were both quite relieved to have a break from the inane chattering of Géraldine and Annette – and every now and then we'd pause to jot down a few notes. I was sketching the ancient fortress with its turrets, which overlooks the entrance to the harbour, and Papa had wandered on a little way when I became aware that two men in dark blue police uniforms had approached him. I could see that he smiled pleasantly at them at first. I also noticed that he slipped his notebook back into his jacket pocket in a very relaxed manner. But the manner of the two men wasn't very relaxed at all. In fact they looked pretty angry and then they suddenly pushed him up against the wall and it looked as if they were demanding something from him.

I quickly closed my schoolbook and walked towards him. He was shaking his head and protesting in a jocular manner, as if the whole thing was just some unfortunate misunderstanding, but the policemen were being pretty insistent. The shorter of the two reached out and grabbed the lapel of his jacket and at that point Papa held up his hands, trying to placate them. But then the man very rudely stuck his hand right into the inner pocket and pulled out the notebook.

I reached them at that point, ignoring the fact that Papa started shaking his head even more when he caught sight of me and was trying to signal with his eyes that I should stay back. However, in the split second that I'd seen what was happening, I'd realised that if ever camouflage was needed, now was most certainly the time.

I didn't have time to come up with any kind of a plan for saving Papa, but I knew I had to save him from being arrested. Poor Maman's nerves were already frayed enough after last time and she'd only just begun to look a little more relaxed on our lovely holiday, so I desperately racked my brains for the right thing to do. That was when those words of Lord Peter Wimsey's popped into my head about nobody ever believing it when you tell the truth.

I tugged at the sleeve of the short policeman who was holding the notebook and smiled my sweetest and most innocent smile. '*Bonjour, monsieur*,' I said, opening my schoolbook and holding it out to him. 'My papa is trying to help me with a project that my teacher has made me do, even though we're supposed to be on holiday. You see, I have all these questions to answer about the geography of the harbour. Papa has promised me an ice cream when I've finished but it's taking ages finding it all out. I don't suppose you might be able to help us?'

There was a completely stunned silence from all three of them for a moment. The man holding Papa's notebook looked at me and then leafed through a few pages. His colleague reached over and took the schoolbook that I was holding out to them and then he started to laugh.

'It's just a kid's homework,' he said. His partner was still suspicious, though, and glared at me in a most unfriendly manner.

I made my smile even sweeter. 'Look, *m'sieur*, I have to count all these cannons and also the boats in the harbour. I don't suppose you might have those figures to hand? It really would be the hugest help if you did and then we can go and get an ice cream much sooner.'

'Are you joking?' the short policeman asked. 'You seriously want me to give you that sort of information?' He was sort of spluttering the words because he was so angry and outraged.

I frowned, pretending to look puzzled, and then opened my eyes as wide as they'd go, as if realisation was dawning. 'Oh, monsieur, I understand what you must be thinking! Of course, you must imagine I'm really a spy, on the lookout for strategic facts and figures that I'm collecting in my schoolbook.' I was mentally crossing my fingers and counting on Lord Peter Wimsey's wise advice to work.

The short policeman's face was an absolute picture. And Papa's turned an interesting shade of pale green.

I took my book back from the taller man and pointed to the open page. 'Strategic facts like this . . .' I began to read what I'd written: 'The Portuguese arrived in Mogador in the 1500s and built the fortress at the entrance to the harbour. The islands offshore, which provide shelter from the ocean currents, are known as the Purple Islands because a dye can be made using the mucus from the glands of carnivorous sea snails, called murexes, that inhabit the islands, which the Romans used to use to colour the robes of their emperors.'

The tall policeman was laughing again now, even though the shorter one was looking extremely cross. 'Come on, Régis, let's give the poor kid a break. Holidays should be about having fun, not having to do schoolwork. You and I both remember what it's like.'

The shorter one shook his head, but I could see he was wavering a tiny bit. 'We should confiscate both of these' – he waved the notebook in the air and grabbed my schoolbook from my hand – 'and destroy them.'

I managed to look very disappointed then and my chin was trembling as I said, 'Oh no, not my project. After all my hard work. I'll be in terrible trouble with my tutor.' A big tear fell from my eye and I wiped it away with the back of my hand.

That seemed to do the trick because he gave his colleague a very exasperated look and then handed me back my book.

'All right, all right, you can keep your homework, I suppose. But I'm going to destroy this.' He flapped Papa's notebook in the air. 'If it fell into the wrong hands this information could be misused. And also, while we can see you're simply helping your daughter with her homework and you're clearly not spies' – he shot me another annoyed glance – 'not everyone is as reasonable as we are. There are some who will shoot first and ask questions later.'

I gave him my most angelic smile and restrained myself from pointing out that if someone was to be shot at such close range they would therefore most probably be dead, in which case there wouldn't be much point in asking them any questions at all.

Instead, I thanked the policemen and the nicer one wished me good luck with my project. They marched smartly off to go and destroy Papa's notebook and I turned towards the harbour and started counting boats.

'What are you doing, Josie?' Papa asked. His voice sounded a bit weak and when I glanced up at him he still looked a little green.

'I'm counting boats. For my project. And then I think we could probably both do with a little refreshment at a café, don't you? That way, we can work out what else there was in your notebook that I haven't already written down and we can try to remember the

184

details. After all, two heads are better than one, as the saying goes. Wouldn't you agree, Papa?'

He just stared at me for a while and then he reached out his hand and stroked my cheek very softly, saying, '*Ma p'tite*, what an extraordinary child you are.' Once again, just like when we were in the cave, there was so much love in his expression that for a moment I could hardly breathe. But we had work to do, I reminded myself sternly, and so I returned to my counting.

When we'd sat down at a café and Papa had taken a large gulp of brandy to calm his nerves (I find chocolate ice cream has a similarly soothing effect), we worked out that I'd collected pretty much all the information he needed. The only thing that was missing was which ports had a telegraph line. He could remember that he'd seen them at El Jadida and Safi but not Oualidia, and so I added that information to each of the relevant sections. There was no sign of a telegraph line in the port there at Mogador either, so I noted that down in my schoolbook too.

After he'd sipped the rest of his brandy a little more slowly, Papa looked at my project thoughtfully, turning the pages. 'Where did you find out all these other things?' he asked. 'The purple islands and the sea snails and everything?'

'I don't only take novels out from the library, you know, Papa. You can read all sorts of interesting things in books.' Then I gave him a very stern look. It was time to lay my cards on the table. 'So,' I said in a businesslike tone. 'On the basis of what I've found, I have deduced that if I were contemplating an invasion of this coastline, I would choose Safi as the best place for a landing.'

He gave me a startled glance again, but then a smile crept slowly across his face. The brandy must have been taking effect, I think. 'And why is that, *ma puce*?' he asked.

'Well, El Jadida is closest to the north, which is where the fighting is, but it's too much of a stronghold to invade easily with

185

that big fortress. The harbour there is fairly small too, and the boats I counted were all little ones, which tells me the channel into the port is probably not very deep, so we can rule it out. Oualidia is completely out of the question because it's much too small and of course the harbour is all silted up. I wouldn't want to disturb the flamingos there, either.'

I paused to take another spoonful of my ice cream and then turned the page. 'Here at Mogador the harbour is quite small too, although there are a few larger boats so the channel's probably a reasonable depth. But at Safi there's a good-sized port for all those sardine boats and some of them were huge. That means the channel must be deep enough to accommodate larger vessels so, if I was invading, I'd be able to get troops and equipment in fast. As I'm sure the Portuguese found back in 1488,' I added with an innocent smile, pointing to the date that I'd jotted down in my book.

Papa nodded, digesting what I'd said.

'I wouldn't bother looking any further south either,' I added. 'On the map the next port is Agadir, which looks quite large but it's too far from the north. Any invaders wouldn't be too keen on a long journey by land where they could be attacked and pinned down by an enemy.'

Papa nodded some more, thinking about that too. Then he smiled at me again and said, 'I think we should go back to the hotel and put your schoolbook away in a very safe place now. I'm quite sure Miss Ellis will be extremely satisfied with your work.'

'I hope so,' I replied. 'And Mr Reid as well.'

Here are some words from the thesaurus to describe the expression on Papa's face when I said that about Mr Reid and he realised I knew pretty much everything that he was up to: startled, amazed, astonished, astounded, flabbergasted, dumbfounded.

I particularly like those last two and intend using them in conversation whenever possible.

Zoe – 2010

My Tree of Life quilt blocks are coming on well. I've spent hours stitching the stacks of starched triangles together, transforming the scraps of fabric into the larger squares that will form the central design of my quilt. Every now and then I take a break from sewing to stretch my back and shoulders and ease the stiffness out of my fingers from gripping the needle, and I lay out the completed blocks on Grace's bed. I'm on the tenth one now. Just three more to go and my little forest of trees will be complete, ready to place in their matrix of sashing strips. But I'm going to need to consult Kate again about the next steps, so I give her a call.

'Come over,' she says. 'It'll be easier for me to show you. I've got some spare backing fabric, too, that you might like, and we can discuss what you'll need in the way of setting triangles and a border.'

Like me, Kate has appropriated the attic rooms of her house to use as her studio. She sets down the tray and busies herself pouring coffee while I admire an example of her work, which has been hung on the gable wall. It's simply stunning. The colours of the quilt are as vibrant as jewels and they seem to glow with a light of their own. The pattern is more complex than the one I'm attempting. Each block looks like a four-petalled flower, with feathery, finely pointed petals. It's dramatic but delicate at the same time.

Kate comes over to stand beside me, handing me a fragrantly steaming mug.

'What's this pattern called?' I ask her. 'It's gorgeous.'

'It's a Bear Paw quilt. See, the quarters of each block are stylised, six-pointed paw prints.'

When she points it out, I can see how the design has been built up. The prints radiate from a central square – which I now know to call a setting stone – with a cross of sashing strips framing them. The geometry is quite simple when you look at it in that way, but the overall effect is complex. The way Kate has chosen the colours and juxtaposed her blocks creates harmony and a sense of progression through the quilt, drawing the eye along a path that weaves from left to right and back again, from the top to the bottom of the wall hanging, rather like reading a book.

'I particularly like this pattern,' she says, 'because it's supposed to be one of the designs that were used by the Underground Railroad.'

I look quizzically at her, then return my gaze to the quilt. 'Wasn't that the secret network that helped American slaves to escape their owners?'

She takes a sip of her coffee. 'That's right. There's a story often told in quilting circles about how the designs were used to help communicate the routes to follow and the times when it was safe to go.'

'How did they work then?' I ask.

'Each plantation would have had a seamstress or two who worked for the owners. First of all, a sampler quilt would be sewn as a way of learning the patterns. This would be used to show the other slaves on the plantation how to recognise the different kinds of blocks. Then the seamstress would sew a couple more quilts. First, using this Bear Paw pattern, she would create a sort of map, showing a coded version of the route that the runaways should follow. It's easier to memorise a map by visualising it than it is to try to remember a series of written or spoken directions. And the African tradition has always relied on signs and patterns to communicate.'

I nod. 'Like the designs woven into Berber rugs?'

'Exactly. Whole cultures can be recorded through methods of traditional weaving and painting. In North Africa this could range from the tattoos on women's faces to the embroidered crewel work on their shawls. In other countries, tribes use beadwork or printed fabrics or even designs painted on to their bodies to tell the stories of who they are and where they belong. So you can see that it's possible they extrapolated this to use quilting when scraps of fabric might have been all that were available to them in their captivity.'

I always like spending time with Kate. I'm not surprised Tom so enjoyed her company at Claudine's dinner party the other evening. He's mentioned her name once or twice since. And if that makes me feel a little uneasy, I tell myself again firmly not to be paranoid: she's my friend, first and foremost, not the sort of woman who would betray my trust with a flirtation with my husband, let alone an affair. This is the first time I've been in her house and I'll admit I was just a tiny bit curious to see whether she might show any reluctance at inviting me over or any sign of feeling uneasy in my company since that night, but she seems relaxed, her smile as open and warm as ever. She's a natural teacher and I could listen to her all day as she shares her knowledge of crafting techniques from different cultures around the world. It's more than just a hobby for her – it's a passion.

She pulls a book from one of the shelves that line the other walls of the room, which hold bolts of material and baskets of binding tape and sewing thread as well as a small reference library. 'The quilt with the route map could be hung out of a window for a few days, as if to air, so that those who were going to attempt to escape had time to memorise the information on it. You could give directions, pointing north, south, east or west, for example, and show where there were rivers and where there might be sources of food. You could also show with the setting stones where there might be safe places to stay or where a guide would meet you to show you the next section of the route. And then, when it was time to go, a different quilt would be hung from the window. It's said that they used this one' – she turns to a bookmarked page – 'called Wagon Wheel, or perhaps this one called Tumbling Blocks. That would be the sign that they should leave once darkness fell, that the next delivery along the railroad was expected. I guess in some cases,' she continues, 'a traveller might even have carried a rolled-up quilt on their journey. It would serve a dual purpose, as a map and as something to keep you warm if you were sleeping rough or bedding down on the floor of someone's shack.'

'What a wonderful idea. And they were also carrying some-thing of their culture with them – a visual representation that held in it something of the family they'd left behind, perhaps?'

Kate nods. 'It's also said that sometimes a quilt would be hung out of a window to air at the safe houses along the route, to indicate that travellers on the Railroad would receive a warm welcome there. So there was a whole conversation being conducted in a secret language. Every quilt tells a story, as we know. Now then, how are you getting on with yours?'

I show her the blocks I've finished so far. I know they aren't perfect, and in many places I've had to unpick my stitches and redo them (although I'm pleased to say that's happening less and less often nowadays as I've become more practised).

She turns the squares over and examines the backs. 'You can always tell how careful someone's been by looking at the parts that will be hidden.' She smiles. 'You've done well, Zoe. This is neat work.'

190

I breathe a big sigh of relief that my sewing's passed the test, and show her my ideas for setting the blocks.

'That'll work well, I think. Just plan the order carefully when you've finished the last three blocks. Then you'll need enough fabric for sashing strips to go between the thirteen of them and you might want to think whether you wish to use a contrasting material for your setting stones and your corner stones. Your border could be made with some more of the sashing fabric if you like, which will give a sense of cohesion to the whole design.' She shows me some examples in the book, and another piece of her own work too, and we discuss blocking, backing, batting and binding.

My head is spinning by the time we're done. I thought once I'd finished sewing my blocks there wouldn't be much more to do, but I was wrong. At least for some of the next steps I'll be borrowing an old sewing machine of Kate's, though, so it will be faster than painstakingly sewing everything together by hand. 'Keep it as long as you like,' she says, once she's given me a tutorial on how the machine works. 'I never use it these days. I've only been hanging on to it as a backup.'

Before I leave, a thought occurs to me. 'Kate, might it be possible for me to borrow the Bear Paw quilt one day? I'd like to show it to someone.'

'Of course,' she says. 'Just let me know when you need it.'

I return home feeling fuelled with enthusiasm (or perhaps it's just the large mug of very strong coffee I've drunk). As I sit and begin to sew the final three blocks of my quilt, I sing to Grace and she claps her chubby hands and waves at the silver moon and stars that hang over her bed, as if she's cheering me on towards the finish line.

Josie's Journal – Thursday 14th August, 1941

Today was Nina's birthday. We're both teenagers now. I went with Kenza to their house in the medina so I could give Nina the present I'd got for her, a polished shell that I'd bought from a fisherman on the quayside when we were in Mogador. It was as white as the feathers of a seagull and it glowed like the moonlight and the minute I saw it I knew she'd love it, even though I had to haggle very hard for a long time to get it as I only had a few francs of my pocket money left by that stage of our holiday.

She did like it very much and she put it on the little shelf in her room where she keeps her most precious treasures – a beaten silver bangle and an amethyst geode.

I always find the geode fascinating. The first time I saw it, I thought it looked like half of an eggshell made from very plain and rather dull-coloured stone. But then, like a magician performing an astonishing trick, Nina turned it over and in the hollow centre of the rock was a cluster of gleaming purple crystals. I couldn't believe that something could look so very ordinary and unremarkable on the outside and hide such a beautiful treasure within.

When I said that to Nina she replied that many things in her culture are like the geode. For example, Moroccan houses often present a windowless stone façade to the street and it's only when you enter through a narrow doorway that you discover a hidden courtyard within, richly decorated with colourful tiles and filled with flowers and fountains. Because rich people and poor people can live side by side in the medina – unlike the *nouvelle ville*, where everyone is wealthy, or the mellah, where everyone seems to be quite poor – those who are wealthier here like to keep things plain on the outside and hide their good fortune on the inside so as not to rub their poorer neighbours' noses in it.

Nina also said that people can be like that too – sometimes the ones who look the plainest are the ones with hearts of gold. I thought of Felix, and Madame Bénatar, and I knew that she was right.

For Nina's birthday, Kenza had made gazelle horn pastries and a honey cake covered in caramel-gold almonds. Several other members of the family popped in to give Nina their birthday wishes, including the dreamseller. Once she'd finished hugging Nina, she smiled at me, showing the gaps in her teeth, and then wrapped me up in a hug too. Her arms felt as fragile as the bones of a bird, although there was a deceptive strength in them. Her skin smelled of patchouli oil and spices and I thought about the geode and what Nina had said. I could tell the dreamseller had a heart of gold beneath the tattoos and her toothless smile and the wrinkles of her leathery skin.

Kenza gave us each a slice of honey cake and we settled ourselves on piles of cushions to enjoy it. Then Nina asked her auntie to tell us one of her stories. She looked at us both for a few moments, those fierce, bright eyes darting from Nina's face to mine and back again as if she was looking into our souls and reading what she found there, choosing the right story from the whole library that she carries in her head. And then she began:

'Once upon a time, when the world was very much younger, the waters of the sea were sweet and fresh. The sea itself was very proud of this and it grew too arrogant. It decided it would flood the whole world. But a tiny mosquito saw this and began to drink the sea. It drank and drank until every drop of water was gone and it was drinking sand. Then it threw up all the water again. And because the smallest creature in the world had drunk it up and humbled it, the sea became calm. From that time on, the waters of the sea have been salty since they've passed through the stomach of a mosquito.'

I liked the story very much but it was only later, when I got home, that I thought about it some more and understood the message in it. Sometimes the war and everything else that's happening in the world, like the bad things that are being said about Jewish people, can feel like they are huge and overwhelming. But even tiny mosquitoes like me and Nina have the power to do something about it.

I like the way the dreamseller's stories have the knack of helping you to feel so much better about things that feel impossible. I think that is a truly magical talent.

Zoe – 2010

Bit by bit, my confidence in being able to navigate my way around Casa is growing. I've met Kate at local cafés on a couple of occasions and now know to ask for a *nuss-nuss* – a half-and-half – if I want to order a milky coffee. We both enjoy chatting about Bristol, reminiscing about the Clifton coffee shops and the rows of pastel-coloured houses in Montpelier, where Tom and I used to live and Kate had rented a room as a student.

We both worked as primary school teachers back in the UK too – another thing we've discovered we have in common. It's not easy to find work in Morocco with our foreign qualifications, but Kate has a part-time job at a language school, giving English lessons to businessmen and students. She says she loves having the opportunity to break out of the expat bubble now and then and meet Casawis. 'I miss the kids, though,' she said, and I agreed.

'All those hilarious things they say and do . . . I once asked my class if anyone could name the four seasons and one little boy stuck his hand up and said, in all seriousness, "Salt, pepper, vinegar and tomato ketchup." His mum was one of the dinner ladies.'

Kate laughed, almost choking on a mouthful of honey cake. 'That's priceless. I asked my class if anyone could tell me what "benign" means and one girl said, "Please, Miss, we will be nine next year, once we've finished being eight." They could be a handful too, though, couldn't they? I told one of my pupils to stop messing around while my back was turned, without turning around while I was writing on the whiteboard. It was just a hunch, you know that sixth sense you have – I had no idea what he was up to really – and he said, "Oh, Miss, how do you *always* know what I'm doing?" He truly believed it when I told him that teachers have superpowers and can see everything that goes on, and from that day on he behaved himself.'

Reminiscing with Kate makes me miss my old job. I've toyed with the idea of trying to go back to teaching somehow, but I know I'm not strong enough yet to take on that level of responsibility again. The thought of not being able to wash my hands as often as I need to fills me with an anxiety that I know is unreasonable, but the fear cripples me, making me unable to face going for an interview, let alone handle a class. And, besides, Grace needs me right now. It's spending time with her that soothes my frayed nerves. I love being a mother to her, more than anything else I've ever done in my life. Plus, I need to finish making the quilt. Sewing the Tree of Life blocks helps me feel more at peace than I have done in a long time, so I think I'm making a little progress.

Visiting the library and walking back through the Habous is getting a bit easier for me too nowadays. Admittedly, I tend to stick to my familiar routes – there've been no more crazy marathon hikes across the city to the corniche – but I'm starting to feel more relaxed on my daily walks with Grace, which do us both good. The Parc Murdoch is our favourite place. Its peaceful green spaces in the midst of the city's chaos never fail to calm and soothe the jangle of my thoughts as I sit on the bench I've come to think of as ours, tucked between two tall Aleppo pines that shelter us in their ink-dark shade. Grace loves to watch the bulbuls flit from branch to branch above us, and the liquid notes of their songs seem to help cool the air. It's a secluded corner of the gardens, where we're rarely disturbed by the tourists and the local workers who visit the park. Occasionally, the man who sweeps the paths with a palm frond comes by, but he simply nods and leaves us be, intent on his task.

I've begun venturing a little further into the Habous, too, encouraged to do so by Monsieur Habib, who knows where the best shops are for anything I might need. I was delighted to find an antique crewel-work shawl the other day. The shopkeeper was surprised when I wanted to buy it, rather than one of the newer ones hanging from the ceiling of his shop. It's frayed at the edges and slightly moth-eaten in places, but I was immediately drawn to its stylised pattern of leaves and flowers. And when he told me it's a Berber Tree of Life design (warming to his task when he realised my interest was serious and I wasn't to be dissuaded by the poor condition of this particular shawl), I knew I'd found the fabric for my quilt's sashing strips and border.

In the same shop, as I was waiting for him to wrap my purchase, I came across an amethyst geode like the one Nina had that Josie had been so taken with. It was just as she'd described. The egg-shaped outer crust was a rough, nondescript shell, but it encased a cluster of crystals whose astonishing purple depths sparkled in the dim light at the back of the shop. I picked it up, strangely unsettled by a thought that dawned on me as I held it. Nina had told Josie that life in the medina was like the geode – plain on the outside but with hidden treasures within. It made me realise that my life in the *nouvelle ville* is the opposite: all the glitz and sparkle of my expat life is on the outside, for show. A beautiful home, a luxurious lifestyle, a perfect-looking marriage. But hidden behind it is a hard, dead core. That realisation made my heart feel as heavy as the lump of rock I held in my hand. I replaced it quickly on the shelf, shaking my head as the shopkeeper tried to persuade me to buy it too. Although the curio was beautiful in its way, it represented a painful emptiness to me and I didn't need that constant reminder in my home. One woman's treasure is another's burden, I guess.

How I wish I had a bit more of Josie's irrepressible optimism and Nina's gentle innocence. I'm sure I used to view the world differently, but I seem to have lost both of those traits somewhere along the line.

After buying the antique shawl, I retraced my steps to Monsieur Habib's shop to show him my purchase, knowing that he, too, would see the beauty in its threadbare folds. I think I needed the reassurance of his calm, thoughtful presence too, knowing that life wouldn't seem quite so empty once I'd spent a few more minutes sipping tea from a worn glass and hearing the latest news from the shelter.

I'm going to visit it with Madame Habib again next Friday. And this time I shall have a story to tell the women as well as the children.

Josie's Journal – Monday 22nd September, 1941

This evening is the beginning of Ramadan, which Nina has been explaining to me. She and her family will be fasting during the hours of daylight for a whole month until the next new moon appears and then it will be a time of feasting and celebration called Eid al-Fitr. Before the sun comes up, each day will begin with prayers and a meal called *suhur*, which is sort of like supper; when the sun sets, her family will eat an evening meal called *iftar*, which is sort of like breakfast. It seems that during Ramadan the days are turned upside down. Until this year, Nina has only fasted for some of the time but now she's 13 she's going to go the whole day without food and water. It's part of being grown-up.

I'm in my room writing this and listening to the call to prayer. The muezzin's voice is resonating on the evening air and it sounds even more solemn than usual to me, knowing that this is the start of a very holy month for my friend. I've decided that when she comes to the house I won't have anything to eat or drink either, so that I can support her in her fasting. After all, it would be pretty mean to eat cakes and drink lemonade while she's not allowed to. But she's promised that I can come to her house when the Eid celebrations begin and we'll have an amazing feast.

We've taken a large supply of books out of the library as I think reading will be a good distraction for Nina if she's feeling hungry or thirsty and will help the time to pass more quickly. When I told Mademoiselle Dubois about this plan, she suggested we might enjoy the works of Jules Verne as they are exciting tales of fantastic adventures. We have *Journey to the Centre of the Earth* and *20,000 Leagues Under the Sea*, and she's promised to reserve a copy of *Around the World in 80 Days* as soon as it comes back in.

I've also been working on a new project with Miss Ellis, studying the history of the United States of America. She says it's always important to understand the background of a country if you're going to live in it. There was a war in America called the Civil War and the President at the time was Abraham Lincoln, a very tall and kind man who wanted to abolish slavery. He made a famous speech at a place called Gettysburg, where more than fifty thousand soldiers from both sides of the divide lost their lives in a terrible battle, which Miss Ellis says actually still has great relevance for the war that's going on in the world today. The newspapers report that many, many soldiers are being killed in the fighting. There are also some really terrible stories beginning to emerge about what the Nazis are doing to the Jewish people they've sent to camps in Europe – they make our time in the Aïn Chok refugee camp sound like a holiday in a nice hotel in comparison. I've been having quite a lot of bad dreams again and I keep thinking about the girl I saw in Marseille who didn't get on the ship. I still look out for her, hoping to spot her face in the crowds when I go to the library or the Habous. I wonder where she is now. There's still been no word from Uncle Joseph either and Maman's eyes grow dark with sadness whenever his name is mentioned. It's very frightening to think that so many people can just disappear. I never used to imagine it could ever happen to us. These days I'm not so sure.

But when Miss Ellis read me the words of Abraham Lincoln's address at Gettysburg, they made me feel a bit stronger. I've decided to copy them out here in my journal to remind myself that I can make a difference – even to events that seem so enormous – just like in Nina's very ancient auntie's story about the mosquito drinking the sea. Because words can inspire people, whether you are the President of America or the Dreamseller of Casablanca:

> 'It is for us the living, rather, to be dedicated here to the unfinished work which they who fought here have thus far so nobly advanced. It is rather for us to be here dedicated to the great task remaining before us – that from these honoured dead we take increased devotion to that cause for which they gave the last full measure of devotion – that we here highly resolve that these dead shall not have died in vain – that this nation, under God, shall have a new birth of freedom, and that government of the people, by the people, for the people, shall not perish from the earth.'

Miss Ellis has a way of making you see that everything is connected, just like with my project on the harbours of Morocco from El Jadida to Mogador. She took my schoolbooks away for quite a long time when we returned from that holiday and when she gave them back to me she said I'd done an excellent job. I got an A+ for it. She also said, with a bit of a twinkle in her eye, that Papa had informed her how especially hard I'd worked. From that, I deduced he'd told her about nearly being arrested by the policemen and how they'd confiscated his notebook but my project had saved the day.

Since we got back, Papa sometimes gives me messages written on his blue notepaper to give to Felix. He knows he can trust me now. If there's ever another message to be delivered to Miss

Josephine Baker, I hope Papa will entrust that task to me too. Although, according to Felix, who seems to know an awful lot about these things, she's been very unwell and is being looked after in a private clinic here in Casablanca. I hope she gets better soon. I'd like to see her again and ask her how the animals are getting on these days.

Josie's Journal – Wednesday 22nd October, 1941

Two things have happened in the last 24 hours.

The first is that last night I was allowed to go to Nina's house to celebrate the great feast of Eid al-Fitr. The thin sliver of the new crescent moon appeared in the sky just after sundown, which meant that Ramadan was over and the fasting was at an end. Nina has managed to do it for the whole month even if sometimes she's had a bad headache and felt very tired. The stories of Jules Verne definitely helped, though, and we both agree that Phileas Fogg and Passepartout are our favourite characters. We'd like to travel the world by boat and train ourselves one day, and have all sorts of adventures like them.

Anyway, at Nina's house all the lamps were lit and the rooms were full of members of her family. I said, '*Eid Mubarak*' to them all, as Nina had taught me. Everyone was dressed in their best clothes – Kenza was wearing a beautiful kaftan embroidered with silver thread and Nina had on a very pretty new dress called an *abaya*. Both of them had their hands painted with henna patterns, which I admired very much, although I don't think Maman would allow me to have mine done. I wish she would. It's not really all that different from the way Annette paints her face with rouge and lipstick, after all.

We broke the final day's fasting in the traditional way with a glass of milk and some dates, but that was just the beginning. Nina and I helped Kenza bring out one dish after another and set them on the low table in the middle of the room. Then everyone tucked in. We ate and ate until our bellies were filled with all the good things Kenza had cooked. First of all we ate bowls of *hrbil*, a sort of sweet and creamy porridge made with cracked wheat, and then *m'semmen* pancakes with honey and preserves. Next came the lamb dishes. The family had bought a lamb from the butcher and had given a proportion of it away to the poor so that they could have a feast too, which is another tradition at the end of Ramadan. There was a big platter of rather strange-looking bits of grilled meat and Nina told me these were chunks of the lamb's liver and heart wrapped in fat from the animal's stomach. I didn't find the thought of that very tempting, but I politely ate a small morsel and said how delicious it was because I didn't want to hurt Kenza's feelings. What I did really love, though, was the special lamb tajine she'd made with figs and almonds in, and so I had two helpings of that. Once we'd cleared away the main course, Kenza brought out trays of beautiful sweets and cakes and, even though I thought I probably wouldn't be able to manage another thing, I ate one of each kind: a pistachio and rosewater *ghoriba*; a gazelle horn pastry filled with almonds and cinnamon; a sweet and sticky slab of caramel studded with nuts and seeds; and a sugar-dusted *ma'amoul* stuffed with dates. By the time Papa came to fetch me home at the end of the feast, I was very full and very sleepy.

I slept deeply and woke late, my dreams of flying through the air with Nina and Felix in a hot air balloon having been disturbed by the sound of excited voices floating up the stairwell. I got out of bed and shoved my feet into my leather slippers, then went downstairs to see what was happening. And that's when I discovered the second amazing thing.

Annette was shrieking with joy so shrilly that I had to put my hands over my ears. Maman seemed to be laughing and crying at the same time. And Papa was waving a sheaf of papers triumphantly above his head. When he caught sight of me, he tousled my hair and gave me a big kiss. 'Guess what, *ma puce*? Our papers for America have finally come through!'

I had some very confusing feelings when I heard that. On the one hand it's what we've been waiting for all these months and it means we can escape from the war and begin our new lives on the other side of the world. On the other hand, the thought of leaving behind Nina and Kenza and Felix and Miss Ellis and Mademoiselle Dubois has made me feel completely devastated.

I looked at Papa and Maman and Annette, who were all so happy, and I tried to make my expression as excited as theirs. But I felt a huge emptiness inside and tears sprung into my eyes. Luckily, I think Papa and Maman assumed they were tears of happiness as I didn't want them to think I'm ungrateful for everything they've done for us. I couldn't help but feel that the world was ending, though. And while I know there will be a new beginning, right now there's more grief than gladness in my heart.

So I thought I would come up to my room and write this down in my journal, to try and get my thoughts in order.

But it hasn't helped much yet. I still feel pretty confused.

Zoe – 2010

The children at the refugee centre recognise me now and look up from their drawings to ask what book we're going to read today. I'm pleased to see their pictures aren't only of the brutality and trauma they've witnessed: one little girl is busily colouring in her picture of the lazy grasshopper and the hard-working ant, and her sister proudly shows me a drawing she's done of the Wisest of Cats – an African folk tale I read to them the other day from one of the new books.

They all loved that story. It concerns a very small cat who realises he needs a bigger, stronger friend to look after him. He tries the other animals, one by one, but discovers that the zebra is scared of the lion and the lion is scared of the elephant. Then he finds that the elephant is scared of a man who carries a gun. So the cat goes home with the man, thinking that he has at last found the biggest and strongest friend of all. At the man's house, though, his wife comes and takes the gun from her husband, giving him a kiss, and the cat realises that the woman must really be the strongest one of all if she can disarm a man so easily. From that day on, the Wisest of Cats stays in the kitchen with the woman because he knows she will keep him safe. When I'd finished reading, I looked up and saw that Madame Habib and some of the other women had been listening too and they were all smiling as I put the book of fables away.

But today I tell them, 'We're not going to read a book this afternoon. However, I do have a story to tell you. It's in here.'

The children gather round, curious to see what's in the holdall I'm carrying. There are little gasps and murmurs of amazement as I unzip it and bring out Kate's Bear Paw quilt.

The children touch it carefully, reverentially, stroking the softly padded blocks, tracing the outline of the design. The colours of the quilt glow against the stark grey of the breeze-block walls and the cement floor.

Once everyone's had a chance to examine it closely, I drape it over the stacks of boxes that form the shelves of our embryonic library and the children settle themselves, cross-legged on the floor, as I begin to tell them the story of the Bear Paw design and the part it played in communicating a difficult, dangerous journey to those who sought to escape fear and oppression and follow their dreams to a better life.

I've brought Kate's book with me too, and I show them some of the other quilting patterns that tell their own stories – Log Cabin, Double Wedding Rings, Flying Geese and the Tree of Life.

As I talk, the women draw closer, to listen and to admire the intricate design of the quilt. Once I've drawn to a close, an excited babble breaks out. One of the women unwinds the length of fabric she wears over her hair and shows it to me. Her French is heavily accented and mine is poor, but I understand that she's explaining the patterns printed on the cloth. They, too, tell a story.

Madame Habib, attracted by the flurry of chatter, comes over to help translate. 'This lady is from Mali,' she says. 'Her people – the Bambara – also have a tradition of using patterns like this to record their culture and their history. She is curious because the design of the quilt is quite similar to some of the motifs on her headcloth.'

The woman nods vigorously and points to a diamond pattern on the cloth. 'She says the designs are created using mud,' Madame Habib explains. 'The brown and black are the everyday colours but this rust-red is special. It signifies her marriage. But her husband was working as a guard, protecting wildlife in the region from poachers, and he was killed in an attack on their home. The house was burned down by the gang. Her husband fought them off long enough for her and her children to escape and hide in the bush. Afterwards, when she returned, there was nothing left of their home. She found her husband's body in the ashes. She was terrified that the gang would return, and she had nothing and no one left in Mali, so she fled north with her two children, hoping to find a place where they could be safe and she could earn a living. She is still looking and still hoping. And she wears the cloth every day as it ties her to the things she has lost – to her husband and to the land she so loved.'

More of the women show us the patterns on pieces of their clothing, eager to explain the stories behind them. And as they do so they talk and laugh together, reminiscing about their homes and their families, about the traditions they've left behind. The children chip in here and there, asking questions about histories and cultures that have become lost along the hard and dangerous paths they've been following on the journey towards their dreams.

The Bambara woman points at me and says a word that I don't understand, but the others nod and clap their hands. I look to Madame Habib. 'She says you are *une griotte*. It is a great compliment – it means a female storyteller, who is much revered in African society. The oral tradition of keeping cultures alive is so important for them, although they have many other ways of telling their stories too – song, dance, carvings and the patterns on fabrics like these are just a few of the things they use.'

The women chatter excitedly among themselves and then turn to us again. 'You have given them inspiration,' Madame Habib translates. 'They say, unlike the Underground Railroad, they don't need a quilt made into a map to get to Europe, these days they just use a trafficker. But they want to make a quilt to tell their story. They'd like to create something beautiful like the one you've shown them today, to make a representation of the cultures they've left behind and the families they've lost. It would hang on the bare walls of this place and help to brighten it up, for them and for the others who will come after them. Could we help them do this, do you think?'

I smile at the women. 'I think it's a wonderful idea. But I'm a beginner myself and I don't feel confident enough to be able to teach them. I'll speak to Kate. She might be prepared to help out.'

'Very good,' says Madame Habib. 'Perhaps your friend would come with us next Friday afternoon and help us to get started?'

'I'll ask her. And in the meantime, tell them to start collecting together any pieces of fabric they can spare. They don't need to be very big.' I take a piece of scrap paper from the pile the children use for their drawings and fold it to the size of a ten-inch layer cake square. 'Anything this size will be perfect. Then we can work out the shapes they want to work with from here on.'

'What other materials will they need?' Madame Habib asks. 'If you can tell me then we'll see if we can get some donations.' Together, we draw up a list. I'll bring my cutting mat along next week and I'm sure I can ask Kate if we can borrow hers too. With so many pairs of hands eager to set to work, I think the women's quilt is going to make far more rapid progress than my own much more modest effort.

The women and children begin to sing and dance, celebrating their plans. And the centre seems to fill to the rafters with something new. It's the sound of joy, I think. Accompanied by a chorus of hope.

Josie's Journal – Sunday 9th November, 1941

Now that we have our visas for America, Papa has been spending time queuing at the Portuguese consulate to get our transit permits. He says the queues are just as long there, but the people in them are generally happier and more positive because they know they've cleared the main obstacle to leaving the war behind and can start letting themselves picture their new lives in America. He says hope is a great pick-me-up, even better than a glass of brandy. We have 3 months to get the next lot of paperwork sorted out. After that, the health checks that we underwent for our American visas will expire and we'll have to start the whole process all over again. When I asked Papa about that he said not to worry, it's not going to happen. I hope that's not another one of those promises that he makes just to be reassuring. I dread to think how Maman and Annette would react.

When he's not queuing at the Portuguese consulate, Papa still seems to be going to the mellah a lot. Sometimes he takes me to a café in the *nouvelle ville* afterwards for an ice cream. I can tell I'm providing camouflage again on those occasions (not that I'm complaining about the chance to eat ice cream), because inevitably some stranger comes up to us to ask the time or see if they can borrow Papa's newspaper for a minute or two and one of those notes on blue writing paper is slipped over. I'm very good at pretending we're just there for a run-of-the-mill father-and-daughter outing and there's nothing suspicious to be seen. There are quite a lot more German soldiers around these days and once or twice we've seen men in long, dark overcoats getting out of cars with swastikas painted on the sides so I know they are members of the Gestapo. As Maman says, it's high time we were getting out of here, although I will always be proud to know that my papa and I have secretly helped do our bit to fight the Nazis, and we have resolved that those who have died shall not have died in vain, as Abraham Lincoln would say.

A few days ago, Papa had just arrived back from the mellah and he asked me if I'd like to go to the café again. We were just about to set off when there was a knock at the front door. Because I was standing next to it, waiting for Papa to fetch something from his study (i.e. to write an important note for us to take to the café, most probably), I opened it. I got the shock of my life to see none other than Monsieur Guigner, the vulture-man-cum-scorpion of Taza, standing right there on our doorstep in Casablanca. He grinned his wolfish grin and his teeth were just as yellow as ever. 'Well, well,' he said, leaning forward into the hallway and much too close to me for comfort, so that I could smell his disgusting breath. He definitely doesn't brush his teeth often enough. 'If it isn't the younger Mademoiselle Duval again.'

Fortunately, Papa appeared at that moment and I could see he was very cross that Monsieur Guigner had turned up at our door. 'What are you doing here?' he asked, not even pretending to be polite.

'That's no way to welcome an old friend now, is it, Guillaume?' replied Monsieur Guigner. 'Aren't you going to ask me in?'

'I'm afraid not,' said Papa. 'Josie and I are just on our way out for a coffee. Won't you join us, though?' I could tell he was trying hard to find a way to get Monsieur Guigner away from our house. And so the Vulture Man came with us to the café, which completely spoiled our outing. He ordered a glass of pastis even though it was only 3 o'clock in the afternoon. Then he told Papa that he had been told to meet us here at the café all along, but he'd been curious to see our home in the Boulevard des Oiseaux so he'd taken it upon himself to call on us first. Papa looked even more furious at that.

I asked Monsieur Guigner how his friends were and asked if he'd been calling on them too, but he looked completely blank, which showed he was lying all along about knowing anyone in Casablanca, let alone living in the same street as us. Anyway, Papa discreetly handed over the sheet of blue notepaper and then downed his *p'tit noir* and said we must be getting back as Maman would be waiting for us.

Before we could leave, though, Monsieur Guigner put out a hand to stop Papa. 'I don't suppose you could lend me a little something to tide me over, could you, Guillaume? Times are hard right now and I'm going to need to cover a few unexpected expenses while I'm in Casablanca.'

Papa shook his head. 'I'm sorry, no. Times are hard for all of us.'

Monsieur Guigner showed his yellow teeth in what was supposed to be a smile, but his eyes were as chilly as splinters of ice. 'Oh dear, that's a great shame. I quite understand, living in that grand house and keeping your lovely wife and daughters in the manner to which they're accustomed can't be cheap. But what a great pity it would be, wouldn't it, if anything were to happen to them?' He fixed his cold blue eyes on me when he said that and very deliberately tapped the corner of the folded blue note on the table. Then, very slowly, he tucked it into the folds of his black robe, still not taking his eyes off me as he did so, and then at last transferred his gaze to Papa again.

My papa's face was furious. But he couldn't fail to understand the threat and I guess there was nothing he could do. Very reluctantly, he said, 'I don't have much money on me. Here, take this, it's almost all I have.' He took out his wallet and handed over a small sheaf of notes to Monsieur Guigner.

'Why, thank you, Guillaume. That's most kind of you,' said the vulture, as if this had come as a lovely surprise. 'But I'm sure you could spare some more if I was to come to call on you again at the house, couldn't you?'

Papa looked utterly miserable and I could see he was struggling to decide what to say. But Monsieur Guigner took the note out again and very deliberately tapped the corner of it on the table once more in a way that was clearly a threat. So in the end Papa nodded. 'Come to the café again tomorrow at 3 o'clock and I'll see what I can do. But I'm warning you, if you call at our home again I won't give you another *sou*.'

With a grimace of a smile, the vulture took the money and stood up from the table. '*Au revoir*, Mademoiselle Josie,' he said. 'It's been a pleasure, as always.' He put a particular emphasis on the words *au revoir*, in a way that made my skin creep.

Well, it most certainly wasn't a pleasure for me and Papa. I don't think either of us felt at all happy about seeing Monsieur Guigner again.

True to his word, Papa left the house again the next afternoon to go to the café with the extra money for Monsieur Guigner. Just before 3 o'clock, I heard him in the hall putting on his jacket and telling Maman he was going out for half an hour or so. I started to come downstairs, thinking he might need me for camouflage, but I stopped in my tracks when I heard Maman say, 'I hope you're not meeting that horrible man again, Guillaume. I saw him at the door yesterday. You know how much I hate you having anything to do with him.'

Papa didn't answer her. I suppose he didn't want to tell her a complete lie. And then he glanced up and saw me and quickly shook his head, so I retreated back to the drawing room. Annette was there, flicking through the pages of an old copy of *Movie Monthly* that she's already read about a thousand times, but it's impossible to buy new magazines from America in the shops now.

I couldn't stay still over the next half-hour. 'Sit down,' she snapped at me, as I went to look out of the window for the tenth time to see if Papa was coming back. 'Honestly, Josie, you're being even more annoying than usual today.' Of course I couldn't tell her and Maman why I was on tenterhooks.

At last Papa appeared again, walking back from the café, and I ran downstairs to open the door for him. 'Is everything okay?' I asked him.

I could see he looked out of sorts, but he pulled himself together and tried to give me a cheerful smile as he ruffled my hair and said, 'All is just fine, *ma puce*. Don't you worry, your papa has everything under control.'

At least now we have our visas and will be leaving soon, so hopefully it will be the last time we ever have to have anything to do with that ghastly Monsieur Guigner.

When I told Nina about having got the visas she tried hard to look happy for us but I could see she was attempting to hide her real feelings, which were pretty much the same as mine. Then I told her I'm going to give her my bicycle and that made her smile properly again. She said she'd only be looking after it until I came back, though. I laughed and said I'd definitely come back to Morocco someday in the future, but by that time we'd both have grown out of that particular Steel Steed. Then she said something a bit strange. She told me her old auntie has seen that I'm part of their family (as she said the first time I met her), and that I belong in Casablanca. I was very flattered that they all feel that way, but I know it's just a kind thing the dreamseller must have said to Nina so she wouldn't be sad about us leaving. But maybe I will come back one day when I'm a lawyer and I can do good works here like Madame Bénatar. Anyway, I think the dreamseller's words did make us both feel happier, knowing that we'd still be friends and would always keep the feeling of being sisters even if we are really separated by an ocean as wide as the Atlantic.

It's very strange to think that in 3 months' time I'll be living a completely different life. If we're still here at Christmas I think I'll give Nina the bike then, with the ribbon tied to it that I've kept from when Papa and Maman gave it to me for my birthday. We'll still be sharing it anyway, if I'm here for any longer after that.

Speaking of birthdays, tomorrow is Annette's. She'll be turning 18 and she seems to think that makes her completely grown-up and therefore has the right to criticise me even more than usual. She's forever telling me I need to scrub the ink off my fingers and stop burying my nose in books all the time. Today she even said that if I'd let her curl my hair and pluck my eyebrows then I might look more like a young lady and less like the First Mrs Rochester, which is what she loves to call me, as she still likes making frequent references to *Jane Eyre* and the mad woman in the attic where I am concerned.

She's chosen a dinner-dance at the Hotel Excelsior to celebrate and we all have to go, no ifs, no buts, as Maman says. Olivier will be there, of course. Maman asked me if I'd like to invite Felix to come too so that I'd have someone to dance with. I turned down the offer on his behalf as I know it would just make him feel very uncomfortable and he won't have the right things to wear, even though from my point of view the evening would be a lot more fun if he were there as we could laugh about the dopey way Olivier moons around when he's with my big sister. I'm looking forward to the food, though, and hoping there may be some Coca-Cola too.

With Maman's help, I've bought Annette a leather writing case. It will be something to remind her of her birthday in Morocco and also somewhere to keep her letters from Géraldine, who she's been corresponding with ever since our holiday in Mogador. And her letters from Olivier too. I suppose there's going to be the same carry-on when we leave Casablanca as there was when we left Paris, with her moping about and everyone having to be very nice to her. She seems to have managed to get over her broken heart at leaving Édouard behind pretty well, although she definitely didn't appreciate it when I pointed that out the other day. I was only trying to be helpful and look on the bright side of things.

Zoe – 2010

Kate agrees to come with me to the refugee centre the following week, to help get the women's quilting project up and running. 'It's a wonderful idea, Zoe,' she says. 'Quilting has always been a way to bring people together. We can help make something beautiful that will have great significance for everyone who needs the sanctuary the centre provides. And perhaps the women who make the quilt will feel empowered, that they've been able to create something at a time when they have so little.'

She's brought with her a box of spools of thread and some packets of needles, and has also promised to donate the batting to pad the quilt once each woman has sewn her block and we're ready to assemble it.

She's a natural organiser, and she and Madame Habib get on well as soon as they meet. I think they share a sense of community spirit, despite being from such different backgrounds, and I can see she's genuinely interested in how the centre has been set up to meet the immediate needs of the women and children.

Kate has prepared squares of unbleached cotton, marked with a seam allowance, which the women can use as the basis for their blocks so that each will be the same size. As she hands them out, there's much excited discussion about their ideas. The women show us the scraps of fabric they've collected, and tell us of the significance of the patterns and colours. Kate encourages them to be as creative as they like when making their blocks. They can use whatever materials and techniques they choose. She's very knowledgeable, too, about the different cultural backgrounds the materials represent. 'Look,' she tells them, 'this Igbo lady from Nigeria will use her pieces of ukara cloth, with their designs of the crocodile, the serpent and the hand of God, while you' – she points to another woman – 'will use your mud cloth from Mali with its diamonds and crosses. And this lady here, from Benin, will know how to do some beautiful, bright Abomey appliqué, *n'est-ce pas*? So every square will be unique and represent your own culture. But when we bring them all together to make the quilt, we will have shown how our different backgrounds can sit side by side, in harmony, and how something truly beautiful can come out of the difficulties that have brought you all here.'

She gets the children involved, too, making colourful felt flowers, which the women will be able to appliqué in place on the sashing stones and cornerstones when they come to assemble the quilt.

Madame Habib smiles her approval. 'You know, Zoe, it is so good to hear this place filled with noise and laughter. That was missing before. It took a storyteller to come and open all our eyes to other possibilities. I've been talking to the other volunteers and we are all thinking that perhaps we can do more in the way of arts and crafts here, make it a sort of collective where the women can express themselves in their own traditional ways. I've discussed it with my husband, too, and he has agreed that he could sell some of the items in his shop to raise more money for the centre. In this way we'll be able to help many more women and children.'

'You already do a great job of helping them,' I tell her. 'But, yes, imagine how much more we could do. It would be a good way of raising some more funds.'

'I like your friend Kate very much,' she says. 'Do you think she might be prepared to come and help out on a more regular basis?'

'Why don't you ask her,' I reply. But it appears Kate is already well and truly immersed in this new project, as she helps the women look through a book of block designs for inspiration.

I know none of this is a solution to the underlying problems the refugees face. And I know they will still either attempt the hazardous journey northwards or return to uncertain and arduous futures in their own countries. But, while we find ourselves in Casablanca, just for a few hours a week we will all gather here and forget the fears and the grief that overshadow our lives, shutting out the cruelty of the world and the pain that it can inflict, as we talk and laugh together and sew a patchwork quilt.

Josie's Journal – Tuesday 9th December, 1941

Something very terrible has happened and we're not sure yet how it's going to affect our chances of getting out of Casablanca. Yesterday the news came through on the wireless that the Japanese attacked an American port called Pearl Harbor early on Sunday morning and they sank battleships, cruisers and destroyers that were anchored there, killing more than two thousand men and injuring over a thousand more. This means that President Franklin D. Roosevelt has announced that America has decided to join in the war.

Papa says it's a good thing as now the Americans will not only fight Japan but also Hitler's Germany and this will surely help the war to end more quickly. Maman said, 'But what about us getting across the Atlantic? Does this mean there won't be any ships to take us now?' Papa looked a little bit worried, but he tried to reassure her by saying he was sure it would all be fine. He said he'd speak to his friend Mr Reid in the American consulate and try to find out a bit more about what was going to happen. Of course, it will take a while because everyone else will also go back to queue there now and the Americans will be very busy with this new turn of events. So it looks as if we are going to be celebrating Christmas in Casablanca once again this year.

With the war going on and on and growing worse and worse, my nightmares seem to have come back with a vengeance. Perhaps I should ask Nina if I can go and see her ancient auntie again to get some better dreams, because she certainly helped me out before. Occasionally Monsieur Guigner appears in them, grinning his ghastly grin and breathing his terrible-smelling breath over me and I can hear his voice, saying '*Au revoir*, Mademoiselle Josie' in that horrible creepy way he did at the café.

We hear that in Europe there's bitter fighting between the Germans and the Russians and many, many more soldiers have lost their lives. Here in North Africa, the Germans and British have been fighting in the desert again but this time Rommel's troops seem to have the upper hand and have advanced into Egypt. And all the time I'm thinking about the people who've been sent to work camps, and what might happen to us if the Germans decided to do that here and the kind Sultan was no longer able to stand up to them.

We have until the 20th January before our American paperwork expires and we're back to square one again. Papa is redoubling his efforts at the Portuguese consulate.

Josie's Journal – Thursday 1st January, 1942

Happy New Year. It's a whole twelve months on from when I first started writing in this journal and we're STILL in Casablanca. But we have some news. Mr Reid has told Papa that there's a ship due in from Portugal in a couple of weeks' time and we should be able to leave on it. Papa says he will go and sit in the middle of the Portuguese consulate next week, and refuse to move if need be, until someone sorts out our transit visas. Then he just has to go to the Préfecture de Police with all the paperwork to get our exit permit, but he says that should be a mere formality.

I've just realised that my New Year's resolution still needs to be to stop biting my fingernails. Maybe now is not the best time.

Zoe – 2010

I sit beside the window in Grace's room, with the stack of twelve hand-sewn blocks that I've finished beside me. I'm stitching the thirteenth – and final – one. By now, my fingers have grown accustomed to the sewing and I'm able to work on assembling the neatly cut triangles into the Tree of Life design almost automatically. Concentrating on my needlework has helped me avoid worrying with my teeth at the sides of my fingernails and the skin has healed a bit, making it less sore to hold the needle. My hands are still cracked and dry, and the rough, scaly patches burn and itch, but when I'm sewing the pain fades into the background a little and my mind feels calmer, having something else to focus on. Each triangle of material needs to be stitched to its neighbour, once I've considered how best to arrange the colours and prints so that they sit together harmoniously as a whole and yet allow each piece to tell its own individual part of the story.

The memories ebb and flow as I sew. Sometimes they make me smile. And sometimes a tear runs down my cheek and I brush it away with the back of my hand, the salt stinging the rough, red skin. I think of the day Tom and I met, for lunch in the pub with a group of friends, and how we ended up, just the two of us, deep in conversation after everyone else had left. We didn't want the day to end and we walked for miles along the river, while Tom told me about his work and his plans for the future in a world with limitless horizons, as the autumn leaves tumbled around us. We ended up back at my flat, hugging mugs of tea to warm our chilled hands, and I knew, as he very deliberately set his down on the coffee table, that he was going to lean over and kiss me and that our lives would never be the same again once he did.

I remember my first day in my new job, when thirty six-year-olds filed in to my classroom and sat down at their places, as excited as I was on the first day of the new school year. I'd already pinned some bright posters to the board behind my desk and filled the little set of shelves in the reading corner with books I loved and wanted to share with my pupils. Their faces, filled with joy and curiosity, float before my eyes as I sew. I also see the faces of the children in the refugee centre, their eyes filled with so many other things, things no child should have to endure. And yet there are glimpses of that same innocence and amusement when they listen to my stories and laugh at the ridiculous antics of the characters in them.

Picking up another triangle, I remember the day Tom and I married and the way the wind caught my veil and made it stream out behind me, as though it was my spirits and not a gust of wind that made it soar. We had everything before us then and it felt as if we were setting sail, together, on the ocean of our dreams.

And I remember my pregnancy, the way my belly took on a life of its own as Grace grew and somersaulted and flexed her feet against the warm, cocooning walls that constrained her and how she arrived in our arms, perfect, scarlet, yelling in outrage at the indignity of birth, and then immediately grew calm as we held her and laughed and cried, our love for her and for each other spilling over as I covered her tiny face in kisses.

I turn the block I'm sewing so that I can pin the next triangle in place, shifting my chair so the light falls on my lap and I can see what I'm doing more clearly. The colours of the pieces remind me of the photographs on Tom's phone of the sunrises he's encountered, morning after morning, as his feet pound the boulevards and avenues of the sleeping city. I feel a pang of sadness for him on his lonely runs. He's been asking again if I'll consider some sessions with a marriage guidance counsellor. I've told him I'll only do so if he stops drinking, creating a stand-off in which neither of us is able to make the first move. We seem to be arguing more and more these days, following the same old well-worn tracks, going round and round over old ground – his drinking; my suspicions; his frustration at my inability to move on from the blows our marriage has already suffered; my frustration and anger at his past mistakes, his absences, his need for company that I can't fill. I know he's as unhappy as I am. But talking to a stranger won't change what we've been through. The wounds we both carry will never heal, but that's no reason to stick a knife into them all over again. I still can't bear the pain. It's all I can do to get through each day as it is. My coping strategy may be avoidance, mixed with a large dollop of what the professionals call denial, but it does help me to cope. I'm too scared to admit the truth to myself, let alone to a counsellor in a featureless office, a box of tissues sitting on an otherwise empty table between us. I know my refusals frustrate Tom and only make him turn all the more often to the comfort and numbness he finds at the bottom of a bottle of whisky. I suppose he means well and he's only trying to do the right thing. But I'm afraid nothing can make it all right, ever again. And I'm even more afraid that trying might only prove that to both of us.

The light shifts and I pick up the pieces and begin to sew again, soothed by the repetitive action and the need to think only of forming one neat backstitch after the other.

At last I reach the end of the last seam and finish it off with three firm stitches, tucking the end of the thread under itself before snipping it with the tip of my scissors. That's the thirteenth block completed. I hold it up, showing it to Grace, who gurgles her approval.

Next, I'll need to carefully work out how I'm going to cut the Berber shawl into the sashing strips I'll use to set the blocks. But the sun is sinking beyond the rooftops of the city now, dropping slowly towards the distant waves that crash beyond the breakwater, and the shadows have lengthened across the floorboards, dimming the worn colours of the rug.

'Time to pack up for today, I think,' I tell Grace, and she reaches her arms towards me as I bend to pick her up, giggling as I kiss the soft curve of her neck and inhale the scent of her innocent perfection. 'And time to get you ready for bed.'

The distant sound of the call to prayer mingles with the contemplative murmuring of the doves as I hold her close and hug her so she knows she is safe here with me in our sanctuary, tucked away from all the hardship and pain of this world in our attic room.

Josie's Journal – Friday 23rd January, 1942

We're all feeling pretty shocked after the events of this week. I'd expected to be on the ship to Portugal now, but here I am back in my bedroom – so there's still a mad woman in the attic of the house in the Boulevard des Oiseaux.

Papa managed to get our transit visas for Portugal and the exit permit for Morocco and so at last we had all the bits of paperwork in place to leave. The ship that Mr Reid had told Papa about – the *Esmeralda* – arrived into Casablanca on the 14th of January and was due to leave for Lisbon 3 days later, just in time for our papers for America to still be valid. We packed everything up and I said my goodbyes to Nina and Felix, sad that it was all such a rush in the end after those long months of waiting. I gave Nina my library card and told her that Mademoiselle Dubois would be expecting her. She said that her auntie, the dreamseller, had sent a farewell message for me, to remind me of the words she'd said before: when the moon shines on one hundred bowls of water, every one of them is filled with moonlight. We agreed that those words would help us feel better even though we were apart – we could look at the moon, whether we were in Morocco or America, and know that it was shining on us both, reminding us of our friendship.

Kenza stood on the doorstep to watch us leave. She gave me a massive hug, which made me cry a lot even though I'd promised myself I wouldn't, and as she held me tight she whispered, 'Be brave, Green Eyes.' And then we got a taxi to the port.

The queues were enormous there and everyone seemed very nervous and short-tempered, waiting to get on the *Esmeralda*. At last we were allowed to board, once our paperwork had been checked very thoroughly by three different officials at three different desks. The final one looked over the American visas and the doctor's certificate and made a note of the date. 'Just in time, eh?' he said grimly, as he handed them back to Papa. He wasn't smiling and his tone really wasn't very friendly at all.

We found our cabin – which reminded me of when we left Marseille all those months and months ago because it smelled stale and we were all feeling pretty anxious – and tried to make ourselves comfortable in our bunks. Maman told Annette and me to go to sleep because then the time would pass faster and we wouldn't feel so sick, which would be a serious risk once the ship got out into the Atlantic waves, which were going to be bigger than those in the Mediterranean. 'When you wake up tomorrow morning, we'll be well on our way,' she promised.

Well, that turned out to be yet another one of those promises that didn't come true. I opened my eyes in the grey light of the dawn, expecting to hear the thrum of the ship's engines and feel the pitching and rolling of our progress, but there was an eerie silence. Papa wasn't in the cabin, but he appeared a little later to tell us what was happening. He looked worried.

The ship hadn't been given clearance to leave the port because some sort of military manoeuvres were taking place off the Strait of Gibraltar. That meant the ship would have had to sail further out into the Atlantic to avoid them and apparently the captain had neither the authorisation nor the fuel to do that. So we were stuck, and nobody knew how much longer it would be before the *Esmeralda* could sail.

We waited for two days and two nights, by which time my fingers were bleeding as I'd bitten the nails so much. And then the grim-looking official who'd noted down the expiry date of our doctor's certificate came and rapped on the door of our cabin and told us we had to disembark. He had a list and he put a line through each one of our names with his pencil in a very definite way, which made me feel as if our lives were being crossed out. Then he told us to bring our belongings and report to the main deck where police were waiting to make sure all ineligible passengers got off the ship to make way for those who did have all their papers in order. We sat in stunned silence when he left, not moving.

We heard him walk along the narrow corridor and knock on the door of another cabin a bit further on. And we heard the wail of a woman and the sound of her begging him to let her stay on board and his voice very gruff and angry telling her to bring her belongings and report to the main deck before he had to call in the soldiers.

At that, Maman pulled herself together and wiped her eyes on her handkerchief. Then she stood up very tall and very straight, without saying a word, and began picking up our things. Annette and I followed her example, trying not to look at the expression on Papa's face. It was utterly wretched.

Fortunately, Madame Bénatar had not yet found new tenants for the house on the Boulevard des Oiseaux, so we could move back in.

At least Nina will be pleased to see us, even if it does mean having to share the bicycle and the library card with me again.

Zoe – 2010

The quilt they're making at the refugee centre is progressing far faster than the much smaller one I've been working on at home. So many of the women have contributed a block that it's morphed into a sizeable piece of handmade art that will cover at least half of the longest wall of the makeshift building once we've assembled it. And, with Kate's help, the children have made a whole meadow of bright felt flowers that will be added as embellishments between the blocks. We started laying it out this morning, spreading clean sheets on the floor as we don't have a table big enough to accommodate the whole thing.

Each woman knelt to place her block within the outline that Kate had roughly marked out with strips of binding. Every individual square is unique, lovingly pieced together to tell one person's story. Geometric Log Cabin, Bear Paw and Friendship Star blocks are interspersed with free-form designs, and motifs of exotic birds and animals in needle-turn appliqué. Plain sashing strips will frame each one, and the children's flowers will be scattered among them, drawing the eye through the quilt so the viewer reads the individual stories represented there and the piece of history that they tell as a whole.

The blocks are testament to shattered lives, to families torn apart, to cultures fragmented and crushed. These scraps of fabric have survived dangerous journeys where even more has been lost along the way. But now, in an ugly, bare-floored building on the edge of a shanty town, a group of women have triumphed. Gathered from starkly different backgrounds, they have picked up the pieces and, with love and the support of new-found companionship, have carefully pieced together something new. They've turned their heartbreak into something beautiful. It will cover the dead, grey blocks of the wall of the centre with a reminder that it's possible to find joy in the midst of devastation, that the human spirit is indestructible.

Eventually, the women who've made this quilt will move on, trying to find their way to a home – out there somewhere – that offers a life filled with dignity and empty of fear. But more women and children will come, and they'll see the wall hanging and read its message of triumph in the face of what's been lost. They will understand, then, that they're not alone, that there is kindness in this world and that they should be proud of the people they are and always will be.

May McConnaghy came along to the centre today. She spent ages talking with Madame Habib and the other Casawi volunteers. She's involved with a committee that raises funds for local projects and thinks she'll be able to make a strong case for the award of a grant to help get the quilt-making enterprise up and running. The women have already come up with a name for it – *Sawianaan*, which is the Arabic word for 'together'. To my ears, it sounds a little like they're saying 'sewing' and when I tell them that they laugh and clap their hands in delight. May has asked Madame Habib to come and talk to one of the other groups she's involved with as well. The volunteers here have such a wealth of knowledge and experience to share.

On the way back through the city, I ask the taxi driver to drop us at the entrance to the Parc Murdoch so I can walk the rest of the way home, stretching my legs and giving Grace a breath of fresh air. I feel happier than I have done in ages. I smile at Grace and she picks up on my mood, gurgling and chortling, trying to mimic my words as I point out a pair of rust-breasted redstarts who scold us indignantly from their perch in the branches of a jacaranda tree.

I take a slight detour, following our usual path towards the bench beneath the pines, intending to pause there for a few minutes to sanitise my hands and give Grace a drink. But as we approach, I'm disappointed to see the seat is already occupied by a couple. They sit close, heads inclined towards one another, deeply absorbed in their conversation. And then I stop in my tracks, half concealed behind a cluster of mock-orange bushes. Instinctively, I draw my shawl closer, covering Grace in its folds. Because the blonde-headed woman is my friend Kate. And the man she's sitting so close to, with her hand on his arm in a gesture that's at once intimate and comforting, is not her husband.

She says something and draws back slightly, and I catch sight of his profile. This is no stranger. No, it isn't her husband. It's mine.

I stand there, frozen with shock, my heart pounding and my stomach constricting in a tight knot. As I watch, Tom pulls his phone from his jacket pocket and Kate leans closer to him again as he appears to type something into it before putting it away.

I can't bear to watch them together like that – closer than he and I have been to each other in months. I know the sensible thing to do would be to walk up and say hello. Perhaps there's a perfectly innocent reason for them to be here or maybe they've just bumped into each other. But it certainly doesn't look innocent from the way they're sitting, the way his eyes never leave her face as he talks to her. My legs feel as if they're about to give way beneath me and my every instinct is to get away from here, to put the sight of them behind me. I don't think I can deal with this. The one person I thought was my friend here has deceived me in the cruellest way possible.

I've never felt so alone.

I turn away, walking fast towards the nearest gate, clutching Grace to me so tightly that she begins to cry.

I almost break into a run as I head for the safety of the house on the Boulevard des Oiseaux, where I can scrub furiously at my hands as if that might somehow wash away the shame and humiliation of Tom and Kate's betrayal.

Josie's Journal – Monday 27th April, 1942

Somehow I haven't had the heart to write in my journal for months, since we got back from the port after so nearly leaving. The house has been quieter, and even Annette is pretty subdued these days. Olivier and his parents left last week on a ship bound for Lisbon, so of course that made her feel even worse. We are still waiting for Papa to get our paperwork organised again. It's taken so long to get the American visas updated that our Portuguese transit visa has expired too, so it's back to square one.

Life feels like a game of snakes and ladders for everyone right now: we were almost at the one hundredth square but we landed on the head of the huge snake that lurks at the top of the board and slithered all the way back down to the start. I don't think I'll ever want to play that game again if I have the choice.

The war is also a bit like a snakes and ladders board: sometimes the radio reports that the Germans and the Japanese have won battles and they shoot up a ladder towards victory; the Allies seem to be slipping down a lot of snakes, if the newsreaders are to be believed. At the moment, it feels as though everyone is struggling somewhere around the middle of the board and it's not at all clear who is going to be the eventual winner.

Maman has got very thin. All her dresses seem too large for her these days and her hair is turning grey. I've always thought of her as being as strong as a stone fortress, but the constant buffeting of the waves of war are eating away at her, just as the ocean eventually wears away the strongest fortifications, like the ones I saw in Mogador.

Even Annette seems to have given up hope. She's stopped curling her hair now that Olivier has gone, she just pins it back and mopes around the house. I've tried lending her books to read, but she can't seem to concentrate for very long before it's time to write another letter to Géraldine complaining about how tough life is. To try to cheer her up, I pointed out to her that if she thinks life in a nice townhouse in Casablanca is tough then she should try going back to France, where there are Nazis running the country and the people are starving, or living in a work camp in Germany or Poland from where, according to Miss Ellis, rumours of things even worse than starving to death have been coming through. As usual, Annette didn't seem to appreciate my encouragement and she threw my copy of *Murder on the Orient Express* across the room at me so hard that it broke the binding. So now I'm going to have to explain that to Mademoiselle Dubois and there may be a fine to be paid. If so, I told Annette, she'll have to cough up for it. That made her scream for Maman, yelling that I was being annoying again. So I've retreated upstairs to my room for some peace and quiet.

Papa has gone back to his old routine, standing in queues and spending time at secret meetings in the mellah.

It's good seeing Nina and Felix again, at least that's a silver lining to still being stuck in Casablanca. Felix is busier than ever with his deliveries, and not just of bread. He confided in me that, since America joined the war, there have been more notes than ever going back and forth between the port, the *nouvelle ville* and the mellah. The other news is that Miss Josephine Baker is still in poor health in the hospital here in Casablanca. According to Felix, in spite of the many operations she has to have, she's in pretty good spirits and is visited often by officials from the American consulate and also Moroccan leaders. I said they must be very worried about her being so unwell, but he shook his head and said that wasn't the only reason such important people gathered there. When I asked him what he meant he got all puffed up with importance again and said he couldn't tell me, but that there were plans afoot. He can be quite pompous sometimes. And he shouldn't try to keep secrets and then drop hints about them because I can deduce exactly what's going on, although I didn't tell him that because then he would clam up and not say anything.

I'm glad that Papa is still helping the people who are trying to fight back against the Germans in any way they can. A few times he's asked me to pass messages on to Miss Ellis when he has to go out for a meeting or to stand in another queue, which shows how much he trusts me – otherwise he'd wait and do it himself. He also still takes me with him to the café quite regularly, although there's rarely any Coca-Cola these days and things like ice cream are very scarce and very expensive. Once, to my utter dismay, it was Monsieur Guigner who turned up again at our table. He didn't even pretend to ask Papa the time or to borrow his newspaper, just sat himself down and waved to the waiter to bring him a *p'tit noir*, grinning all the while and showing those yellow teeth. He made no mention of the money Papa had loaned him and gave no sign whatsoever that he meant to repay it. After he'd downed his coffee, he slipped a piece of paper across to Papa and then waited, expectantly, his hand resting, palm up, on the table. Very slowly, Papa reached into his pocket and handed over a rolled-up wad of notes. I hated seeing what passed between them so much, not just the money but also my papa's humiliation and Monsieur Guigner's smug glee. After that, the vulture got up and left. Papa even had to pay the bill for his coffee as well.

It's getting hotter every day in the city. We can't afford to go to the farm for horse-riding lessons any more.

Josie's Journal – Thursday 11th June, 1942

Today is my 14th birthday. Little did we think, this time a year ago, that we'd still be here in Casablanca for it. Unlike last year, I wasn't able to have a party in the courtyard to celebrate. I know our money must be running low, even though Papa and Maman never talk about it in front of Annette and me, so when Maman asked me what I'd like to do I said I just wanted Nina to come over and we'd ask Kenza to bake a nice cake that we could all enjoy. There is no Coca-Cola left in Morocco, even if we could afford it. There's no champagne either.

But the other reason that we couldn't have a party in the courtyard – even if we had been able to afford it – is the locusts. The whole city has been overrun by a plague of them and they're eating everything in sight. There's not a leaf or a blade of grass left in the Parc Murdoch and all the colourful flowers that make the city so beautiful have gone. Casablanca looks like a ghostly copy of itself. It's horrible going out, the locusts are everywhere, crawling and flying, and they get into your hair and crunch under your feet. The palm trees, which are now missing their crowns of leaves, look like telegraph poles. Miss Ellis says the locusts have even eaten the moss on the sea walls around the port. She told me they breed on the banks of Lake Chad on the other side of the Sahara Desert and usually, when people know that's going to happen, they cover the sand with oil to keep the eggs from hatching. But this year all the oil is needed for the war and so the locusts have won that particular battle for once. They've marched and flown across the miles and miles of the desert to descend on Casablanca.

I find that unsettling for more than one reason. If insects can do it, then I can just imagine how easy it will be for the German army with its tanks and aeroplanes once they've finished fighting the British in Egypt. There've been reports of heavy losses since Rommel and his tanks have advanced into what they're calling 'the cauldron' on the BBC.

The way the young locusts crawl along the ground reminds me a little of the scorpion we saw in the hotel in Taza and that, inevitably, reminds me of Monsieur Guigner. He, too, seems to find it pretty easy to cross the desert and pop up where he's not welcome. The other day when we were at the café, I asked Papa if he'd seen anything more of him and he assured me that he hadn't. Then I asked Papa if he thought Monsieur Guigner might turn up again sometime and he shrugged and said, 'There are many Monsieur Guigners around at the moment – the war seems to have brought them out from under the stones. We may not like them, *ma puce*, but they have their uses. Beggars can't be choosers of the company they keep.'

Anyway, we may be beggars these days, but at least I've been able to choose the company I've kept on my birthday. I've had a nice day really, in spite of the locusts and everything else that's going on.

Happy birthday to me.

Zoe – 2010

I'm reading to the children at the refugee centre when Kate walks in on Friday afternoon. She's late. I suppose she's probably been having another cosy lunch with Tom on a secluded park bench somewhere. For a moment I struggle to catch my breath as my chest constricts with pain and rage and humiliation, and I lose my place on the page. How dare she turn up and so coolly pretend nothing's going on behind my back? She smiles and waves across the room at me before turning her attention to the quilt. Regaining a little of my composure, I focus on the book again and try to summon up a smile for the children, who are looking at me a little quizzically, wondering why I've stopped so suddenly in the middle of the story of 'The Fisherman and the Genie'.

I deliberately spin out my storytelling and readily give in to the children's requests for another, to try to avoid having to be anywhere near Kate. But by the time I finish, she's come over to stand to one side of the group. She hands me a cup of mint tea and then asks the children to collect their felt flowers and bring them over to the long trestle table that she's set up to make it easier for the women to work on the quilt. I set the glass down on the floor beside my chair and busy myself putting away the books.

'Are you okay, Zoe?' she asks me as I turn my back on her.

I bite the inside of my lip and taste the metallic tang of blood. Then I turn to face her, my neck and cheeks burning with rage.

'No, Kate. As you will know very well from your cosy chats with my husband, I am most definitely not okay.'

She frowns slightly, pretending not to understand.

'Don't play the innocent,' I hiss, keeping my voice low so that the others won't hear. 'I saw you and Tom together in the park the other day.'

'Oh, Zoe, we need to talk . . .' she begins, extending a placatory hand towards my arm. I shake her off.

'This is hardly the time or the place for that,' I retort.

'But we're only trying . . .'

I cut her off again in mid-sentence, her use of the word 'we' making my anger surge again. 'It was perfectly obvious what the two of you were up to. Do me a favour, don't insult me by trying to justify yourself, on top of the humiliation and damage you've already caused.'

She reaches for my arm again and this time I wheel away from her, the heel of my shoe catching the glass and kicking over the tea as I do so. She stoops to pick up the glass, pulls a tissue from her sleeve and tries to mop up the spill. 'Leave that,' I say, so sharply that several heads turn towards us. 'I'll sort it. Go and get on with your work – they're waiting for you.'

Tears spring to her eyes and she winces at the sudden harshness of my words. But she seems to realise she's already made enough of a scene. Madame Habib is approaching and so Kate backs away, reluctantly returning to her place at the quilting table.

As I kneel and blot up the puddle of sweet-smelling liquid with a wad of paper towels, I surreptitiously wipe the hot tears of rage and pain from my cheeks too. Then I tell Madame Habib that I'm going to leave early today as I have a headache. She fusses over me, telling me her husband will gladly drive me home, but I refuse the offer and tell her I'll take a taxi. I can't bear to be in the same room as Kate for a second longer.

My hands itch and burn, feeling dirty and contaminated, and I run upstairs to the bathroom on the top floor the minute I get home, washing them again and again, as if that will help calm my troubled mind.

Eventually, I pat them dry on a towel and go through to pick up Grace, hugging her close, the soft weight of her in my arms comforting me far more than I am able to comfort her. She picks up on my distress and begins to fret, pulling away from me as she strains to be put down. Her rejection stings my already bruised nerves and I am suddenly overwhelmed by the urge to shake her violently and scream. I quickly put her down on the bed, horrified and frightened by the powerful impulse. How could I ever feel like that about Grace? I disgust myself. Is it any wonder Tom doesn't want to be with me any longer?

She reaches for the pink rabbit that sits on her pillow and begins to chew an ear, watching me warily. 'I'm sorry, I'm sorry, I'm sorry,' I sob. She reaches a chubby hand to my cheek in forgiveness, and then holds up the cuddly toy to share it with me. I lie beside her, stroking her hair until we are both soothed. Then I reach for the sandalwood box of Josie's treasures and bring them out, one by one, to show Grace, distracting myself from my torment. She chuckles and murmurs at the sight of them, her coos as soft as a turtle dove's, and I dangle the gold Star of David above her, letting the light catch its angles as it spins slowly at the end of its fine chain.

'I wish she was here,' I say. And I mean it with all my heart.

Later, once I've fed Grace and she's fallen asleep, her lashes fluttering on her cheeks, which are as rosy as a sunrise after her bath, I settle myself in the armchair by the window and listen to the evening sounds of the city. The call to prayer floats on the warm air above the background hum of the traffic. As those noises fade,

I can hear the soughing of the ocean wind over the rooftops and I turn my head a little to let the breeze caress my cheek. I feel wrung out, exhausted from my anger and my grief and the tears I've shed today. But most of all I feel alone.

I reach for the leather-bound journal, hoping to find solace and distraction in the company of the girl I've come to think of as a friend. I leaf through the pages, rereading the last section about Josie's fourteenth birthday in a city stripped to its bones by a plague of locusts in a time of war. Her words make me smile and they give me strength, her indomitable spirit shining through.

Then I turn to the next page of the journal and I freeze.

The words written here aren't at all what I was expecting to read and I'm unable to take them in properly at first. I read them again, more slowly. My heart pounds in my ears and my hands tremble.

'No,' I whisper.

But there's no denying the words on the page, written in Josie's looped handwriting, a little smudged here and there. Could she have been crying as she wrote this?

I imagine her, here in this very room, alone and scared.

And I wish more than anything that I could reach out across the years to put my arms around that frightened girl and comfort her in her pain.

Josie's Journal – Tuesday 30th June, 1942

This is the very worst day of my life. Without Papa, how can we go on? Without Papa, I'm not sure that I want to go on. Every minute seems to last an hour as we watch and wait for him to be returned to us.

It is so hard to write these words, but I know he would tell me to put them down on paper so that they aren't in my head, and then I might be able to sleep a bit tonight. I don't think I will ever sleep again, though, not until he is home with us where he belongs.

On Sunday, Felix arrived at our door, having cycled over from the mellah. He was out of breath, gasping to get the words out, and Papa pulled him and his bike into the hall and closed the door behind him. Maman and Annette were in the drawing room, but I'd started to come down to see who was at the door, so I stayed on the stairs and listened.

'Don't come this afternoon. The meeting is cancelled. They're arresting everyone,' Felix said. Although I couldn't see his face, it sounded as if he was sobbing.

Papa calmed him down a bit. 'Take a breath, son. Are you all right? And your parents?'

'Yes, we're okay. But the Gestapo have made a move. There are police everywhere. They've taken hundreds away.'

'The others . . . ?' Papa didn't mention any names, but I guessed he was referring to the people who were at those meetings he'd been going to.

'Gone,' said Felix. 'I think one or two may have managed to hide, but they're raiding houses, arresting Jews, anyone they suspect of being in the resistance.'

Papa hushed him then and said, 'Do you want to stay here? We could hide you and your parents. Of course, nowhere is entirely safe but it would probably be better for you here than in the mellah.'

Felix refused. 'No, Monsieur Duval. But thanks all the same. It would put your own family at even greater risk if we were here. The baker will shelter us.'

'Stay a while. Get your breath back. At least wait here until the worst is over,' Papa urged.

But Felix wouldn't stay. 'I need to get going. There are others I need to alert. And then I want to get back to be with my parents.'

'Be careful,' Papa said. And then he opened the door and Felix and his bike disappeared.

I ran down the stairs and put my arms around Papa as tightly as I could. He smoothed my hair with his hand and kissed the top of my head. 'There, there, *ma puce*. Don't worry, it will be all right. We're safe here.'

I nodded, resisting the urge to tell him I'd just heard him say that nowhere was entirely safe. I wanted to believe him. I wanted it to be true. I didn't want Maman and Annette to know what I knew. But it was very hard to try to be brave then and I felt terribly scared, knowing that the wolves and the sharks had begun closing in and that they were starting to snap up the little white mice.

-x-

We were sitting around the breakfast table this morning when the knock at the door came. There was nothing particularly out of the ordinary in that, although we were all a bit more jumpy than usual – it could have been someone begging for food or asking if we had any odd jobs that needed doing in return for a few francs – and Papa went downstairs to answer it. But then we heard the sound of a guttural accent, loudly demanding to know whether he was Guillaume Duval, asking to see his papers, and I knew something was wrong. Maman froze, her coffee cup halfway to her lips, and Annette put down the knife she'd been using to peel an apricot and her eyes grew very wide indeed. I jumped up from the table and went to the window, using the folded-back shutter to hide behind.

In the road below were two large black cars, painted with the emblem of the Nazis, and my blood froze in my veins. I could hear voices from the doorstep, Papa's tone soothing and placatory against the perfunctory snapping of the officials.

Maman got up and came to peer out too, standing so close behind me that I could hear the shallow gasps of her breath. I thought perhaps the pounding in my ears was the sound of her heart beating like the wings of a trapped bird against glass, but then I realised it wasn't her heart but mine. Instinctively, she put out an arm as if to shield me from what we could see, but I ducked out from under it and bolted for the stairs.

'Josie, come back!' Maman's voice was high and thin with fear, but I ignored her. My mind was racing as I ran down the stairs, desperately trying to think of what I could say this time to help protect Papa. If ever camouflage was needed, now was the moment. But I couldn't think of the right thing to do to save him.

As I reached the hallway, Papa turned to glance at me over his shoulder. It looked as if the two men were holding him by the arms. He opened his eyes wide when he saw me and I read so much in them in that split second – love, fear, pain and grief. But the most awful thing of all was the look of defeat that I saw there too, a realisation that the game was up.

He shook his head at me, so gently that it was almost imperceptible.

But I couldn't give up, I couldn't let them take my papa away. I reached for him, but one of the men stepped between us and pushed me away.

'No!' I shouted. 'He's done nothing. Why are you taking him?'

The men's mouths were set in grim lines and they didn't answer me, they just marched Papa down the steps to the waiting car. I started after them, but Papa looked back at me once more. 'Stay there, Josie. Look after Maman and Annette for me,' he said. His voice was low, so filled with emotion that the words sounded thick in his throat.

I was expecting him to say that he promised he'd be back soon: I desperately wanted him to say those words, to make one more promise and be able to keep it this time. But there was no time for him to say anything more as the two men bundled him into the back of the car and slammed the door. Then the driver pulled away and I couldn't see Papa, even though I tried desperately to catch one more glimpse of him through the window, because the German who'd climbed in after him was in the way.

The second car drew forward, following the first. And then I caught sight of one of the passengers travelling in it and sickness and anger flooded my guts. He was looking straight at me. I recognised the sand-coloured hair, the sunken eyes and the vulture-like hunch of the shoulders, even before Monsieur Guigner opened his mouth in a grin that looked to me like the grimace of a skull.

With an effort, I swallowed the acid bile that had filled my mouth along with the urge to scream. Then Maman appeared on the steps behind me and I collapsed into her arms. She held me tight and I sobbed into her shoulder. And then, very firmly, she pulled me inside and closed the door.

I can't write any more tonight, although I don't think I'll be able to sleep. Instead, I'm sitting by the window, watching the moonlight cast its silver shadows on the tiles of the roof where the turtle doves are roosting for the night. I remember the dreamseller's words: when the moon shines on one hundred bowls of water, every one of them is filled with moonlight. I hope that, wherever he is tonight, my papa can see the moonlight and he can feel my love shining on him too.

Goodnight, Papa.

Josie's Journal – Monday 6th July, 1942

I'm struggling to find the right words to put down what has happened. But I know that if I want to be a writer I have to record everything. And even though I can never again be carefree I have to trust in Papa's advice to put things in my journal and get them out of my head when they are too hard to bear. So I will try . . .

When Madame Bénatar and Miss Ellis both appeared on the doorstep this afternoon, I knew what they were going to say before they opened their mouths. Their faces already told me the answer to the questions we'd been asking ourselves every second of every day for the past week.

Maman had plucked up all her courage and been to the Préfecture de Police to ask for information about the abduction of her husband, but the stony-faced French policeman behind the desk couldn't – or wouldn't – give her any information. He simply said it was a matter for the German authorities and that it was nothing to do with him, even though Felix had told us that the French police had been helping the Gestapo with the round-ups in the mellah the previous weekend. He'd cycled over, looking for Papa, and I think he was as devastated as we all were to hear he'd been taken too.

Maman knew it was too dangerous for her to pursue things further with the Germans. They might arrest her as well and then Annette and me. So she'd asked Miss Ellis to let Mr Reid and Madame Bénatar know, as she hoped they might be able to hold some sway with the authorities.

When the two ladies came to call, Maman showed them upstairs to the drawing room, as if it were a social visit. With all of my heart I wished it was. I wished we could sip cups of mint tea and make small talk about the weather and the progress I'd been making in my lessons. I'd have been happy to make polite conversation for once. But I already knew that wasn't what they'd come for. I don't think any of us wanted to speak, because until the words were said we could cling on to a tiny shred of hope and still believe that Papa would come home one day soon.

Miss Ellis came and sat next to me and Annette on the chaise longue and Madame Bénatar knelt on the floor at Maman's feet and held her hands very tightly. 'Delphine, I'm so sorry. It's the most awful news. We tried very hard to get him released. But yesterday they found twenty of the men they rounded up guilty of spying for the resistance movement. I hate to have to tell you this, but Guillaume was among them.'

A noise came out of Maman's throat that wasn't a word, it was more like the strangled cry of an animal in pain. Madame Bénatar gripped her hands even harder – I could see her knuckles go white.

I was the one who found my voice first. 'Is he . . . ?'

Miss Ellis reached over and put an arm around my shoulders and there were tears running down her cheeks. 'Josie, I'm so terribly sorry. All twenty of the men were executed at dawn today. The Gestapo wanted to make an example of them, to deter others.'

My ears were filled with noise then, and my brain couldn't seem to register what it was or where it was coming from. It took a few seconds for me to realise that it was the sound of Annette's screams, filling the room and echoing in the vast emptiness that I felt within my heart.

It's still there now, that emptiness in my heart, as I write these words in the journal that my papa gave me a year and a half ago in order that I could write down the thoughts that were in my head and stop being so anxious. But there aren't enough pages in the world for me to express the way I miss him.

I'm trying to remember the dreamseller's words. She said I'm stronger than I know. She also said it's only when you let go of fear and grief that you will find your freedom. I don't feel strong at all tonight. And my fear and grief close in around me like the bars of a prison. I wonder whether Papa was held behind bars. I wonder whether he was able to stay strong until the end. I can see his eyes now, when I close mine, trying to say so many things. But mostly telling the story of his love for me and Maman and Annette.

I think I understand the dreamseller's words about the moon shining in one hundred bowls of water differently now. Perhaps she was also saying that when someone dies, their love is still there, bathing you in its light. The only trouble is, it doesn't feel that way at all to me at the moment.

Yes, my heart is empty now. How can it hold the moonlight when it's been shattered into a thousand pieces? Because without Papa our lives seem as bleak and desolate as the Sahara Desert.

Zoe – 2010

I hear the faint whispers of the Duvals' story in every room in the house now. As I come in through the front door, on my return from the library or Monsieur Habib's shop in the Habous, I shudder, picturing the Gestapo standing on the steps and Guillaume Duval glancing back over his shoulder towards Josie, his eyes trying to communicate so much to her in those final moments. I can hardly bear to sit on the couch in the drawing room, imagining that terrible day when Hélène Bénatar and Dorothy Ellis arrived to break the news to Delphine, Annette and Josie that Guillaume had been executed. I can find little peace indoors, now I know what these walls have witnessed. The plasterwork surely still holds resonances of the women's words and the echoes of Annette's screams.

How did they manage to keep going, Delphine, Annette and Josie? Their money was running out and the clock was ticking for the refugees in Casablanca.

There are only a couple of places I can bear to sit. One is upstairs in Grace's room, keeping watch over my sleeping daughter and bearing witness to the phantom presence of Josie, alone and afraid without her papa.

The other place is outside in the courtyard and it's to here that I now retreat, bringing my sewing to sit beneath the jasmine-covered trellis. I settle Grace on her play mat, which I've surrounded with cushions from the garden chairs so it's safe for her to practise her crawling. It's a skill she's seemed to be in no hurry to acquire, preferring to sit and thoughtfully survey the shade-dappled leaves rather than being tempted by the toys I put just beyond her reach to try to encourage her. She knows I'll give in sooner or later and come and kneel beside her, handing her the pink rabbit and the brightly coloured jack-in-the-box that are her current favourites.

When she settles for her nap in the shade beside my chair, I pick up the quilt and begin to stitch through the layers, outlining each block so it springs into relief. Assembling the blocks and sashing strips didn't take long with Kate's sewing machine, but I want to finish it off by hand. There's not much more to do – just the quilting and then I'll hand-stich the border with the binding that will frame the whole thing.

The quilting project at the refugee centre is almost finished too. This Friday, we'll kneel around the yards of fabric and begin this same task, hand-quilting the blocks. The women talk and laugh as they work, happy to have the companionship and a welcome distraction from the harsh realities of life beyond the centre's walls. Sometimes one of the women will begin to hum as she sews and, one by one, the others will join in, layering on harmonies of their own until the hot air reverberates with the waves of sound. The tunes are sometimes mournful, sometimes joyous, but always a welcome alternative to the despairing silence I encountered on my first visit to the centre.

As I sit and sew in the courtyard, I think about Tom. Seeing him and Kate together in the park like that was a huge shock. But it was also a wake-up call. I suppose, if I'm being honest with myself, I'm not surprised he's sought out the company of other women. I haven't been much of a wife to him: neither the friend he deserves, nor the lover he desires. I ought to be feeling anger at his betrayal, but I don't any more. I just feel defeated. We came to Casa to make a fresh start, to pick up the pieces of our broken relationship and try for a new beginning in a place where the reminders of what we once had wouldn't be waiting to ambush us around every corner. But I've come to realise I just can't do it. It feels like an ending now. The final, faint traces of the dreams we once shared have gone, evaporating in the blaze of the Moroccan sun.

I've finally had to admit to myself that my marriage is over. Seeing Tom with Kate wasn't even all that astonishing, once I got over the initial shock. I'd been expecting it from him, after all, watching and waiting for it to happen. I just thought it would be with someone like Suzette from the dinner party at Claudine's, or a woman I didn't know from his work perhaps. Not with someone I'd come to think of as a good friend.

We both deserve better, Tom and I, than this marriage that we're trapped in. It's time we admit to ourselves and to each other that it's finished. Time to let each other go.

Perhaps, one day, I'll be able to dream anew. Perhaps Tom has already found another dream to follow. Maybe he's discovered his next sunrise, with Kate. But for the moment I have to accept that he and I have tried and failed. I've made up my mind. Once my quilt is finished and the project at the refugee centre has been completed, I'll leave.

Just as I'm nearing the end of Josie's journal and the pages remaining unread have dwindled to a thin sheaf, like the last fragile leaves clinging to the trees as winter approaches, I have to face the fact that an ending of my own story is approaching. As I work on my quilt, outlining each of the blocks I've stitched together with such care, I remind myself that the Tree of Life represents the hope of new beginnings, even as the leaves relinquish their hold and flutter to the ground in the autumn wind.

For the moment, I'll keep my eyes cast down to the sewing in my lap. But as I push the needle through the layers of material and make one tiny, precise stitch after another, I am all too aware that one day soon I shall have to lift my head and – at last – face the reality of the truth that's been waiting there, just beyond the limits of my peripheral vision, all along.

Josie's Journal – Monday 31st August, 1942

We have received our updated American visas back today. Maman had to go and queue at the American consulate but Mr Reid stepped in to help, which was only right. After all, it was because of him that Papa got involved with the resistance network and so I imagine he must have that on his conscience. I don't blame him. It's not his fault – it's the fault of the war, the fault of the unkindness in this world, the fault of cruelty and injustice, the fault of my papa's good heart, which meant he couldn't just sit by and watch while people were persecuted and humiliated for their faith. Especially knowing that his own wife shared that faith, even if she had lapsed. Mr Reid has also promised to help us get our exit permits for Morocco as soon as we've managed to get our new transit visas for Portugal. Apparently he knows people at the Préfecture de Police. I just hope they're not the same people who helped round up the Jews in the mellah, nor the unhelpful man who Maman spoke to when she was trying so desperately to find out where Papa had gone after the Gestapo took him away.

Anyway, Annette has promised to go with Maman to queue at the Portuguese consulate while I'm having my lessons with Miss Ellis. She only comes to teach me twice a week now. We can't afford to pay her at all any more, but she very kindly offered to keep tutoring me for free and Maman was so grateful that I couldn't protest, even though I really find it quite hard to concentrate on studying things like maths and history these days.

Also, Miss Ellis has another motive for carrying on tutoring me, but I can't tell Maman about that or she'd hit the roof with fury and fear. It was my decision, though, and Miss Ellis was pretty reluctant when I first told her of the plan that Felix and I had made.

Felix came over on his bike a couple of weeks ago and I could see there was something on his mind. We went and sat in the courtyard for a while and tried to talk about the weather and the bakery and the fact that the locusts had gone at last, although there's not a leaf to be seen and the city is going to take quite some time to recover. There were several awkward silences and after one of them he finally plucked up the courage to ask me how I was doing. I shrugged and picked up a feather that had fluttered down from the roof, where the turtle doves were murmuring softly to each other, smoothing the grey filaments between my fingers.

'Your papa was a very brave man, you know,' Felix said in a low voice. 'He's helped establish a resistance network here in Casablanca and, even though they caught him, his work will continue. It's important that it does, so that he and the others who died with him won't have given their lives in vain. I shouldn't really be telling you this, but I just wanted you to know.'

His words, like those of Abraham Lincoln, were a call to arms. They startled me, jolting my soul, so that I felt as if I was waking up from a deep sleep and opening my eyes to the life that continued to go on around us. '*It is for us the living to be dedicated to the unfinished work which they who fought here have thus far nobly advanced,*' I whispered to myself.

'What did you say?' Felix asked.

I shook my head. Then I let the feather fall back to the ground at my feet and turned to face him. 'What can I do, Felix? Tell me what I can do to help. I want to keep my papa's work going. I can pass on messages, ride my bike across town, come and visit you in the mellah. Tell me.'

He refused at first, saying my maman would kill him if she thought he was involving me. But I can be pretty persistent when I'm determined about something and, in the end, I managed to persuade him to give me a job. It's only passing on messages from him to Miss Ellis when she comes to teach me my lessons, but he says they are important. He says he doesn't know exactly what's happening – and he wouldn't tell me even if he did, but I can tell he really doesn't. After all, we are just two little white mice in this war between giants – but he thinks the Americans and the British are planning something big. It's important that the lines of communication, which my papa helped to establish, continue to pass information back and forth so that the resistance here on the ground in Morocco can be ready to help when the call to arms comes.

Miss Ellis wasn't too keen on our plan at first, but then she admitted it would be a help as it would look much more natural if Felix visited me now and then as my friend and she just happened to be continuing as my tutor. I feel a tiny bit less helpless knowing I'm playing a small part in Papa's 'unfinished work'.

When my papa was murdered (I refuse to call it by anything other than its true name), Maman, Annette and I were frozen with grief and fear for several weeks at first. I didn't want to see anyone, not even Nina, but one day Kenza persuaded me to go and sit in the courtyard with her for a little while and she fed me *ghoribas* and told me that Nina was missing me terribly and wanted to bring me some books from the library so that we could read together again. Just as she said that, a pair of turtle doves fluttered down from the roof to peck at the crumbs I'd scattered on the ground beside the pomegranate tree. A few tiny green shoots have begun appearing on it after the locusts ate all the leaves. I said I'd like to see Nina, but could the three of us go to the beach one day soon because there was something I needed to do there. Kenza looked at me with her lovely dark eyes and they looked very sad, even though she was smiling in an understanding way. I could see she knew exactly what I was talking about and she nodded and said she'd ask Maman if it would be okay to organise a taxi to take us again.

And so Kenza, Nina and I went to the ocean so that I could write my papa's name on a stone and throw it into the waves. I was crying a lot when I did it because I really didn't want to have to let him go like that, even though I knew I had to.

We can't go to Papa's grave because the Nazis won't tell any-one where they buried the twenty so-called traitors that they shot. Madame Bénatar is still working on it, but Annette says we may never know and we need to stay strong for Maman and not show her how much pain we truly feel as that would just make it even worse for her, if such a thing were possible, which I doubt. But for once I didn't want to argue with Annette and so I decided the best thing would be to go to the ocean instead, where I could remember Papa and say goodbye in my own way.

Before I could let it go, I held on to the stone with Papa's name on it for a long time, and Kenza and Nina were very kind and patient and let me take as much time as I needed, standing beside me and supporting me, but not saying anything while I cried. My tears were as salty as the sea and I thought about the mosquito drinking it all up. That seemed to me to be an impossible task, just as impossible as letting go of the stone I was carrying.

At last, though, I felt brave enough and strong enough and I threw the stone as far out as I could so that the currents of the ocean, which are as powerful as love itself, would carry it away into a place as deep as the love that I will always have for my papa in my heart. I couldn't see anything for a while, because my eyes were too full of tears. But the wind from the sea dried them at last. And then a glint of something caught my attention in the wash of foam among the pebbles at my feet. When I looked more closely, I saw it was a piece of jade-green glass, worn smooth by the waves, and I bent down to pick it up. As I held it in my hand, it felt as if the ocean had given me back this sliver of smooth glass as a gift in exchange for my papa's name. The memories came flooding back. I remembered how Papa had looked at me with so much love that time in the cave near Taza, and the time at Mogador when I'd managed to save him from the police.

Kenza smiled at me and I think she had guessed what I was thinking, because she said, 'It is the same colour as your eyes, *Khadar Ini*. He was so proud of you.'

I'm keeping it in the sandalwood box, along with my other treasures.

Josie's Journal – Saturday 12th September, 1942

Ramadan is just beginning. I've been sitting at my window, watching the sun set out over the ocean. As the sky darkens, the evening star appears and then the first sliver of the new moon rises and the muezzins start to sing.

I wonder whether I'll still be here in a month's time to see the first glimpse of the next new moon, which will mark the beginning of Eid al-Fitr. We have all our papers in place again now and are ready to leave Casablanca. We have to wait for a ship, though, and there are so few of them these days. Maman has told us it's looking as if we'll have to be patient for a few more weeks. But in the meantime we've pulled the suitcases out from the cupboard under the stairs and begun to pack the things we don't need at the moment. We're determined to be ready to go if a berth on a ship becomes available at short notice.

Annette asked Maman why we couldn't catch a plane to Portugal. There's still one flight a day out of Cazes airfield, but apparently that's out of the question. The seats are reserved for diplomatic personnel and VIPs. Even if, by some miracle, three places were available then we wouldn't be able to afford the tickets. It's all Maman can do to pay the rent now. Although none of us has said it, I know we're all thinking the same thing: if we don't manage to get out of Morocco this time, we'll have to move to the mellah by Christmastime. The threat looms on the horizon like the dark wall of an approaching sandstorm. I can't get the thought of Madame Adler's poor sore eyes out of my head.

As I watch the moon climb higher, until it hangs directly above the minaret of the mosque, I send up a silent prayer to whichever god may be listening. It will break my heart to leave this place: the place where my papa's body lies who-knows-where, perhaps in a hastily dug grave entangled with the corpses of 19 others, or in the ocean, where his bones will be picked clean and turned into the shells of sea creatures; the place where my friends Nina and Kenza have taught me so much and stood beside me on the beach to give me the strength to say so many hard goodbyes. But I know we need to leave now, because I fear for Maman's health. Like the waning of the old moon, she's fading day by day. It's not a physical illness, but something harder to diagnose – a dullness in her eyes; an expression of exhaustion when her features are in repose; a mixture of fear and grief and hopelessness that silently eats away at her. I don't know how much more she can take. Even though life in an America at war with the world holds great uncertainty for the three of us, I know it will be best for Maman if we can get to a place where there are other members of her family to help support her, even though they are only distant relations and we have never actually met them.

It's too much for Annette and me as well. We need to be in a place where we won't be living in constant fear, just because of our mother's birthright.

-x-

Yesterday, Miss Ellis asked me if I'd be prepared to perform an important task for her. I thought it would just be delivering another message to Felix, which I still do at least a couple of times a week, but this time it was something a little different. She explained that the information that she'd copied from my project on the Atlantic ports had already been useful. But now some people of great importance had asked to see the source material. Would I be prepared to hand it over, knowing that it would be put to good use? She explained that all I'd need to do was take my schoolbook and rendezvous with a courier in the Parc Murdoch at 5.30 p.m.

'Not Felix?' I asked her.

'No, it won't be Felix this time.'

I hesitated for a moment then. 'I know I'm not supposed to ask questions, but I have to know this one thing – will it be Monsieur Guigner?'

At the mention of the name, Miss Ellis looked very angry. Her mouth set into a thin line and her cheeks flushed red. 'Josie, I can absolutely assure you of one thing: it most certainly will not be the agent who used to call himself Guigner. He was discovered to have been a turncoat, responsible for betraying many of the men who were arrested, including your father. He bargained with the Gestapo, trading the lives of other, far better men in return for his own. But luckily the network that people like your papa had managed to put in place has been strong enough to survive the loss of so many of their number. On Guigner's release, there was a band of *résistants* waiting for him. They have made sure that none of us will ever see anything of that treacherous snake ever again.'

I felt a surge of anger myself when I heard it was that horrible, despicable man who had betrayed my papa. I remembered how annoyed he'd been when I appeared at the door of our hotel just behind him and stopped him from hurting Annette any worse than he already had done. I suppose he'd borne a grudge against us ever since. I knew I ought to feel pity for him – a traitor who had been unceremoniously killed by the comrades he was supposed to be helping – but the truth is I didn't. I just felt glad that he was gone because if I ever saw him again, I would have killed him myself. So I agreed, in that case, to deliver my project to the Parc Murdoch at 5.30 that afternoon.

At the end of my lesson Miss Ellis gave me a hug, which surprised me. As an Englishwoman, she is usually far more formal. 'Your papa would be so proud of you, Josie. What you're doing today may seem like just another small task to you, but it's of crucial importance. You've done more than you will ever know in the fight for what is right.'

I put my schoolbook in the basket of my bike and cycled through the streets to the park. As I walked over to the bench beside the drinking fountain, where Miss Ellis had told me to wait, the swifts were performing their displays of aerobatics, soaring and swooping as they caught flies in the cooling air of the late afternoon against the forget-me-not blue of the sky. The colour reminded me of the flowers that grew beside the stream on the farm when we used to go for our horse rides. I wonder how Najima, Marguerite and Malik are doing these days. I hope they're still safe in their peaceful paddocks, eating the daisies.

It was a quiet time of day and the park was almost empty. The only sounds were the dripping of water from the drinking fountain and the occasional calling of the bulbuls from the branches of the fig trees. The park is still suffering in the aftermath of the locust invasion. The trees are leafless and the once-green oasis is stark and bare. The tyres of my bike whisked up little clouds of dust as I wheeled it over to the bench and took my project from the basket. As I sat down to wait for the courier, I flipped through the pages of the book. The sketches and details of each of the harbours reminded me of that holiday we'd had – our last one as a family of four. With a sigh, I closed the book before the memories it evoked could overwhelm me. I ran my fingers over the cover, tracing the outline of my name and the A+ that Miss Ellis had written there with her fountain pen in the green ink she favours for marking students' work.

I was so lost in my thoughts that I didn't notice the figure approaching until she had almost reached the drinking fountain. At first, I thought it was an old, old woman, as ancient as the dream-seller, only dressed in more fashionable clothes. She was skeletally thin, bent almost double over the stick on which she leaned heavily as she took shuffling steps along the dusty path towards me. But as she neared the bench, she looked up and smiled. I'd have recognised those huge dark eyes anywhere.

'Miss Josephine Baker!' I exclaimed.

She sat down beside me, moving carefully, as if any sudden move might break her in two. 'And you are Josie, my almost-name-sake,' she said. 'I've heard a lot about you. I think perhaps we've met here once before, *non*?'

I nodded, hardly able to speak. Then I came to my senses and said how sorry I'd been to hear of her poor health and that I hoped she was recovering now.

'Progress is frustratingly slow. They've opened me up so many times, I told the surgeon to install a zipper in me next time to make things easier for all of us.' Her eyes regained a little of their old sparkle when she smiled. 'But, as you can see, I'm just about back on my feet. I like to try and get out of the hospital for a little while every day, if I can manage it, to come and walk here and breathe the evening air.'

'I'm glad to hear it,' I replied. 'I hope one day you will be able to sing and dance again. And may I ask how your animals are?'

It was her turn to sigh then. 'I've had to leave them in Marrakesh, I'm afraid. They wouldn't let me have them in the hos-pital, and of course Glug-Glug and Gugusse would have caused all sorts of havoc and Bonzo would have been miserable there. But don't worry, my staff are taking good care of them all and one day soon I hope I'll see them again.'

We watched the drips from the drinking fountain for a few moments. 'Look there,' Josephine Baker said, pointing to where they'd splashed on to the dusty ground. A faint shimmer, like tiny stitches of green silk thread on a blank canvas, was just visible. She smiled once more. 'You see, the grass is beginning to grow again. And if it can rise again from the dust, then so can we, *n'est-ce pas*, Josie?'

Another squadron of swifts swooped above us, so low that we could hear the sound of the scimitar-shaped blades of their wings slicing through the air.

Miss Baker roused herself. 'I must be getting back to the clinic or they'll be sending out a search party. They are so very bossy, those doctors and nurses, although I know they have my best interests at heart. But before I go, I think you have something for me perhaps?' She nodded towards the schoolbook in my lap. I handed it over and she glanced at the cover. 'An A+, hey? Excellent work, Josie Duval. No wonder your papa was always so proud of you.'

I was pretty surprised to know that she'd heard of my papa and me. How strange it is to be famous – even in secret – to someone who is so famous herself.

I sat for a while and watched as Josephine Baker shuffled away along the path back to the hospital. The stooped, wizened figure, with my schoolbook tucked under one arm, looked spectral against the bare twigs in the fading light and for a moment I thought, 'She has turned into a ghost of herself.'

Maybe that's what we've all become now. The war has taken thousands of lives. And even those of us who are still living have been turned into ghosts of our former selves.

Josie's Journal – Friday 6th November, 1942

At last we have news that our berth has been confirmed. Our ship, the *Esperanza*, is due to arrive in port today. We sail for Portugal on Wednesday next week, which is the day after Annette's birthday. I like the fact that the Portuguese have sent a boat whose name means 'Hope'. Perhaps they understand it will be carrying not just refugees but a cargo of hopes and dreams as we look forward to our new lives.

So I have just a few days to finish packing and to say my good-byes. I've put most things in the suitcases already. I'm only leaving out the clothes I'll need. And I'll keep my box of treasures and this journal in their hiding place until the last minute, so that I can carry them with me when I go and there'll be absolutely no chance of them falling into the wrong hands.

It's going to be a busy few days, I think. I need to buy a present for Annette and return the last of my books to the library. Kenza is planning to bake some special cakes and pastries for Annette's birthday as it will also be our chance to say our farewells to her and Nina and Felix.

Maman seems to have a little more energy, now that the end of our time in Casablanca is almost upon us. I can be thankful for that at least.

Zoe – 2010

I turn the page, expecting to read something more. But there is nothing. The last few pages of the journal are blank. And then, as the significance of this sinks in, a fear begins to grip my guts. I should have thought of it before.

Why was Josie's journal left behind? What happened to her and her mother and sister? Surely she wouldn't have left it on purpose? She'd never have forgotten to pack it. And there's no way she would have forgotten her box of treasures either. I open it again and take out its contents: the little gold Star of David that she was told by her mother not to wear in case it invited trouble; the carved length of stick that mimics the call of the turtle doves, evoking Felix and Nina; Josephine Baker's autograph; the faded flamingo feather from the visit to the lagoon on the family's final holiday down the coast; and most importantly of all, the sliver of jade-green sea glass that the ocean gave Josie in return for her father's name. She'd never have left them behind deliberately.

My fear gathers strength as I set them all out on the quilt and my sense of doubt becomes more concrete. Something must have happened to prevent Josie from taking them with her. I imagine a knock at the door, a large black car waiting in the street below, men in greatcoats with Nazi insignia on their lapels coming to take the family away just as they were about to leave for safety.

Then I look at the date of the final entry in the journal once again: the 6th of November. They were due to sail on the 11th. But I know from my research that Operation Torch, the American invasion of North Africa, began three days before that, on the 8th – a couple of days before the farewell party they'd planned for Annette's nineteenth birthday. Very slowly, I set down Josie's journal on the bed beside me. I recall now that I read that the main landings of US troops took place via the port of Safi, the harbour that Josie identified in her project as being the optimal one for an invasion. At the same time, attacks were launched on the other main cities along the Atlantic coast.

Casablanca, the port where the *Esperanza* lay at anchor, came under fire from sea and sky. The attacks were short-lived, but fierce.

So, as the war arrived at the walls of the city, what on earth happened to the Duvals?

Zoe – 2010

I grab my laptop to try and piece together what happened to Josie and her family, searching the internet for information about the attack on the harbour at Casablanca. I learn that the naval battle raged for a few days when French fighter planes and battleships engaged the American forces as they attempted to land at Fedala, a few miles up the coast. The French finally surrendered on the 11th of November, the day the Duvals had thought they would be leaving Morocco for good. But there's no mention of the *Esperanza*, just the fact that several ships lying at anchor in the port were sunk. It's going to take a bit more digging to unearth the details. Then the internet connection drops and I slam the laptop shut in frustration.

I pull on my trainers and strap Grace into her sling, then hurry to the library. I speak to the librarian and she manages to unearth copies of local newspaper reports covering the events. Most of them describe only the military vessels that were involved and it takes me a while to find any mention of other ships. But then I see it. The *Esperanza*, mentioned almost as a footnote to one of the articles. She took a direct hit during the fighting on the 8th of November 1942 and was sunk, still at anchor in the harbour. All the civilian passengers and crew on board were believed to have been lost.

My hand trembles as I set the paper down on the table in front of me. Josie. Annette. Delphine. They'd been through such a lot and were so close to getting away. I can't bring myself to believe they didn't make it. The *Esperanza* – filled with its cargo of hopes and dreams – should have sailed, carrying them safely to Lisbon. From there they should have transferred to another boat, one that would carry them across the Atlantic to their new life in America. I've pictured Josie as a grown woman in the many roles she'd dreamed of in her journal – farmer, lawyer, librarian, reporter, scientist, doctor. Instead, now I have an image in my head of the burning carcass of a ship, the bodies of its passengers strewn into the dirty water of the harbour, struggling for life, losing the fight, sinking without a trace. All that's left of the Duval family's story is the secret journal that Josie hid beneath the floorboards in her attic room. Somehow, in the scramble of their departure, it must have got left behind. And I am the only person in the world who knows.

My heart breaks with the weight of this knowledge. Josie, above all, has become so real to me. And now I have to let her go.

But I can't quite do that yet. Then something else occurs to me. I go back to the desk, where the librarian sits.

'Did you find what you were looking for?' she asks.

'Yes, thank you, you've been so helpful.'

'It wasn't the news you were hoping for, though, I think?' Her expression is concerned and kindly. 'You look as if you've had a shock.'

I shake my head. 'Not the news I was hoping for, no. But I wonder if I could ask you another favour? It's a long shot, I appreciate, but I'm wondering whether the library records from the 1940s still exist? Details of who took out which books and so on?' I just want to know whether Josie returned her library books, as she'd been planning to do in the final entry in her journal. It's a tiny thing, but the only one I can think of that might give me one more clue about her last days in Casablanca.

The librarian beams. She's a true custodian, well suited to her work. Fact-checking and record-keeping are obviously something of a passion for her. 'We have all the old ledgers in the basement. Is there a particular year you're interested in?'

'Yes, 1942. Especially November of that year.'

'Wait here,' she says. 'I'll be right back.'

The black linen cover of the ledger is worn and fraying at the edges, the corners dog-eared with use. As she opens it, I catch a faint whiff of mildew. She turns the pages carefully, searching for Josie's name. 'Look,' she says triumphantly. 'Here she is – Josiane Duval. She took out two books by Dorothy L. Sayers on the 29th of October and returned them on the 7th of November.'

I reach out a finger to touch the name. It's not Josie's handwriting, it must be that of Mademoiselle Dubois, but it still feels like one last tenuous link to her.

The librarian turns the pages. 'Here she is again,' she says.

I look politely, expecting it's a previous reference. But I do a double take when I see the date. 'The 23rd of November? But that's impossible. She was on a ship that was sunk in the battle of Casablanca.'

The librarian continues to flip over pages. 'And here again, in December. It looks as if perhaps she may have survived.'

The wave of hope that surges in my chest subsides again suddenly. Of course. Josie gave Nina her library card. Mademoiselle Dubois must have continued to record the books in Josie's name, even after she'd gone. I shake my head. 'Thank you. I think I know the explanation. But I don't think it was possible that she survived.'

'Are you sure? We do take a pride in keeping accurate records in my profession, you know.'

'The newspaper reports say everyone on board was killed. The ship exploded, you see, while it was at anchor in the harbour.' I show her the article.

'Oh well, a bit of a mystery then. But as you say, a tragedy as well.'

I thank her again for her time and her help. Grace is getting restless now and so I hurry home.

I struggle to sleep. When I do, my dreams are haunted by Josie. She's here in the house, pleading with me to rescue her. I reach out to grab her hand as she reaches for mine, but her fingers are covered in a black, oily slime and she slips out of my grasp and seems to be drowning in the darkness as I open my eyes, gasping for breath.

I'm wide awake then, so I reach over and switch on the bedside light. My arms are burning where the dermatitis is worse than ever, and I carefully dab a little more cream on to the worst of the wheals. It's torture, trying not to claw at my skin to relieve the agonising itch. I know it'll help for a few seconds and then make it burn all the more, the skin broken and bleeding. I have to resist, for my sake and for Grace's. She needs me. I can't let her down. But I know, too, that I'll be exhausted in the morning and I'll have to force myself to go through the motions of the day. Losing Josie has broken me. I'm not sure I can go on.

At last an idea occurs to me. I'm so desperate to sleep that I'll try anything. And so the next morning, while Tom is catching up with some work in his study, I go to find Alia in the kitchen. She's chopping herbs for the couscous she's making for us to eat tonight and the smell of mint and coriander are pungent on the air. The knife flies beneath her hands as I come to stand beside her, on the pretext of fetching myself a glass of water, watching as the pile of leaves subsides into a neat, finely shredded mound.

'I can bring you a jug with ice in to the drawing room, if you would like, Mrs Zoe?'

I take a gulp and shake my head. 'No, thanks, Alia, this is fine. Actually, there was something I wanted to ask you about. Do you know whether there is someone in the medina called a dreamseller? I think she could be some sort of a storyteller? A woman who might be able to help people when they are struggling with their thoughts?'

Slowly, she lowers her knife, placing it alongside the little heaps of dark green herbs on the chopping board. She fixes her eyes on mine and I'm unnerved by the intensity of her gaze.

'The dreamseller?' she repeats. 'What do you know of the dreamseller?'

'It's just something I read about. I found a journal, you see, and there was a mention of this woman, a kind of fortune-teller or something, who is able to see what people need and help explain it to them through her stories.'

'A journal?' Her voice is sharp, suddenly, very unlike her usual gentle lilt. 'What journal?'

'It belonged to a girl who once lived in this house. I can show you if you'd like?'

'I'd like very much to see this journal, please, Mrs Zoe.'

'Come,' I say, and we go upstairs together.

We sit side by side on the chaise in the drawing room. I open Josie's journal at the first page and show Alia the words. 'See? She began writing this in 1941. But it ends the following year, very suddenly. I found this, too.' I show her the inlaid box, opening it to reveal the treasures safely concealed inside.

Alia's eyes shine. 'Mrs Zoe, can you come with me to my home in the medina? I need to show these things to someone there. Someone I'd like you to meet.'

We step through the nondescript door and into another world. The small riad that is Alia's home is an oasis of beauty and greenery tucked behind high walls within the maze of narrow streets. The walls of the interior courtyard are whitewashed, creating a peaceful sense of space, and overhung with the leaves of potted palms. The scent of jasmine fills the air. Low settees face one another across the geometric tiles of the floor and I can imagine the inhabitants of this home, whose rooms are arranged on the two upper floors, looking inwards on to this quiet space, gathering here in the evenings to share a meal and enjoy each other's company.

Alia gestures to me to take a seat and then hurries away. I clutch the leather-bound journal and the sandalwood box, wondering whether someone is going to demand them from me. I know I'm not their rightful owner, but I've come to feel I'm keeping them safe in memory of Josie and I couldn't bear to give them away to a stranger.

Alia reappears, followed by a woman who's wiping her hands on a dishcloth, evidently having hurried through from the kitchen.

'Mrs Zoe,' she says. 'I am pleased to introduce you to my mother. You already know much about her. She is Josie's friend. She is Nina.'

I look up and find myself gazing into a pair of warm brown eyes. They are smiling, welcoming, and yet at the same time there is a look of something else there. I'm so taken aback that it takes a moment for me to register what it is: anxiety, I think.

I stand, setting the box and journal carefully on the cushion beside me, and reach out both my hands. 'Nina,' I say. 'Nina who loves reading Dorothy L. Sayers books, and skipping? Nina who stood beside Josie in some of her hardest moments? Nina who was given a flamingo feather by her best friend many years ago?'

She smiles more broadly. 'I still have that feather.'

I open the box and bring out its twin. She takes it from me and gently strokes the coral fibres. 'Mine has faded much more than this one – I guess being in the box undisturbed for so many years has helped preserve its colour. Alia tells me you found a journal written by Josie too.'

I don't feel quite so reluctant to pass it to her, knowing that in Nina's hands it will be safe.

Alia says something to her mother in Arabic, a rapid stream of words that make Nina frown and shake her head. Alia seems to be persisting, though, trying to convince her mother of something. Nina glances at me and her eyes are filled with that same look of anxiety again. At last, reluctantly she nods at Alia and turns to face me fully.

'Alia tells me you asked about the dreamseller. Apparently you read about her here in this notebook. Of course, my mother's aunt died many years ago. But there is still a dreamseller. And Alia feels you should meet her, because you yourself are in need of help.' There's still a hesitancy in her expression and I sense there's something she's withholding. She glances at my hands and I nod, self-consciously pulling my sleeves down to cover the raw patches on the backs of them.

'Very well. Please come with me.' Nina hands the feather back to me and I replace it in the box. She carries the journal carefully, almost gingerly, and leads me up a narrow staircase to the balcony overlooking the courtyard. The room we enter is dark after the brightness of the whitewashed walls outside, and it takes a few moments for my eyes to adjust. A tortoiseshell cat is curled up on a low couch. It lifts its head, regarding us with inscrutable golden eyes, then blinks and yawns, stretching luxuriously before tucking its head into the crook of its shoulder again and going back to sleep.

Sitting on a chair at a desk in one corner is an old woman, hunched over a piece of paper on which she appears to be writing.

Her face is partially covered by the richly embroidered Berber shawl she wears draped over her head and shoulders. Nina knocks on the door frame, announcing our presence, and she turns to look at us. As she does so, the shawl slips a little and I stifle a gasp. The woman's face is like the melted wax of a candle, the skin distorted by what appear to have been terrible burns. She raises a henna-painted hand to readjust her shawl and smiles at us. And that's when I see her eyes.

They are still bright and lively within the ruined beauty of her face. And they are the clear green of a piece of jade-coloured sea glass.

Nina puts a hand on my arm. 'Go gently,' she says softly as she hands me back the journal. 'Her mind comes and goes. Today is a good day, but we don't want to give her a shock.' Then she says a little more loudly, 'Josie, you have a visitor. Someone who wants to talk to the dreamseller. Her name is Zoe.'

Josie nods and beckons me forward. I kneel beside her chair and set the journal and box in her lap. She looks down at them in blank surprise at first and then a smile slowly spreads across her face like a sunrise. 'My treasures.'

I take her hands in mine. 'I found them. I've been keeping them safe for you,' I say, my voice low, trembling with all the conflicting emotions I'm trying to hold in. 'I hope you don't mind, I read your story. I thought you were lost, like them. But now I've found you, too.'

The backs of her hands are covered in ornate henna designs and I stroke them very gently with my thumbs. 'And look,' I say, with a smile. 'You no longer bite your fingernails.'

She turns my own hands over and inspects the raw, scaly skin, taking in the scarlet welts and the painful cracks across my knuckles. 'Zoe,' she says, as if trying out my name. 'Zoe, who has read my story. But I see you have a story of your own to tell. And so you've come looking for the dreamseller.'

'I don't have a story, really. I just haven't been sleeping too well lately. Partly because I was searching for you in my dreams, I think. And now that I've found you and I know that you were saved, I'll probably be fine.' I push to the back of my mind the knowledge that I'll be leaving both my marriage and Casablanca soon, and the thoughts of how hard the future will be as Tom and I go through the cold formalities of a divorce.

She fixes her piercing green eyes on my face and shakes her head. 'These hands do not belong to a woman who is "fine". I'll make a deal with you. I'll finish telling you my story.' She pats the journal in her lap. 'After all, I didn't get the chance to complete it in here. And the ending turned out to be somewhat different from the one you'd probably expected, as real-life endings so often do. Would you like that?'

I nod.

'And then,' she continues – and something in the tone of her voice tells me this is not a question but a statement of fact – 'when you've finished listening to my story and you feel ready, you will tell me yours.'

Zoe – 2010

Nina is highly protective of Josie. When I return to the riad a few days later, she brings us mint tea in the courtyard and hovers anxiously until Josie tells her to stop fretting and come and join us, patting the cushions beside her.

Josie turns to me. 'Nina worries that you will tire me out. My mind can be a little treacherous at times. Not for nothing did my sister christen me the mad woman in the attic! It turned out to be prophetic.'

Nina protests. 'Now Josie, you know we don't think you're crazy. You just have to be careful not to overdo it.'

Josie pats her hand fondly, then continues, 'Trauma can do strange things to the mind, can't it, Zoe? Sometimes mine simply shuts itself down when I try to approach things that are too much to bear. That's why I can become a bit vague at times. It's a sort of safety valve, I suppose. But necessary, I think, until we find other ways to bear the pain.'

I squirm a little under the piercing gaze of those sea-green eyes and try to resist the urge to pick at the frayed edges of my fingernails. She's talking about herself, but it's as if she's reading my mind as well. She knows nothing about me and yet she has a disconcerting way of talking to me as if she's known me for years.

'Thank you for giving me back my journal,' she continues. She's had it for a few days now, to give her a chance to reread it before telling me what happened to prevent her from taking it with her when she left the house in the Boulevard des Oiseaux. Nina insisted it would be wise to give her some space to do so, to allow Josie some time with her memories first. 'It's been good reminding myself of my previous life. How privileged we were! And yet we were stuck here along with all the other refugees fleeing the war. As helpless as little white mice. But you will want to know how I came to leave behind my most treasured possessions, and what became of us all.' She opens the journal at the last page, reminding herself where she left off, almost seventy years ago. Then she nods and begins.

'On the Saturday evening, Nina and I went to the library on my bike, to return my books. Back at home, my suitcase was packed. All I'd need to do was put the last few things in a bag I'd carry with me on board the ship the following week. But, although Maman had everything well organised, we hadn't reckoned on the Americans attacking. I was in the library, returning the last of my books and saying my goodbyes to Mademoiselle Dubois, when Annette came tearing in. Maman was in a taxi waiting outside. The news had come through that the Americans were about to invade further along the coast and the ships in the harbour were preparing to leave immediately. We had to go, right now. I protested, of course, that I needed to go back to the house, to fetch my most treasured belongings. But Maman said there was no time, we had to get to the port straight away. She had my suitcase in the taxi, that was all I could take. I think Annette must have known how desperate I was feeling because she gave my hand a little squeeze of sympathy, but there was no going back.

'It was chaos at the harbour, but we managed to board the *Esperanza*. Darkness was falling and we spent the night cooped up in a stuffy cabin yet again. All us passengers were under strict orders from the captain to stay put. Nobody seemed to know what was going on, but our ship's departure appeared to have been delayed by the manoeuvring of military vessels in the port. I argued with Maman to try to persuade her to let me dash home and pick up my journal and my sandalwood box, but she was adamant that it was much too dangerous – the ship could leave at any moment. Early the next morning, waking up to find we were still in the harbour, I was so miserable that I couldn't bear to stay in the cabin one more moment – captain's orders or not – so I slipped out while Maman and Annette were still asleep and went up on deck. Suddenly, there was a tumult all around, with men running and ships being made ready, and everyone was far too busy to notice me. Imagine my joy and amazement when, among the melee of faces on the quayside, I glimpsed Felix! Somehow he'd managed to slip past the guards in all the chaos and confusion. He was shouting something, but I couldn't make out what he was saying. Everything was in turmoil, with people panicking and horns blasting and all the carry-on that goes with making ships ready to sail. There were several French naval vessels in the harbour too, I remember, and one vast battle-ship called the *Jean Bart*. They were starting up their engines and frantically preparing their guns. I ran to the stern of the *Esperanza* to try and hear what Felix was saying. I even thought I might perhaps be able to ask him to cycle back to the house, to try to fetch my things for me if there was time. But that was the last thought I had before, out of the blue, I heard the sound of gunfire and the scream of the bombs. The ship was hit and it exploded.'

Nina puts her hand over Josie's at this point, and I see how it trembles, but she takes a shaky breath to steady herself and continues.

'I only pieced together what happened later, of course, from what others told me. The force of the blast knocked me

280

unconscious and threw me into the water. Felix was still there and he saw what had happened. He jumped in to save me. If I hadn't gone up on deck and if he hadn't raced to the port to try and warn us of the imminent attack on Casablanca itself, I wouldn't be here telling you this today. So it's funny, isn't it, that indirectly it was my journal that saved me?' She strokes the leather cover with her henna-painted fingers.

'The water was covered in a sheet of flames, with all the fuel leaking from the sinking ship, and I was badly burned, as you can see.' She draws the edge of her shawl a little closer to the side of her face that's most badly damaged.

'What about your mother and Annette?' I ask, although I already know what she's going to tell me. Nina squeezes her hand a little tighter.

'They were trapped in their cabin when the ship went down, along with most of the other refugees who were leaving that day. None of them made it.'

We're silent for a few moments and Nina reaches to pour the tea, providing a welcome distraction from the pang of grief I feel at hearing these words from Josie. How she must have suffered, and not just from her physical injuries. It must have been terrible for her, in a way, to have been the only member of her family to have survived.

When she's ready, she continues. 'Anyway, Felix leapt into the burning water and pulled me out. He was lucky he only suffered minor burns himself, the foolish boy. He managed to find a navy medic on the quayside, who did enough to save my life. I was in hospital for many months.'

'The same one Josephine Baker was in?' I ask.

She laughs. 'No, hers was a very smart private clinic. I was in a far more modest hospital. And then, when I was well enough, Kenza and Nina came and brought me here to their home. We'd always felt like sisters, hadn't we?' She smiles at Nina. 'And, after all, the dreamseller had always insisted that I was part of the family – remember, she'd seen it when we first met.

'Miss Ellis and Hélène Bénatar tried to track down other members of my parents' families who might take me in, but everything was in such chaos that it was impossible.'

'What about your uncle and aunt and the annoying cousins who fled Alsace before you left Paris? You mentioned them at the very start of the journal.'

Josie's eyes cloud with sadness. 'Theirs was one of the threads Madame Bénatar followed, which ended with deportation to the camps in the east. Joseph, Paulette and their two sons died in Belsen. It was certainly not a time for me to return to France, and attempting to get to America again was impossible by then. No one came looking for me. I suppose my mother's American relatives – if they were even expecting us – would have read about the attacks on Casablanca and assumed we'd all been killed.'

As I listen, I'm reminded of the story of 'The Dream' from the *Thousand and One Nights*. 'So you didn't need to seek your future elsewhere after all? It was right here, all along, just as the dreamseller had seen.'

Josie chuckles. 'You know how the story goes, don't you, Zoe? That's right – and secretly I was relieved. I didn't want to have to face leaving Casablanca again. Having already gone through that twice was more than enough. In any case, once the Americans were here everyone was even more preoccupied with fighting the war. I felt safe and happy with Kenza and Nina, who were all the family I had left, so here I stayed.

'Nina spent hours reading to me while my body and my mind mended. She'd go on the bike to the library and take out books.'

I nod. 'I saw your name recorded in the ledger at the library. I thought it might be Nina.'

She chuckles. 'I think we reread every single one of the Lord Peter Wimsey novels during that time and it was a comforting distraction for me. Something familiar when my mind wasn't able to make much sense of anything else. My memory seemed to be full of holes.'

'Is that why you didn't tell Kenza where you'd hidden the journal and box so she could fetch them from your old house?' I ask her.

She nods. 'I was in the hospital for so long and my mind shut out a lot of what happened – there were places I just couldn't reach, even though I kept trying because I had a sense of certain important things being missing. Besides, the house was very soon let to new tenants and Kenza no longer worked there because she was so busy caring for me, so even if I had remembered it would have been difficult to gain access and retrieve my things.' Once more she pats the cover of the journal, which lies in her lap. 'It's been wonderful reading this all over again. You've given me back so many happy memories and reminded me what my papa and I did. We weren't just helpless little white mice, after all.'

'And Felix? What happened to him?'

She smiles broadly. 'He and his parents got out in the end. They went to America. And guess what? He became an orthodontist! He spent the rest of his days fixing people's smiles, having had his own fixed first, of course. I have a photo here, look.'

She rifles through a folder of letters and postcards and draws out a photo printed on to a card along with the words *Happy Hanukkah from the Adlers!* In it, a grey-haired man stands with his arm around a smiling woman and they're flanked by three children, all with perfect white American teeth. 'Sadly, he passed away a couple of years back. His wife still writes occasionally, though. They visited – when was it, Nina? About ten years ago? That's right, it was a special trip they made for the millennium. He wanted to show his wife and kids where he'd been in the war years. They retraced the whole journey, from Vienna to Casablanca.'

We talk for hours, and the years seem to fall away as Josie and Nina relive the time that marked the end of their childhood. Alia sits beside me on one of the settees, entranced, watching them laughing together and becoming more animated as they dig up more of their memories.

'It's wonderful, seeing the two of them like this,' she says. 'Josie's mind seems to have grown stronger just in the past few days, ever since she got her journal back. You can see the girls they once were, can't you?'

The two friends sit close, heads together as they pore over another page, recalling how Felix tried to teach them to juggle. 'Can you still do that?' Alia asks them. 'Here, have a go.' She takes three oranges from a bowl on a low table.

Josie's hands are stiff, her fingers bent into talons, and she fumbles the fruit, laughing as they roll across the mosaic tiles of the floor. But Nina hasn't lost the knack and we applaud her, cheering loudly.

Later, when Josie has grown tired, I help her upstairs to her room. She sinks into her chair with a sigh. 'How annoying the side effects of ageing can be! I'll have to practise my juggling and see if I can improve. Still, I shouldn't complain. Growing old is certainly better than the alternative, as they say.'

She's making light of it, but I'm reminded again of her lost family. 'I hope you won't mind my asking you this, but did you ever give the names of Annette and your mother to the ocean?'

Her expression grows serious again. 'No, I never did. I was too unwell for a very long time and somehow I've never got around to it.' She fixes me with her clear green gaze, reading the things I keep hidden beneath the surface. Then she reaches out and takes my hand in hers, the tips of her fingers very lightly stroking the sorest patches. Her touch is cooling and it feels as if she's drawing the heat out of my burning skin. She continues, 'When I was so badly injured, and Kenza brought me home here to recover, I spent many hours with the dreamseller. She had the time to sit with me, to talk to me and to listen. She helped heal many of my wounds – the ones on the inside as well as the external ones. She taught me a lot, telling me her stories, enabling me to see life in a way that would help me be able to bear my pain. I asked her whether she thought it would be possible for me to become a dreamseller myself one day and she smiled. She had a smile that lit up her face, you see, transforming the ravages that life had wrought on her features into something truly beautiful. She made me feel that my ruined face, too, had its own beauty. And then she told me that I already had the power to become a dreamseller, not just because I had stories of my own to tell but also because I could hear people. Being a dreamseller is a two-way process, you see. But she didn't just mean that I was a good listener, she meant that I could really hear what it was people were trying to say, even when their words were saying something else.'

She looks at me searchingly again and I drop my eyes, avoiding her piercing green gaze. She puts one claw-like finger beneath my chin and raises my face again. 'I can hear you, Zoe, even when you don't say a word. One of the things I learned from the dreamseller was that we all need to be able to speak our own truth, to have it heard. Sometimes we can feel there's no one listening and then we must find other ways to make ourselves heard. But I am listening to you now, Zoe. I am ready to hear your truth when you are ready to tell it.'

I nod slowly, reluctantly. 'What if my truth is something really unbearable? What if telling it means I will lose something for ever? Wouldn't it be better not to speak? After all, you told me yourself that the mind shies away from the things it's impossible to bear.'

'I did. And I also know the value in facing those things when the time is right, when you are strong enough to do so. But we can't do it alone. We need the help and support of people we love and trust, both to be able to begin to face the truth and to see it through.'

I nod again, but she can sense my reluctance. Very gently she says, 'Remember our deal, Zoe. I've told you the whole of my story. Now it's your turn.'

'All right,' I say. 'But not today. You're tired and I must be getting back.' I glance at my watch. Grace is restless and hungry, and I know she'll begin to fret if I don't get her home for her supper soon. 'May I come back tomorrow?'

Every cell in my body is longing to get away, to run as far and as fast as I can from the truth that I've avoided for so long. My hands itch and prick and the urge to scrub them clean is overwhelming. Even as I say the words to Josie, I'm not sure I'll be back. I can find a reason not to return tomorrow, I think. I can make my excuses. Everything can stay just as it is.

She smiles at me, her eyes as clear as the green waters of the ocean, and I get the impression she's listening to my thoughts. 'How would it be if I came to you instead?' she says. 'Back to the house in the Boulevard des Oiseaux? I haven't been near the place for almost seventy years. Maybe now it's time.'

She can read me like a book. There is no escape. Like the refugees arriving in Casablanca all those years ago, I've reached the end of the line. There is nowhere else to go. And suddenly I realise how tired I am of running away from the truth. A feeling of deep exhaustion seeps into my bones along with that sense of recognition: maybe now it's time for me, too.

Zoe – 2010

Alia brings us a tray of tea and then tactfully retires, leaving the two of us alone in the drawing room. From the folds of her shawl, Josie produces a little paper bag. 'I made you some *ghoribas* – thought you might enjoy them.'

'Kenza's recipe?' I ask.

'But of course.'

'I wanted to show you this.' Fully aware that I'm playing for time, I slide the section of an obituary photocopied from a newspaper across the table. The words are accompanied by a grainy photograph of a slender woman with cropped hair and sparkling brown eyes.

> *During her time in North Africa, Josephine Baker worked tirelessly to support the French Resistance movement, carrying messages written in invisible ink on sheets of music back and forth between Morocco and Portugal. Her efforts provided invaluable information about conditions on the ground to the Free French under General de Gaulle and helped with the co-ordination of resistance activities in the run-up to the American invasion in 1942, which established an Allied bridgehead into Europe.*

In 1943, de Gaulle himself arrived in French Morocco. Ms Baker performed at a gala in Algiers to raise funds for the cause of French liberation. The day before the show, she had planned a grand finale: she commissioned nuns in a local convent to sew a vast French flag emblazoned with the symbol of resistance – the Cross of Lorraine. Ms Baker graced the stage in a simple white gown, singing before an audience of the great and the good, including General de Gaulle and his wife. At the end of the evening, she delivered a rousing rendition of 'La Marseillaise' as the 18-foot-high flag descended from the ceiling above her. The crowd roared their applause.

During the remaining years of the war, she travelled around North Africa and Italy performing for the Allied troops and helping to raise more than three million francs for the Free French. She was made a sublieutenant by the Women's Auxiliary wing of the French air force, was awarded the Medal of Resistance and the Croix de Guerre, and was made a Chevalier of the Légion d'honneur by de Gaulle.

Despite lengthy struggles with poor health, in the decades that followed the war Josephine Baker continued to perform and became a prominent activist in the civil rights movement. Desperate for a family, but unable to have children due to her health problems, she adopted twelve children from a wide range of ethnicities and backgrounds, whom she nicknamed her 'Rainbow Tribe'.

Ms Baker died in Paris on 12th April, 1975, aged 68. She had performed on stage just four days earlier, to glowing reviews, at a gala to celebrate her 50 years in showbusiness.

Josie passes it back to me with a smile. 'She really was something special. Just being in her company made you feel as if your life had been sprinkled with a little stardust. I'm so glad I have her autograph in my keeping again.'

She falls quiet then and the room is filled with her unspoken question as she waits. The silence is loud in my ears. It's my turn to talk. But I can't find the words, knowing that once I begin there will be no going back.

At last I say, 'There's something I want to show you. Would you come upstairs? To the room that used to be yours?'

'Help me up.' I take her hand and help her get to her feet and then together we climb the stairs to the attic.

She hesitates for a moment at the door. 'So many years.' She smiles at me. 'And yet it feels like yesterday.'

I push open the door and she steps over the threshold into her old bedroom.

Grace's room.

She stands in silence, taking it all in – the toys and books, the jack-in-the-box and the pink rabbit, the mobile with its silver moon and stars, the bed with my handmade quilt spread out on it, the baby sling hanging from the back of a chair: everything any parents would want to give their baby girl.

But here's the truth, and it's time for me to face it at last: Tom and I no longer have a baby girl.

This empty room, filled with the things I've bought, has been my way of coping with the impossibility of carrying on, pretending that the unbearable hasn't happened in order to be able to bear it. I've been living two lives: the real one in which I am a lonely expat wife trying to establish a new home in Casablanca and struggling with a failing marriage; and the one in my head, in which Grace is still with me and I spend my days by her side, caring for her.

Josie sits down on the bed in the empty room and picks up a corner of the quilt. 'This is beautiful,' she says. She runs her fingers over the triangles cut from Grace's dresses and romper suits, set in their border of intricate Berber crewel work. The thirteen on-point blocks, each one depicting its own Tree of Life, represent the thirteen precious months that she was with us: there's one made from scraps of her tiny, newborn Babygros and the brushed cotton blanket I wrapped her in to bring her home from the hospital on the day she was born; there are trees made from the colourful, cheerfully printed clothes she wore at three months, then six months – the little smocked dresses and cosy pyjamas printed with flowers and animals and sailing boats; there are triangles cut from the onesie she was wearing the day she began to crawl; and there's a whole tree made from the dress she wore for her first birthday party, embroidered with buttercups and bumblebees.

These are the trees of Grace's life. Just enough to make a quilt for a baby's bed.

'Would you like to tell me about it?' Josie asks softly.

And so I sit beside her and I explain how our baby girl died, coming up for a year ago. I tell her how perfect Grace was, how happy Tom and I were. I tell her how much I loved my daughter, how hard I tried to be the perfect mother to her. But then she caught a cold, nothing much, just a sniffle. I noticed she was running a bit of a temperature, so I called the doctor's surgery and they said to give her Calpol and fluids and call back in the morning if she was still not right. I thought she'd settled for the night, but just as I was getting into bed she began to scream, not just the cry of a hungry baby who was feeling a bit under the weather but full-on, agonised screaming. I snatched her out of her cot. She was burning up with fever, screwing up her eyes in distress when I turned on the light. And on her cheeks and her chest was a livid rash of dark spots.

We drove to the hospital in a blur of panic and I clutched Grace to me, willing her to fight the sickness that was raging in her tiny body, consuming her before my eyes. She fell silent then and the feverish weight of her became as limp as a rag doll in my arms. Her silence was almost worse than her screams. We ran into the Accident and Emergency Department and she was taken from me, whisked away behind a swinging door. A kindly nurse sat with me and told me I'd be able to see her very soon, they were just running some tests and trying to get her temperature down as it was dangerously high.

But when I did see her again it was too late. Despite the lumbar puncture, and the antibiotics they'd pumped into her, within a few hours she'd succumbed to meningococcal septicaemia, a swift and merciless killer in such a tiny child. A few nasty germs in the wrong place at the wrong time.

'WASH YOUR HANDS' said the posters on the walls of the hospital, in the corridors and in the bathroom. And they made me feel it was my fault, that I was a bad mother, that I was dirty and careless and I should have taken better care of my baby girl. But no matter how much I washed my hands, scrubbing them until the skin was cracked and raw, I could never bring her back. I couldn't wash away the guilt.

Tom and I rushed into the hospital that night as a couple of desperately worried parents. A day later, we walked out again so slowly – the longest and hardest walk I've ever taken – devastated and broken, without our baby girl. My heart felt as empty as my arms without her. And then, at the very time we most needed the comfort of one another, Tom and I were separated by the unbridge-able distance of our grief, each drawing into our own worlds as we struggled to go on with our lives without her.

Making the quilt has been my way of trying to turn her clothes into something else, I tell Josie. Because how could I ever throw them out? How could I give them away and imagine another child wearing them? And yet no one will ever wear them again and I can't keep carrying the neatly folded piles of baby clothes with me from one home to another for the rest of my life.

Stitching the Tree of Life pattern has come to symbolise hope for me. Making the quilt has got me through some of my darkest moments here. It's also been my way of trying to reconcile myself to some sense of an ending – my way of picking up the pieces of my shattered life and putting them together again. I know life never can be the same after losing Grace, but sewing this quilt has been a way of showing that perhaps I can transform the pain and the grief into something else, something new and beautiful, from the tattered scraps that remain.

I'd promised myself that once I'd finished sewing the quilt, I'd be ready to face the truth. And in a way I was right, because here I am saying these things to the one person who I think just might be able to understand.

I don't cry as I'm telling Josie all this. It's a relief to be able to speak my truth to someone who understands that a heart can be as empty as the Sahara Desert and still somehow go on beating. I only break down afterwards, when she draws me into her arms and lets me sob into the folds of her shawl, rocking me gently, just as I used to rock Grace to get her off to sleep, singing her a lullaby from long ago.

Zoe – 2010

Tom agrees to drive us to the beach. We pick up Josie and I insist she sits in the front beside him. At first, they make polite conversation about the weather and she asks him a few questions about his job at the port. But I can tell there's an instant rapport between them. I've told him her story and he finds it fascinating too. As we continue through the dirty streets, he asks her about the city in the war years and she points out the fine detailing of the dignified old buildings, still just discernible beneath the modern veneer of tackiness that disguises them these days. I hope there'll be many more opportunities for him to talk to her. I can see how much he respects her, and I know her gentle wisdom would help him as it has helped me.

I sit in the back, only half listening to them, lost in my own thoughts. As we drive past the entrance to the harbour, I picture how it must have been on the day the Americans attacked. I see the flames and hear the ear-splitting explosions as the ships were hit and the *Esperanza* sank, taking its cargo of refugees with it. And in my mind's eye I see the slight figure of a girl thrown from the deck into a sea of burning oil and a boy leaping from the quayside, without hesitation, to save her.

The devastation of the harbour and the devastation of my marriage seem to meld into one. And yet Josie has shown me that, even when the tangled web of life and love and loss and grief becomes too much to bear, it's still possible to keep on living.

On one of our walks in the Parc Murdoch, where we like to go sometimes to stroll beneath the avenues of palm trees and sit on the bench between the pines, I asked Josie how she's been able to move on, having suffered so much and lost so much. She fixed me with her sea-green gaze and thought for a while before she said, 'You know, I used to think of myself as a tiny drop in the ocean of life. But I've come to see that I am not a drop in the ocean: I'm an entire ocean in one tiny drop. There is no answer to your question, Zoe. Some things are impossible to move on from – instead, you have to find a way to live with them. The secret is to open your heart, even as it breaks. Because that's when you discover that you have the capacity to contain it all – the pain and the love, the dark and the light. Just like the ocean. Finding the strength to do so can be quite a challenge, and it takes time. But, in the end, it's facing up to the truth that will set you free.'

Tom and I have talked too, at last. A proper, honest conversation about our relationship, speaking our own truths. He's told me how worried he's been, how desperate he was when he went upstairs to my workroom in the attic one day a few weeks ago and saw all the things I'd been buying. The new toys and books on the bedroom shelves, the bottles of baby shampoo and lotion in the bathroom next door – everything arranged carefully in the rooms under the eaves that had become my retreat. And the sight of the baby sling hanging on the back of the chair shocked him most of all, as he realised I'd been wearing it, concealed beneath my shawl, when I went out on my solitary walks to the park and the library and the Habous. It horrified him, realising just how lost I was as I'd retreated further and further into my imaginary world.

He's been seeing a counsellor on his own, since I refused to go with him – Kate gave him the name of one when she met up with him in the park, someone whose details she'd obtained via one of her students at the language school. Tom didn't know what to do and he had no one he felt he could turn to either. So he contacted Kate to ask for help, knowing she was the closest thing I had to a friend in Casablanca, needing to find out whether I'd confided in her at all and whether she had any idea of my true state of mind.

He says the counsellor has helped him, and he's been able to admit his drinking has become a problem. He hasn't touched a drop in the past few weeks. I've agreed to accompany him now for some joint sessions. Though I doubt anyone, no matter how professional they may be, could help me as much as the dreamseller has done.

Tom's managed to tell me how lonely it's been for him too, how his own feelings of guilt and grief and anger stopped him in his tracks emotionally. He'd been immersing himself in his work, arriving early and working late, because the office was the one place where he'd been able to feel in control, then numbing himself with drink when the work stopped. Being unable to reach me, living like strangers under the same roof, only contributed to his sense of failure and hopelessness.

He still goes running in the mornings. But these days he sends me his photos of the sunrise, sharing his hope with me. And I treasure each one, knowing that I'm still a part of his day and that he wants to try to make this work as much as I do. We still have a long way to go. But at least we are walking that path side by side again, helping one another along, sharing the sunrises.

I've been able to admit the truth to myself fully, at last. With Josie's help – and knowing that she was the one person who might be able to understand, after reading her journal – I've been able to find that strength.

Losing Grace was the worst blow imaginable. We are not built to outlive our children. But in order to unstick myself from the past, in order not to allow the trauma to dictate the rest of my life, I have to let her go now.

Josie and I have even been able to laugh about our shared resemblance to the First Mrs Rochester and have agreed it's time the latest mad woman in the attic of the house in the Boulevard des Oiseaux moved on – although Nina tutted disapprovingly and said we shouldn't be using that disrespectful term to describe people's struggles with mental illness.

'We can when they're our own,' retorted Josie. 'We've earned the right!'

I've packed up the toys and books, the baby equipment and the moon-and-stars mobile, and asked Kate to help me take them to the refugee centre. I'm glad they'll be put to good use. When she came to collect them, she didn't ask any questions about why I had all these things and why I was giving them away. She already knew. So she just gave me a big hug and then loaded them into the boot of her car. She's asked me if, as well as my volunteering at the centre, I might be prepared to help out sometimes at a mother-and-baby group for women who are struggling with postnatal depression. She's been helping May McConnaghy and her committee raise funds for them too. I'm still thinking about it. But I know I'll probably say yes.

I've kept the musical box. And the quilt, of course. As a finishing touch, I embroidered Grace's name along the top border in silver thread, along with a crescent moon and a single star. Tom's making a frame for it so that I can hang it on the wall. I think I'll put it in our bedroom so that Grace will always be there, wherever our dreams take us, watching over us as we once watched over her.

In time, once the wounds we've inflicted on ourselves and our marriage have had a chance to heal, perhaps we'll have another baby. I'd like to be able to tell him or her about the sister who was lost far too soon. I think that would be another good way of keeping Grace with us.

The car slows as Josie points to a dusty track leading from the road to a grove of olive trees. Tom turns off and parks in the shade. He offers to walk the short distance to the beach with us, but I give him a hug and ask him to wait here. He knows this morning is for Josie and me. The few times he's met her, he's grown to like her immensely and he trusts that what we're doing today is something necessary for us both.

I take her arm, steadying her but at the same time drawing strength from her presence beside me, and we make our way down the short, stony path. And even though it's just the two of us now, we know we are not walking this path alone. We are a part of something much bigger. We are the storytellers and the quilt-makers and the dreamsellers of this world. We are the ones who dare to hope.

In the sunshine, the waves sparkle as they curl towards the beach, playfully tossing their heads of white foam in the brisk breeze. Josie and I smile at one another and she says, 'They're happy for us, I think.'

I stoop down and select three flat stones, big enough but not too big. Then I pull the marker pen from my pocket and hand it to Josie. On the first stone she writes *Maman*. On the second she writes *Annette*. She gives me back the pen and I write *Grace* on the third.

We hold those pebbles in our hands as we walk along at the water's edge, their weight as hard and dense as the grief we've carried in our hearts. We don't talk, because words can't express the thoughts that are in our heads right now. The wash of the waves teases our feet and the breeze makes the hem of Josie's shawl flutter. We walk a long way, until we're ready. And then she turns to me, her eyes asking the question, and I nod. We stand side by side, facing out to sea. Beyond the horizon is America, but we don't need to go that far to find our dreams. We know they are right here, within us.

And then it's time to let them go – Delphine, Annette and Grace – and the ocean catches them and draws them into its embrace, promising to keep their names safe for us and never to forget them.

I shade my eyes with my hand to watch as, out across the waves, three white seabirds swoop and wheel. And then they are joined by more and become lost in the joyful, soaring throng. At my feet, a tiny white feather lies on a patch of sand among the stones, as soft as a wisp of baby's hair. I pick it up and hand it to Josie.

'It's yours,' she says, holding it in the palm of her hand.

'I know. But I want to give it to you. It's my payment to the dreamseller. To say thank you. Would you keep it safe in your sandalwood box for me?'

She nods, understanding, carefully closing her hand around the soft curl of it so that the breeze can't snatch it away.

She takes my arm again, gently running her fingers over the rough patches of skin on my hand, which are beginning to heal now. And then the two of us walk back along the beach and up the path, to the grove of olive trees where Tom is waiting.

AUTHOR'S NOTE:
SOURCES AND RESOURCES

Casablanca was a fascinating melting pot during the war years, when thousands of refugees made their way there in the early 1940s, escaping from Europe and hoping to make their way to Britain and America via Lisbon.

Dorothy Ellis, Stafford Reid, the artist Gustave Reynier, Hélène Bénatar and the fabulous Ms Josephine Baker are real-life historical characters, who each played their roles on this extraordinary stage as the drama unfolded across North Africa. Meredith Hindley's book *Destination Casablanca – Exile, Espionage, and the Battle for North Africa in World War II* is an excellent starting point for those wishing to know more about the history of those times.

All other characters in this book are fictitious, and any resemblances to persons dead or living are purely coincidental.

There are many translations of the *Tales from the Thousand and One Nights*. I used the Penguin Classics edition as a reference point, but the interpretation of the story of 'The Dream' is my own. The stories of the princess and the turtle doves and the mosquito who drank the ocean are adapted from *Tashelhiyt Berber Folktales from Tazerwalt (South Morocco) – Berber Studies Volume 4 –* by Harry

Stroomer. The fable of 'The Wisest of Cats' is paraphrased from *The Clever Rat and Other African Tales*, retold by Suzi Lewis-Barned, which also contains the story of 'The Fisherman and the Genie'.

Like Zoe, I'm new to the world of quilting. I hope that those more expert than me in the vibrant quilting community worldwide will forgive any mistakes. *The Quilter's Bible* by Linda Clements was a very helpful starting point in deciphering the language of quilting and explaining how to piece together blocks. Louise Whittle's wonderful shop and website, *The Wonky Giraffe* – www.wonkygiraffe.co.uk – was another source of inspiration for all things crafting. There is also a wealth of resources online, including many different versions of the Tree of Life design. The use of quilts in the Underground Railroad and the links between quilting motifs and African cultures are explored further in *Hidden in Plain View (A secret story of quilts and the Underground Railroad)* by Jacqueline L. Tobin and Raymond G. Dobard, Ph.D.

More information about the global refugee crisis can be found on the website of the United Nations High Commissioner for Refugees – UNHCR.org. I also used the Euro-Mediterranean Human Rights Network's 2012 report on *Asylum and Migration in the Maghreb (Country Fact Sheet: Morocco)* as a source of reference, as well as the March 2013 report by Médecins Sans Frontières (MSF) on *Violence, Vulnerability and Migration: Trapped at the Gates of Europe (a report on the situation of sub-Saharan migrants in an irregular situation in Morocco)*. According to a 2020 report by MSF on *Mediterranean Search and Rescue*, during the course of 2019 there were 123,700 arrivals in Europe by sea: 27% of those attempting to travel were children. It is estimated that around 1,500 people making the crossing lost their lives.

For help and support with bereavement, some of the following may provide a useful starting point:

UK – CRUSE Bereavement Care www.cruse.org.uk ; Child Bereavement UK – www.childbereavementuk.org ; Supportline (UK) www.supportline.org.uk

USA – The American Counseling Association www.counseling.org ; Good Therapy www.goodtherapy.org

ACKNOWLEDGMENTS

One morning, I received an email from a gentleman in America who had read some of my books. He said he wished he had a granddaughter who could tell the story of his wife's time in Casablanca at the outset of the Second World War, having been displaced by the Vichy regime in France. That piqued my interest. Other than the famous film, I knew very little about North Africa in the war years. And so began a journey that would lead to me writing this book. Mr Cohen, I hope you may read it and feel that, in some way, your wife's story has reached a wider audience. Thank you for setting me on the path.

Writing a novel set in Casablanca during a global pandemic gave me a few extra challenges, but I enjoyed 'escaping' lockdown and vicariously spending time wandering the markets and beaches of Morocco.

Thank you to my publisher, Lake Union, and to the whole team who support me through the writing and editing process: Sammia Hamer, Nicole Wagner, Bekah Graham, Mike Jones and Jenni Davis and Sarah Day. Special thanks to Emma Rogers for her beautiful cover design. Madeleine Milburn, my fabulous agent, you are a total star. Thanks to everyone at the Madeleine Milburn Agency for cheering me on and selling the translation rights for my work into all those other countries around the world.

My friend Lesley Singers told me about the use of quilts in the Underground Railway and taught me to tell the difference between a fat eighth and a long quarter. She also listened to my ideas with unerring patience and enthusiasm as we trudged for miles through sunshine and rain on our weekly walks. Thank you for accompanying me on this latest journey, and thanks to Jim and the rest of the Singers family for all their support.

James and Alastair, may you find that the moonlight fills one hundred bowls of water wherever you go in the world.

And to everyone whose lives have been impacted by the extraordinary times we have been living through, please keep dreaming your dreams. Because even the darkest of nights ends with a sunrise.

ABOUT THE AUTHOR

Photo credit: Willow Findlay

Fiona is an acclaimed number one bestselling author whose books have sold over a million copies and been translated into more than twenty languages worldwide. She draws inspiration from the stories of strong women, especially during the years of World War Two, and her meticulous historical research enriches her writing with an evocative sense of time and place.

For more information, to sign up for updates or to get in touch, please visit www.fionavalpy.com.